BAROMETER'S SHADOW

PETER KAUFMAN

For Donna

The author wishes to thank Paul Allen, Charles M. Biscay, Robert Dilgard, John Hiers, the *Kodiak Daily Mirror* and the Cincinnati and Kodiak Public Libraries for their assistance in the preparation of this book.

ISBN 0-615-12604-9

Library of Congress Control Number 2004095956

Printed in the United States of America

CHAPTER 1

"All right," the doctor said. "Drop the table. Let's go."

Billy took up his position by the head. He sat down on his stool, cracked his gloved knuckles one by one and noticed a fly buzzing around the table, banging against the glass, looking for a way out. The fly certainly doesn't want to be here, and neither do I, he thought.

"Let's go, let's go," Dr. Reimers said again as he clapped his hands together. "C'mon, c'mon. I have five cases today." The circulation nurse moved in and released the drop latch so Billy could catch the head in his hands.

Now Billy studied the patient's face. No other choice, really, as the head was 14 inches from his own. It was large and unusually round, maybe 11 pounds, about the weight of a good-sized pumpkin. The head had a day's worth of rough black stubble on its face, with deep-set black eyes looking right through Billy, perhaps at the fly, which was now resting upside-down on the ceiling.

According to the chart, Sam Passalaqua was forty-two years old. He had curly black hair and a round, fleshy face, which along with the small circular scar under his left eye gave him the look of an overweight pirate.

Billy shivered. It was always so damn cold in Room 8. The same familiar chill permeated the sterile cloth, the instruments, and Billy's gown, right through his skin and muscles to his bones. You'd think the room would be warm, with the bright lights and the gowns and the body heat from all of the people, but it wasn't.

The cold air in Room 8 mixed with five distinct smells that Billy could identify: the faint odors of Betadyne, Phisohex, and Cepacol, plus perhaps a sweet whiff of nitrous oxide—a leak from the tubing?—and yes, also a barely perceptible scent of blood.

Looking through the small window of Room 8's door at Sam Passalaqua, an observer might have thought some type of mummification ritual was taking place. Now that the patient was asleep, the team leader placed a plastic-coated wire cage over Sam's chest and then gathered the plastic sheet and tied it off at the neck. A perfectly straight line of metal clips from his toes to his throat sealed off any leaks as air was pumped in through an outlet at the top, the heavy plastic bag compressing and expanding as it cycled along with the machine. The bag had to be completely sealed, or the patient would not be able to breathe well. If there was a leak, his skin would turn a dull sapphire color, and he'd become a Blue Boy, the crash team's name for oxygen-deprived cases. Sometimes those patients died in the Recovery Room if the condition wasn't detected in time.

As he thought about it, Billy felt the old comforting vibrations from the portable iron lung's ascending *whumppp?* and answering *pahhhh!* every eight seconds as he began the difficult part of the operation: trying to pass the time without moving a single inch. He had to think of something, anything to make the forty minutes or so pass as smoothly as possible. There was no getting away from the weight of the head, though; you couldn't rationalize away eleven pounds, that was for sure. Oh, you could attempt to put yourself into the Zone, the place that David Schneider, one of the other surgical techs, had told Billy about—the blissful meditative state where all surgical procedures, even six-hour Whipples, seemed to take took only three minutes; or you could forget about the whole Zen concept and think about the 1962 World Series; you could think about women; you could think about drugs, books, movies, goiters, roller coasters, Niagara Falls; you could think about types of cheeses, sex, anything—only just don't move that head; you know, the one in your hands. The angle has to be exactly correct for the ENT doc to insert the scope down the left or right bronchus. If Billy dropped the head, all of its weight would be on the neck, which would snap instantly, just as if the patient was being hung from a sycamore tree.

To understand what it's like to hold a human head during a bronchoscopy procedure, go to a grocery store and purchase a round watermelon, one that weighs about 8 to 12 pounds. Sit on a stool, relax, get as comfortable as you can, and then hold your hands out, palms up, with your elbows pressed against your body. Have someone place the watermelon in your hands. Then try not to move for the next forty-five minutes or so, depending on the vagaries of the attending ENT surgeon.

If, Billy thought, he could just place himself into David Schneider's zone of semi-consciousness, responsive to the human voice yet detached in his own mind, he could make the time go quickly, but the paradox was he had to exert such a strong physical effort to approach that state of transcendent unknowing that the other techs excelled at doing. Perhaps he simply was unable to turn his brain off; at least that's what Schneider told him.

Now Billy's body came back to him, and he felt the tendons in his arms begin to flutter, as the muscles from his fingertips to his back contracted, all of them focused at the dictatorial brain for ordering them to do something so far outside their normal pick-up-hold-put-down job description. He could already feel the pain beginning deep in his forearms.

His muscles also informed him that it now was time to begin hating Sam Passalaqua. And so he did, with every fiber of his being. Billy hated all of Sam's friends, relatives, any people Sam had ever met, the air he had breathed and every blade of grass that the man had ever bent with his size twelve feet.

Billy looked at Sam's face and he noticed that the patient's lips had turned blue. The patient was not receiving enough oxygen; his breathing was coming in short chuffing sounds. There must be something wrong with the seal, probably a loose connection somewhere.

"Excuse me, Dr. Reimers. The patient looks like he's not getting enough oxygen right now."

The doctor took his hands off the bronchoscope and looked at Billy.

"Who's the doctor here? Last time I checked, I was. You're just a surgical tech."

The doctor looked at Billy for a few more seconds, then moved back to the field.

"Here's a thought. Why don't you just hold the head like you're supposed to do and leave the rest of it to us?"

"But doctor, look at his skin. He's a Blue Boy. He's going to code."

"I'll worry about the patient's goddamn skin. You just hold the head."

Rivulets of sweat ran down Billy's arms.

"Christ's sake," Reimers muttered. "Goddamn two-buck-an-hour tech telling me what to do. Give me some suction."

The Magic Christian, Reimers' personal scrub nurse, dived in over the surgeon's shoulder and ran the tube down, suctioning the mucus from the patient's lungs, Billy watching as the fluid was pumped through the tubing down into the glass jar on the floor. The doctor replaced the scope and rotated it so he could see the tissue a little better.

"Well, boys and girls, I'm down in the left bronchus, and it's a goddamned coal mine in there. Hold on a second. Coming back out. Now the right bronchus. OK," the surgeon said, "it's time for Dr. Reimers' Fearless Prediction: the patient will be dead in two years."

That's wrong, Billy thought. The patient could be dead in ten minutes.

Billy closed his eyes.

"Just another few seconds or so, and we'll be finished. I'll take a biopsy," Reimers said.

He slid a biopsy forceps down the tube, and looked again. The case was almost finished, and now the doctor could afford to relax a little.

"Anybody ever been to the Black Forest in Germany?" he asked, sweat glistening on his brow. A smattering of apathetic "no's" came back at him from Jessie the circ nurse, Dr. Seslow the resident and the Magic Christian. They all hated it when Reimers began to lecture them about his world travels.

Billy wasn't listening anymore. He was too busy fighting the urge to shift his hands, or better yet, just drop the head, break the patient's neck, and run out of Room 8 and smoke a joint. The muscles in both of his forearms began twitching again.

"Well," Reimers said as he maneuvered the biopsy forceps into position, "the Black Forest is called that because it's so dark. Sometimes, you literally can't see ten feet in front of your face.

So if you can imagine the Black Forest at midnight you get an idea of the condition of this man's lungs. He has to be a three-pack-a-day man. Straight Camels, maybe Pall Malls."

He dropped a small bloody piece of tissue into a specimen container.

"We're about done here, Sally. Call Recovery. "

Better be sure and call the chest team as well, Billy thought.

Reimers pushed himself back on his stool and stood up.

Billy said nothing. His eyes focused on a small drop of blood on one of Dr. Reimers' white leather shoes as he heard the fly again. He followed the noise and found the small insect perched on the barium crystals container.

Reimers tossed his gloves with a flourish into the clothes hamper instead of the disposable one and banged through the pale green OR doors. He said hello to Dr. Schwartz and ducked into the doctors' lounge.

As Billy watched the doors settle down, he knew that two things would happen in the next few minutes, both of them bad. The patient's skin color was now a pale violet color and he was going to code any minute. Billy had gone down to Recovery so many times shouting about Blue Boys that the nurses there called him Wolfie because they said that he cried wolf every time he came in with a patient. But he had been right before, and this was a Blue Boy if ever he saw one.

Billy also knew that by the time Sam coded, Dr. Reimers would already be in the doctors' lounge, injecting himself with precisely 175 mg of Demerol into the right quadriceps muscle. Reimers always shot up after his first case. That way, the good doctor could make it through the rest of his cases or at least until lunchtime.

Billy helped put Sam Passalaqua into a bed and wheeled the patient down the hall and out of the OR into Recovery, where Ernestine Baker was the nurse in charge.

"Watch this one, Ernie," Billy said. "He's going to code. I know it."

"Sure, Wolfie," Ernestine grinned.

Alice Tallarico, one of the other Recovery nurses, arched her neck.

"Owooooooo."

"That's funny, Alice. Very original," Billy said.

He went into the techs' locker room and lit a cigarette. Hospitals are the most dangerous places in the world, he thought. You go in for a tonsillectomy and come out with your balls cut off, neatly stitched up in a little cloth bag. He swore that he'd operate on himself rather than go through the shooting gallery at Frey Memorial.

I'd take off my own balls with a pair of tinsnips before I let any of these damn doctors touch me, he thought as he took a long drag.

CHAPTER 2

The day after his Room 8 broncho, Billy arrived at work twenty minutes early, at 6:40 am. Waiting in the locker room was Craig Maxwell, from Central Supply, smiling and shifting his weight from one foot to the other.

"Here are your mediums, Billy," Craig said, handing him a frayed set of green scrubs.

"And here, Craig," Billy said, giving him two small bottles, "is your Cepacol."

Craig cracked open the bottles and drank the mouthwash, one after the other.

"Hey, Craig," Billy said. "Any sign of the SATHO man?"

Craig was obsessed with the mysterious sociopath who ran around with a Magic Marker, writing the words "Shoot All Their Heads Off," on just about every flat surface in the hospital. The anonymous graffiti artist scribbled it on the supply carts, on the glass walls of the coffee shop, on the doors to the ER, across the hood of Dr. Eisenberg's new green Cadillac deVille, and on the polished chrome body drawers down in the morgue. Eventually, the artist abbreviated the phrase to SATHO.

"No," Craig said, wiping his mouth with the back of his hand. "Ain't seen him anywhere. I look for clues every day."

"So do I."

"You see anything strange yesterday?" Craig asked.

"I see something strange every day."

"Well, I'll get him. I'll find him."

"I know you will," Billy said.

"That's right. I'll find him all right. And when I do, I'll tell Dr. Margolis."

Craig tossed the empty bottles into the wastebasket.

"*Oh, have you seen the SATHO man?*" he began to sing. "*The SATHO man, the SATHO man . . .*"

"Oh no, not that shit already," Jack Reynolds said. "Don't start with that, Craig. Don't sing that goddamn song. Once he starts singing it, Billy, you know that he sings it all day long. It's way too early for that shit."

Craig walked out singing his SATHO song. They could hear him down the hallway as he banged open the doors into Recovery.

"That's something, taking advantage of a retard," Rick Spencer, the Magic Christian, said.

"Who's taking advantage?" Billy asked. "Nobody's taking advantage of anybody. He needs Cepacol; I need mediums. It's a fair exchange. Supply and demand."

"Well, I think you're taking advantage of him."

"Didn't you see how he went out? He was happy."

"He's not happy, he's high. He's doing Cepacol, Romilar, Formula 44 too, you know. He'll be drunk by noon."

"That's his business, Rick. So what if he doesn't read his Bible on his break every day like you do? You're just jealous that I can get mediums every day and you can't."

"Yeah, Rick," Jack said. "Not everybody can find Jesus like you did. What the hell difference does it make?"

"Well, it's wrong. It goes against the nature of God."

"Look around, Rick," Jack said, waving his hand. "You see God here right now?"

Jack whistled, "Here, God, here Goddy, Goddy. Here, boy. Herrrreeeeee, God. Here, God. Nope," he said, "there's nobody here. You must not have got the news. God doesn't make house calls anymore."

Billy laughed. He liked Jack.

"You're a blasphemer, Jack, but that's all right. I'll pray for your soul anyway," Rick said. "I'll add your name in with the others."

"List gets longer every day, doesn't it?" Jack said.

Rick turned back to his locker. He finished dressing, kissed a small gold crucifix hanging on the door, and left for Room 8.

"I heard we had a Blue Boy yesterday."

"Oh yeah? Where'd you hear that, Jack?"

"Arcola told me. Some guy went blue after a broncho. He died in Recovery."

"What was his name?" Billy asked, as he felt the hairs on the back of his neck move. He knew who it was.

"Oh, some weird name. Italian, maybe."

"Passalaqua?"

"Sounds about right," Jack said. "How'd you know?"

"Because I saw that one coming."

Billy put his street clothes away, slipped on the medium scrubs, and stuffed his long brown hair into his cap. He tied the bottom of his surgical mask around his neck so that the top dangled loosely in front of him.

Leaning back against his locker, Billy lit a cigarette and watched the techs and orderlies as they came into the locker room. The white clock showed 6:45 when David Schneider walked in.

"Hello, fellow peons," David said, as he swept into the locker room. David was a C.O., a conscientious objector who drove two hours to the hospital each day from his parents' farm near Chillicothe. He was mostly insufferable now, since he had only two months left to serve in his two-year hospital "sentence," as he liked to put it. Right behind David were Chuck Beck, Lance Somers and Terry Buscalia.

"Well," Chuck said, as he sat down by his locker and untied his street shoes, "did anybody listen to the news coming in?"

"I heard it," Jack said. "Nixon came out and said he was a faggot. Turns out the whole goddamn cabinet is—Mitchell, Laird, Kissinger too. All fairies. It's unbelievable, isn't it?"

"Shut up, Jack. No, seriously," Chuck said. "I just heard it a few minutes ago. Hopalong Cassidy died yesterday. You know. Hoppy. Yesterday, September 12, 1972," Chuck said as he put his street shoes neatly in his locker.

"Hopalong Cassidy? The cowboy?" Jack asked.

"Well, it wasn't Hoppy who died, it was the actor," Chuck said. "His name was uh, I can see his face, uh, William Boyd."

"Let's all have a moment of silence for William Boyd, then, gentlemen," David said. "Now, Chuck, just exactly who in the hell was Hopalong Cassidy?"

"Man, I can't believe you, Dave, " Jack said. "What do you raise on your farm—muskmelons? Because you got a muskmelon for a head. Everybody knows who Hopalong Cassidy is. He's the

American West, man—the guy with the white hat and white horse. He stands for decency, not shooting a guy in the back. He's fair, he's . . ."

"He's not real then," David said, spraying deodorant under his arms. "None of those cowboys are real. Did you ever meet anybody like that? I never have, not in Chilltown, not in Hillsboro and sure as shit not here."

He put his deodorant can on a shelf.

"Yep, just one of them there Hollywood cowboys," David said.

Chuck didn't hear him. "Hoppy's dead," he said. "Hoppy's dead. Now what will become of Topper?"

"Hoppy died for your sins, Chuck," Jack said.

A loud knock on the door stopped their conversation. It was Arcola Brown, the OR floor supervisor.

"Come on. Let's go in there. Get to your rooms. It's almost seven."

Billy tied his mask up and followed everyone out to the rooms. He looked at the schedule. Good. His first case in Room 1 was a routine hysterectomy, with Dr. Schwartz.

He went into the scrub room between 1 and 2 and popped open the plastic Phisohex soap. Then Billy began the scrub-up procedure: hold the arms at your sides, bent at the elbow. Turn on the water with your knee. Start with the fingers of the left hand, ten strokes with the soapy scrub brush on each side of each finger—forty strokes per finger. Be sure and hold your arm up so the soap and water run down off your elbow. Now turn the Phisohex pad over and repeat with the right hand and right arm. The procedure took about seven minutes. Billy dipped his left arm from bottom to top under the water to rinse the last of the soap, and repeated with his right arm. He backed into the OR, and picked up a sterile towel from the stack.

The scrub nurse for Room 1 was a short redhead named Polly Rowan, whom all of the male employees at Frey called the Professional Virgin or PV. For years, she had resisted every advance. Once, when Billy had been at Frey for just a few months, the PV came in for some impacted wisdom teeth. After the surgery, she was moved from the table to her recovery bed. Her gown had fallen from her shoulders, she was semiconscious, and everyone realized that it was a simple task for a surgeon, resident, orderly or tech to jostle her accidentally and reveal those perfectly

firm young breasts. But Billy would not permit it. In the fifty
yards between the OR and recovery, he stopped two attempts
to strip the PV's shoulders, grabbing each man's hand before he
was able to touch the soft pink cloth. She made it to Recovery
unmolested. He remembered this incident clearly, since it was
one of the few moments in the past two years when Billy actually thought of himself as a worthwhile person.

The PV was scheduled for Room 1 all day. She ignored
Billy as he dried his hands and slipped into his sterile surgical
gown. George Stone, the only male surgical nurse in the OR, tied
Billy's gown in the back.

Now gloved and gowned, Billy was ready. He clasped his
hands in front of him and waited for the patient, just as the PV
wheeled her into Room 1, a black woman in her fifties, as jittery
as a methed rabbit. Billy bent over and peered at the chart carefully without touching it and read her name and age in blue
ink—Lucretia Wells, 57. The PV locked the gurney down and ten-
derly guided the patient over to the OR table. That was the one
thing about the PV that Billy really liked, she was very gentle
with the patients. She didn't slam them around like some of the
other nurses did.

The anesthesiologist for the room, Gary Meyers, came in and
patted the patient on her shoulder.

"Hello, dear," he said. "How are you today?" He paused to
look at the patient's name. "Lucretia?"

"OK," Lucretia said softly. "I'm OK."

She was so scared the sheet was shaking.

"Sorry? I didn't hear you."

"I'm OK."

"Good," the anesthesiologist said, and drew 200 milligrams of
pentothal from the bottle. He put the syringe next to the ambu bag.

Now Billy heard the heavy Mayo table squeak as it was rolled
up to the field. He walked around the table to the other side of
the patient and stood over her.

"It's going to be all right," Billy said. "You're going to be fine."

Lucretia's teeth were chattering. She was either that cold or
that frightened.

"Can't anybody get her a blanket?" Billy asked.

"What for? She's going to be out in a minute anyway," the anesthesiologist said. He was busy erecting the cloth screen that separated the patient's head from the sterile field. He was all set: pentothal, intubation kit, pen, blood pressure cuff, stethoscope, ambu bag and his book for the week, *Stranger in a Strange Land*. As he busied himself, he began singing a show tune: "*Got my scrubs pressed, got my best vest, all I need now is the doc.*"

A few minutes later, Dr. Schwartz came into the OR.

"Hello everyone," he said. He walked over to the patient and patted her shoulder. "Hello, Lucretia. How are you today, sweetheart?"

"OK," she said in a whisper. She was shivering all over now, her shoulders moving up and down.

"That's great. Great, great, great," Dr. Schwartz said, and walked back to the scrub room.

The anesthesiologist continued to hum as Polly Rowan taped the patient's IV'd arm down to a board. Now he came off of his stool by Lucretia Wells' head and Billy could see that he was holding the syringe with the joy juice.

"Now, dear, I'm going to give you a shot. You might feel a little stinging or iciness in your hand, but that's about all. That's the last thing you'll feel."

Billy watched the cloudy-looking pentothal go into the back of Lucretia's hand. As Dr. Meyers went back to his stool behind the screen, Billy looked at the patient's eyes. They seemed to soften a little as her shivering stopped; she sighed, and then became unconscious.

The two residents, Czernik and Altoonian, banged into the OR. Dr. Czernik looked disorganized—his mask was crooked and upside down, and he had forgotten to tie off his surgical cap, which was perched awkwardly on top of his head. His conductive shoe covers still had their black tails out, and they followed him into the OR, two small snakes at his heels. The other resident, Altoonian, still had some soap running down his left arm.

"You'd better finish rinsing, doctor," Polly said.

"Oh, yes, yes. Sorry," Altoonian said, and backed out into the scrub room.

Billy gloved and gowned Dr. Czernik and the resident positioned himself by the patient's side, then picked up the Betadyne sponge and began to swab the patient's abdomen in round strokes.

"No, no, no," Dr. Schwartz said. He had followed the residents into the OR and was watching them from the suction tubing station.

"You're not a goddamn Rembrandt. Short vertical strokes. How long do you think the incision's going to be? Three feet?"

"No, is . . ."

"Is what?" Dr. Schwartz asked. "Here, give me that."

He snatched the Betadyne prep sponge from the resident.

"Now watch. Short, small strokes, not round. See? Watch and learn. Watch and learn . . . watch and learn. There."

He dropped the prep sponge onto the floor and covered the prepped area with a sterile clear pad.

"Where's Robin?"

"Robin?" Dr. Czernik asked.

"Yeah, Robin. Where's Robin?"

Dr. Schwartz always called his two assisting residents Batman and Robin. He never bothered to learn any residents' names at Frey.

"Oh yes," Dr. Czernik said, "Please. Is still scrubbing up."

"Well, by the time he gets his Armenian ass out here, we'll be through the fascia." Dr. Schwartz was one of the fastest surgeons at Frey. Before he began doing hysters, he liked to brag about doing an inguinal hernia operation, skin to skin, in twenty minutes. Billy had seen him set a timer on some operations.

"Now watch and learn, Batman," Dr. Schwartz said, as he picked up the scalpel.

"Watch and learn. Watch and learn," he repeated, and made a midline incision about six inches long. The blood showed bright through the sterile sheet and Betadyne.

Czernik dabbed at the blood with a 4X4 pad.

"Whoa, not so hard. Don't press so hard. That's it," Dr. Schwartz said, as he reached the next layer. He cut through the subcutaneous. The tough yellow tissue was about two inches thick.

Dr. Altoonian came out through the scrub room doors and was quickly gowned and gloved. He took his place next to Billy.

"Nice of you to join us, Robin. Now look at all this beauti-ful sub-Q. Lady needs to go on a diet," Dr. Schwartz said as he used the electric Bovie to cauterize a few bleeders.

Now here it comes, Billy thought, that horrible stench, drift-ing up from the wound along with a wisp of smoke, right into his nostrils. How come no one else is bothered by it, that smell of burning flesh?

Five layers, Billy thought. First was the skin, subcutaneous, fascia, peritoneum, and the omentum, that strange, scrambled-egg-looking tissue. Finally, the uterus would appear, a glisten-ing pink softball, way down in the wound.

As the surgeon proceeded to Bovie down through the dif-ferent layers, Billy rested his left arm on the patient and wiggled his fingers, relaxing them one more time before he would have to hold the retractor. He really didn't have to worry too much about it on this case, though, since Schwartz worked so quickly. Billy's right hand was beside the surgical tray, scissors ready for quick strikes into the wound to cut the sutures once the team had reached the big arteries and veins.

Billy let his mind wander again. This procedure was easy, as he simply held the retractors and cut sutures. He knew without looking at her chart that Lucretia Wells was a welfare case, from one of the two wards on the second floor. He could tell because a ward case affected the way that Schwartz oper-ated. The surgeon was always quick, but moved even faster and was sloppier with the ward patients, especially once he was on the way back out.

Looking over the sterile screen, Billy could see the chart from where he was standing, and, sure enough, there was a bright red "2D" on it by her name, signifying one of the wards that had six or eight beds to a room with no air conditioning. In the summer, the Cincinnati heat hung heavy over the old iron beds while the big wooden fans in each room only pushed the humid air around.

"Cut," Dr. Schwartz said.

Billy instinctively dived down into the wound with his scis-sors and neatly snipped the excess suture, leaving quarter-inch tails. One thing was for sure: Schwartz was not taking his time on this case. He was operating as though he had a date on the Ohio River. Billy knew that Schwartz was one of the surgeons at Frey who had a boat at Four Seasons Marina, a forty-two footer named *Surgery*. It was one of those cute names doctors loved; whenever Schwartz was on the river, his receptionist was instructed to inform all callers, "Doctor can't come to the phone right now. He's in *Surgery*."

Schwartz had clamped off the last of the blood vessels. There was no doubt about it. He was going for a new world's record, Billy thought. Was it possible to do a total hysterectomy, skin to skin, in thirty minutes? He didn't think so, but Alan Schwartz was certainly willing to give it a try.

"Cut."

Billy swept down into the wound with his scissors. The uterus hung suspended between the clamps, waiting expectantly for the scalpel release.

Down went Billy and cut right above the knot.

"God damn it. Not so short."

"Sorry."

Dr. Schwartz gave Billy The Look.

"You know," the surgeon said, sotto voce, "there is a little receptacle outside this room. And do you know what it's for?"

"No," Billy said, playing along.

"It's for the testicles of anyone who cuts knots. Suction, please, Batman," Dr. Schwartz said to Czernik.

"How's she doing, Gary?"

Dr. Meyers looked up from his fort on the other side of the sterile curtain. Billy could see that he had turned his body away from the nitrous and oxygen tanks. The book was just getting interesting and the anesthesiologist hated all of these interruptions.

Ask him again, Billy said to himself. Ask him to read the dials. Check the goddamned vitals.

"Did you say something, Al?"

"Just watch the vitals, OK?"

But Dr. Meyers wasn't watching any vitals. He wasn't checking her heart rate, nor was he paying attention to the mixture of nitrous and oxygen, and didn't see her slip into hypoxia a few minutes later. And so that is why he was surprised as much as any one else in Room 1 when Lucretia Wells went into full cardiac arrest exactly fifty seconds later.

Her body convulsed and she nearly flipped off the table.

"Jesus Christ," Dr. Myers said, dropping his book. "Chest Team, stat."

Polly called the front desk, the chest team was paged and the Keystone Kops came around the corner, pushing the crash cart crazily on two wheels.

They formed their hopeful semicircle around the patient.

"Clear," Dr. Getz, head of the Chest Team, yelled joyfully as he pressed the red button on the paddle and administered the shock that arched Lucretia Wells' body. He loved shouting "Clear."

Despite the electric shock and the norephinephrine injected directly into her heart, Lucretia Wells died on the table. Her death wasn't a total loss, though, as far as the hospital was concerned, since the Chest Team was able to try out their fancy new $5,000 Cardiocet defibrillator, and for his part, Billy knew the administrators would be pleased that in the interest of hospital efficiency, the patient was tied, tagged and in the morgue within thirty minutes. There was only one slight hitch. That happened when one of the new orderlies had inadvertently taken her to the morgue via the main passenger elevator bank instead of the service one, and so several families visiting their relatives could not help noticing the glazed-over look in Lucretia Wells' eyes, her hands bound with white adhesive tape, fingertips pointed up as if in prayer, and the manila tag neatly tied with a double knot to her left big toe.

Of course, by the time Lucretia was taking her last elevator ride, Billy eyes were glazed as well, because he'd been stoned for more than twenty minutes.

CHAPTER 3

"Two in two days, Jack."

"What do you mean?"

"I said two. The broncho in 8 and an OB/GYN case."

"Billy," Jack Reynolds asked, "why don't you just try to forget about it? Everybody else does. You can't take this shit too seriously."

He took a long drag from the joint and handed it to Billy.

"I can't stop thinking about it, Jack. It's all of their faces. I can still see them floating in front of me. From Joe Kelly—he was the first one, that nine-year-old—to now. I'm beginning to wonder if I can see them coming."

"What do you mean?" Jack asked.

"I don't know. It's almost like I can look at them and tell."

Jack took a drink of beer.

"Look, how long have we been here, two years?"

"Yeah. We both came here at the same time."

"Right, but Billy, think of all the techs who have come and gone since then—Steve Klein, Jimmy Reese, Nick Russo, George Crabb. I guarantee you that none of them ever gave a second's thought about the patients that kick off."

"I'm not talking about all the patients who die. I know they die. Jesus Christ. This is a hospital. People die in hospitals. I'm talking about the ones who die because the doctors screw up. Lately, there's been a bunch."

"I know, but Billy, look. You have to get over it. It doesn't bother me that much. It's all part of the cycle, you know. Even the Magic Christian's got that right—a season for living and a season for dying. If it's meant to be, it's meant to be. Anyway," Jack said, as he took another hit, "what the hell? You better put this shit out of your mind. Because I'll tell you this: each time it happens, it takes a little piece out of you. I can see it."

Jack took the roach and clipped it with a curved hemostat.

"Listen, I got some Jamaican at home. Why don't you stop by after you clock out? Smoke some of that Righteous Shit instead of this shitty homegrown."

Billy didn't need Jack or his RS. He could get high right now if he wanted to do so. He always kept a little bit of hash in his locker, inside an empty suture box. Although he'd been smoking grass and hash since he was in college, he didn't stand out as a pothead at the hospital. Almost everyone smoked, shot, snorted or licked; that's how pervasive the drugs were at Frey Memorial. Some doctors, a few of the nurses, most of the pathology boys, and a handful of X-ray techs, housekeepers and orderlies became stoned every day. In fact, Billy realized that was probably why Reimers had been so testy yesterday—the doctor needed his morning Demerol fix.

At Frey, any drug neophyte could begin in the OR with the blue nitrous oxide or orange cyclopropane tanks. The nox was better than cyclo, although you had to be careful, because too many hits of the sweet-smelling nitrous, the Royal Blue Haze itself, would make you pass out, face first, slammed right down on the linoleum like poor David Schneider, who broke his nose that way last year. He lost consciousness and pitched forward onto the floor in Room 7, which Billy found particularly amusing because 7 was the Rhino Room, where Dr. Pearlman did the rhinoplasties, the nose jobs. They just cleaned up 7, brought in all the sterile gowns and rhinoplasty instruments and fixed David's broken nose right on the spot.

It was David who developed the best nitrous system—two people in the room, five puffs for each of them at a time, no more, no less. That way, one person could sniff through the mask while the other served as a lookout, watching to see if anyone was coming in and standing behind the nox sniffer to catch him if he fell.

David also was the one who came up with the concept of the Perfect Joke. The nox would make you laugh, laugh until you cried, laugh until your sides hurt. David said that you didn't laugh because of the nox, it was because God was whispering the Perfect Joke in your ear.

"God has been working on this joke for a hundred thousand years," David told Billy. "It has this punch line that includes priests, whores, Polacks, morons and elephants. That's why you laugh. You hear God's perfect joke. He tells it to you. It's not the nitrous, Billy."

David's setup worked fine, right up until you felt your knees buckle and your hearing became tinny. Then it was time to stop. You could take the nitrous directly through your mask, on breaks between cases, or at the end of the day before the second shift banged the time clock. The worst nox sniffers were the hollow-eyed vampire techs on the third shift. They were on the bright blue bottle from 11:00 pm to 7:00 am, when the OR was quiet except for the occasional gunshot or knife case.

Prescription drugs were the next level up from nitrous, a little harder to obtain, but a *sub rosa* network of forged signatures and unmarked plastic pill bottles made the locker rooms a banquet hall of Phenobarbital, Nembutal, yellow jackets, red bombers, sopors, percs and codeine. It was an entire *Physicians' Desk Reference,* right there in front of them. One of the techs, Lance Somers, a little ex-Marine medic who liked to hang out in the doctors' lounge, had a well-stocked drugstore in his locker. He knew the dosages better than the hospital pharmacist did and charged five bucks for a bottle of uppers or downers, ten for something really special, like morphine or Demerol.

Billy had tried nitrous, codeine, and a few Secs, but found he preferred the basic grass and hash that was so prevalent in the locker room. After his first case, he generally smoked a joint or some hash and could float through the rest of the day. He was always careful to use Cepacol mouthwash and spray a little Right Guard deodorant around his neck. So far, he told himself, none of the handful of straight docs or nurses had caught on. Then he would take up his position next to the surgeon or resident, smiling and disconnected. And he was not alone. Billy could always tell if the other techs or orderlies were high; their eyes were bloodshot and crinkly, and their masks would move more than the straight techs. The stoned ones were always smiling or giggling. Occasionally, they would drop a retractor or contaminate themselves, but unless you studied their eyes, it was hard to distinguish the stoned techs from the straight ones.

"So how about it," Jack persisted, bringing Billy back. "You coming or not?

"Is Kathryn going to be there?"

Kathryn was Jack's live-in girlfriend. She hated Billy.

"No man, she's out all day at her sister's in Amelia."

Billy took the hemostat and cupped his hand around the roach so it wouldn't go out as he watched the light gray smoke curl through his fingers and drift up to the vents, taking with it any active thoughts.

He let it all go.

"All right, Jack," Billy said.

He reached into his locker for some Cepacol throat discs, but couldn't find any.

"Shit," Billy said. He sat back down on the bench and watched Antonio Mason lock and unlock one of the straight razors from the pre-op room.

"What'd you say, white boy?" Antonio inquired.

"You heard me."

"See?" Antonio said, as he put the straight razor in his locker. "That's one of the problems with you white people. Don't know how to swear. You go around, saying 'Oh shit.' 'Oh damn.' 'Oh hell.' You should be saying, Sheeeeeeiiiiiit. Get some *satisfaction* out of it. Try it again."

Billy cleared his throat. "Sheeeit."

"That the best you can do? Listen. Sheeeiiiiitt. See?"

"Sheeeeeeeeeeeeeiiiiiiiiiiiiiiiiiiiiiiiiiiiiiiiiiiiiiiiiiiiiiiitt."

"That's good. That's good. I like it. Keep working on that."

Antonio reached up in his locker and took a pull from a Romilar bottle. He pointed his finger at Billy. "Tomorrow, we'll work on 'muh-tha-fuk-kah.' "

"Hey, Antonio," Jack called from across the locker room, "Got any more of the RS?"

"No, man," Antonio said. "No more Righteous Shit. Sure could use some, though."

"You finally go through all that stuff you brought back from 'Nam?"

"Oh, yeah. That's long gone, man."

"Hey, White, tell me again why you didn't re-up," Jack said. "With all that dope around 'Nam, I would have been set for life."

"You don't understand it man," Antonio said. "You white boys think that you could just go over there, get high all the time, shoot a few gooks. It wasn't like that. First, you got to watch your ass all the time. I didn't. Best thing that ever happened to me was when Charlie shot me in the ass so I could be rotated home.

"Vietnam is a fucked-up place, Jim. I knew it as soon as I got off the transport. That's when the bullshit started and it hasn't ever stopped. Like when we were in Cambodia. I heard all this shit on Armed Forces Radio about how Nixon says we're not going into Cambodia. I saw the damn road signs—we were already in that goddamn country. See, whatever Nixon says, you got to believe the opposite. So when he tells us that we're winning, I know we are going to lose. The whole muthafucking thing is built on lies.

"One time, the week before I got shot, our company gets this memo from some bird colonel somewhere. It says," and here Antonio stood up and began speaking in a clipped English accent, "It says, 'From now on, we will refer to the enemy as "Charlie" or "Victor Charlie." ' Right there, that's when I knew we weren't gonna win. You know why? Because we were sending out notes on what kind of shit we was supposed to call the enemy."

"Why did you go?" Billy asked. He didn't go because he had a high lottery number. Even if he had been drafted he would have turned C.O. or moved out of the country.

"*Why did you go?*" Antonio mimicked Billy. "Stupid white boy question. I had no choice, man. My ass was drafted, that's why. I didn't go to Canada or Mexico or wherever you sweet little ofays go. So I did my time over there, got shot in the ass for my trouble, too. But it wasn't lost time. I learned a lot in Vietnam."

"Like what?" Billy asked.

"Learned how to smoke over there. How to say 'Yes, sergeant' so that it didn't come out 'Fuck you, sergeant.' And how to get those Saigon whores. Little girls didn't care if I was black or purple. Made no difference to them. Sometimes I'd look at my black skin next to their yellow skin. Mmmm."

Antonio closed his eyes, remembering.

Somebody banged on the locker room door.

"McCord. Get out here."

Billy rose a little unsteadily from his bench and stuck his head out.

"You're to stay out of Room 8 from now on," Arcola Brown barked. "Reimers' orders. And also, from now on," she added with a tight little smile, "I'm going to be watching you."

CHAPTER 4

"So, where should I go, Arcola?" Billy asked.

Arcola looked up from the nurses' station. Her mouth was a thin line drawn crookedly down across her face. She never smiled.

"Check the schedule."

"Oh, come on. Where do I go? Please."

"You're to stay out of 8 from now on," she repeated, and looked down at the schedule, "Six the rest of the day. There are three breast biopsies in there. That will keep you busy for a while."

She paused for a moment. "Unless that's not all right with you."

"It's all right. You don't have to be sarcastic."

"Just do what you're told, McCord."

Arcola turned out to be right; he *was* busy, as each of the biopsies developed into a radical mastectomy. He thought it was a hell of thing for the woman to go into the room not knowing whether she had cancer; not knowing if she was going to wake up in Recovery with a two-inch scar or a seven-inch one. The surgeon would take a small tissue sample, and then everyone, the circ nurse, residents, assistants, techs, orderlies, would stand around silently and wait for the pathologist's report to come back for the frozen tissue section. If the tissue was benign, the patient would be stitched up and in Recovery in about 20 minutes. If the pathologist had seen cancer cells, a new tray of sterile instruments would be brought up to the surgical field, uncovered, and the radical mastectomy procedure would begin. If the cancer was present in the nodes, the surgeon would cut his way down to the chest wall muscles as the breast tissue increased in size under Billy's gloved hands, until the surgeon scalpeled away the last bit of tissue.

Case after case—take one breast, sew another one up, hold
the retractor, suture, suture, help lift the patient back onto her
bed for the trip to Recovery—the whole mad merry-go-round of
the day was finished and then it was 3:00 pm and he was
smoking a cigarette in the locker room. At this time of day, the
room resembled a filthy downtown street, with newspapers
scattered around, mixed in with cigarette butts, ashes, used
alcohol packets, wadded-up lunch bags and empty Mad Dog
2020 bottles. The clock jumpers all lined up against the wall,
watching the big black hands move toward 3:24. They knew that
the time clock broke down each day into six minute segments,
and if they clocked out at 3:24, they were credited for 3:30; as
David Schneider explained to Billy, six minutes each day was a
half hour a week, times fifty-two was twenty-six hours a year—
more than three paid workdays.

Billy smoked another cigarette, punched out at 3:45 and
walked out to his old beat-up '65 Impala in the employee lot.
He drove over to his apartment in a rundown part of Clifton near
the college. Someone was in his spot, as usual, so he had to park
up the street.

He picked up his mail and walked in. The place was neat and
simple, Spartan in appearance, a single bedroom apartment
with a foldout bed, a chair, a small table and a TV that Billy had
bought at the Salvation Army the year before. It looked as if no
one really lived there, especially since all of the posters that he
had collected during his two years of college were gone. He had
thrown all of them away, including his favorite one of Nixon and
Agnew riding Harleys.

The only piece of him that he allowed in the apartment was
a small wooden dresser that he had saved from the house
when his mother and father divorced last year. On top of the
dresser were two photos from his old room. His mother had
given him several more photos, including one 8X10 of Billy and
his father, but Billy had thrown them all out except for these two
pictures. One was a shot of Billy dressed up as a robot on Halloween and the other was of his sister Karen. In that photo, she
was playing with a toy kitchen set but Billy wished he had one
of Karen with the Ouija board he bought her when she was five.

Fingering the frame, Billy ran his hand over her black hair,
remembering her, how they'd spend hours summoning the

spirits of George Washington Carver, Harry Houdini and Marilyn Monroe while Billy wrote down in his spiral notebook what each of the spirits said. They found out that Frank Sinatra had murdered Marilyn Monroe and that Harry Houdini had been trying to communicate with the living, but was now resigned to using the Ouija board to talk to them alone. Karen wanted to call the newspapers but Billy told her no one would believe it.

They always had these seances in a cluster of birch and elm trees behind the house, and even when he went to college, whenever Billy came home from school, Karen was always waiting for him with her Ouija board. He could almost smell the wild onions growing around the trees as he remembered how they both would go into the woods and Karen would put a red handkerchief around her head, a carnival swami with freckles, except that she could never tie it quite right and the bandanna always drooped down over one eye. She used a toy 8-ball as a backup in case she thought the Ouija board was not working well that day.

Then everything began to fall apart two years ago. It started the day Billy quit college, dropping out in his sophomore year. Two months later, his father told Billy's mother that the marriage was finished, that he was having an affair with Risa Janovsky, one of the secretaries at Aristokraft. Billy's dad moved into an apartment in Northside a few days later.

Then in the fall, his sister, who had never been sick before, not even with measles or chicken pox, began to complain about her stomach hurting. After some tests, they learned that Karen had pancreatic cancer. Then her hair began to fall out from the chemotherapy and Billy had to fight back tears when she tied her red hankie on her bald head.

She died that December, two days after Christmas. Billy couldn't remember much from that time, except that he was either stoned or crying.

He looked at Karen's photograph for a long time. Now Billy could feel the leaves crunching under their feet as they walked in the woods with the Ouija board and the smell of her as she would sneak up on him from behind and put her hands over his eyes. He remembered holding her hand in the hospital, how she snaked it through the bed rails.

"Poor Be-oh," she kept saying his old nickname over and over as she squeezed his hand. "Poor old Be-oh."

He put the photo down, changed into jeans and a blue T-shirt and drove over to the cleaners, where he exchanged his dirty hospital whites for clean ones, bought some more cigarettes and beer at the pony keg, and drove over to Jack Reynolds' house.

Jack lived in a three-story red brick house on Maxwell Street that had been divided into apartments. All of the houses on the street were rentals now. Although the 1880's buildings looked charming from the outside, the insides had been gutted and the pegged floors covered with shag carpeting long ago.

It was strange, Billy thought as he parked on the street and walked up to the house, even if he came straight from the hospital, Jack always was there first and made it appear as if he had been there for hours, not just a few minutes. It was one of the little games the two of them played.

Billy walked up the driveway and around to the back of the house. Yes, the yellow and black Triumph motorcycle was there, its engine still ticking from the heat. The motorcycle served two purposes: it took Jack wherever he wanted to go around town, and it functioned as his doorbell. Since Jack was most certainly stoned or in the process of becoming stoned, he never heard Billy knocking, and because the real doorbell was broken, Billy did what he always did. He jumped on the motorcycle, tickled the carb until the gas came out through his fingers, and mashed down on the kick-starter.

The pistons flupped up and down.

Nothing.

Billy tried again. After four kicks, the engine caught and now Billy began counting: "One. Two. Three. Four."

Sure enough, the screen door banged open and here came Jack, barefoot and shirtless, running around the corner barefoot with his Louisville Slugger in hand.

Billy laughed and shut off the bike by placing his hand over the open carb.

"You know, Jack, I do this every day. You don't have to come out with the bat."

"Well," Jack said slowly, a little out of breath, "we live in troubled times. I can't take a chance. Why don't you knock?"

"I used to do that. You never heard me."

"Well, maybe you don't knock loud enough."

"I knock loud enough so they could hear me in Newport."

"Well, I *don't* hear you."

"That's what I said."

Billy followed him up the broken steps into the first-floor apartment, past the parlor and into the large living room, which was furnished in late-twentieth-century psychedelia. A mildewed army parachute was draped across the ceiling with a hole cut out for the overhead light, which was covered by a portrait of Guru Maharaj Ji, the fifteen year-old Perfect Master himself, sporting a Hitlerian mustache on his smooth, round, pubescent face. Posters hung from the walls: a couple locked into a purple paisley Kama Sutra position; the four photos from the Beatles' White Album; Tommie Smith and John Carlos giving the Black Power salute on the podium at the 1968 Olympics; the "Suppose They Gave a War and Nobody Came" poster; a photo of Spiro Agnew, retouched with long hair tied back with a leather headband; Steve McQueen on his motorcycle from *The Great Escape*; a Nixon Halloween mask; a couple of Playmate of the Month triptychs; a page ripped out of the Yellow Pages listing the movie theaters in town, pushpinned crookedly to the wall; "Hopper Bird," with Dennis Hopper giving the finger in *Easy Rider*; and a large piece of posterboard with dozens of photos of Jack's girlfriend, Kathryn from Nantucket. Her real name was Kathy Martz, but she told everyone she was Kathryn from Nantucket, because it sounded like such a romantic place, far better than her actual birthplace of Sandusky, Ohio.

Dust filtered through the yellowed curtains, floating past the cracked windows, and Billy could see the particles suspended in the slanted light. A thin layer of dust had settled over all of the room's furniture, a few rattan chairs, some orange crates, concrete blocks and 2X10 boards, with a broken-down couch that Jack had found over on Klotter Street. Next to the couch stood Jack's electric guitar, plugged in and always ready for its master axeman to play along with whatever song came over the radio. The guitar was his pride and joy—a dark red Gibson SG with a tremolo bar and custom humbucking pickups that Jack had installed himself. The SG was perfect for popping into the amp and playing along with the Hollies or the Beatles. Jack really only knew about five chords but he found he could play almost anything, more or less, depending on how stoned he was at the time.

Billy sat down on the couch and thumbed through an old *Rolling Stone* while Jack was in the other room getting the grass. Hunter Thompson was covering the presidential race. Billy liked reading Thompson's outrageous prose along with Ralph Steadman's behind-the-moon drawings. The opening paragraphs of the lead story in this issue caught his eye: Thompson wrote that Senator Edmund Muskie was probably an ibogaine addict.

Jack came back with a half baggie of grass and half a bottle of Barq's root beer.

"My new *Stone* came today. Guess what? It said that David Clayton-Thomas might leave Blood, Sweat and Tears. Remember when we saw them at the Fieldhouse a few years ago? It was Halloween and they all came out wearing costumes."

"Sure. But why wouldn't he leave? Probably tore his voice up trying to shout over those horns for all these years."

"Well, that would be the end for the band, then. Without Clayton-Thomas, they're nothing."

"I don't know, Jack. They'll still sound great with that horn section."

"But you got to have a good lead vocalist, and, well shit. Here, try this, man," Jack said, as he sank into the rattan chair and jammed a rubber stopper into the bottle. "I bought a new pipe last night. Check it out. It doesn't hurt your throat."

He tossed Billy a box of kitchen matches.

The stopper was connected to a small bowl. When Billy lit the grass and inhaled, the green-gray air bubbled and was pulled down through the root beer and mixed with the air already in the bottle.

Billy held the air in his lungs for a long time.

"Ah," he exhaled. "The pause that refreshes." He slipped back onto the couch.

"Yeah," Jack said. "That fucking pause."

Billy watched Jack inhale and put the bottle on the table.

Neither one said anything for a few minutes. This was good grass, dark green with lots of tops. Maybe Jack was right—it could be Jamaican after all.

"Hey, can you drink that root beer?" Billy asked.

"Do you *want* to drink it? Look at it."

The root beer had changed color. It was now kind of a moldy, brownish-green.

"No, I guess not."

"I got an eight-pack of Little Kings in the icebox if you want one."

"Maybe later."

Billy looked through the gauze curtains and watched the dust moving in the fading light of the day. He had plenty of time.

His gaze fell on the *Rolling Stone*, and as the "Fear and Loathing on the Campaign Trail" headline and Steadman's drawings melted into a black pile of lines in front of him, Billy remembered when he first met Jack two years ago.

It was May 5, 1970, one day after the Kent State shootings. Billy didn't care either way about Vietnam. As long as he had a high number in the draft lottery, the war might well have been taking place on Pluto. One of his roommates at the University of Cincinnati had copies of *Revolution for the Hell of It* and *Do It,* but Billy never read either of them.

He was a sophomore at UC, going against the wishes of his father, who really wanted him to go to Ohio State. Since Billy was the first in his family to go to college, his father insisted he go to OSU so he could brag to the other carpenters down at the union hall. His dad hated all of the local colleges; he referred to UC as the University of Communism, or Ding-Dong School, and it was one of many sore points between them.

Everything changed on May 4, when the Ohio National Guard fired into the crowd of students at Kent. When he heard the news, he knew it had to be a mistake. It was impossible; it couldn't be true. This was Kent State University, just a little college in Ohio's farm belt. It certainly was not a hotbed of radicalism—not like Berkeley or Columbia. This fact wasn't lost on his fellow students. Billy and the others in his dorm thought that if it could happen at Kent State and Jackson State, it could happen anywhere.

The night of May 4, Billy lay in bed and listened to the bonfire crackling in front of the dorm. Students had taken some wooden park benches and chairs from around the campus and stacked them up in a ragged pile. They jacked gas all over, tossed in a few newspaper torches, and the fire burst into life. Billy could hear the wood hissing and popping down in the street. He climbed out of the bunk bed and peered out the window. Hundreds of kids were gathered around the fire, their long shadows dancing around the orange flames, while other students were crouched on the sidewalk, spray-painting clenched-fist stencils onto T-shirts or drawing posters for tomorrow's demonstration. Sparks from the fire flew up past Billy's window and he could smell the burning wood.

The fire burned all night, the figures dancing around it shouting and singing. The next day was a brilliant blue, and except for the charred iron and smoking embers down on the sidewalk, it was as if nothing had happened the night before. Billy woke up and made some coffee. At that point, he still had the idea of going to class, but when he walked into the science building at 8:00 am, he was surprised to see students lying across the halls, blocking the entrance to the classrooms. He tried to step over them. One of them said in a sarcastic voice, "Go to school, machine. Go to work, machine. Go home, machine."

The words were thin silver daggers placed neatly in his heart. He turned around and left the building, following the flow of students walking toward the student union. As he turned the corner, Billy saw the grassy commons jammed with a thousand students and professors. The campus cops were in clumps of two or three around the edge of the crowd. One of the students had a bullhorn and was shouting about a protest march downtown while others off to the side were chanting and singing simultaneously in a cacophony of songs and screams. The T-shirt makers from the previous night had moved to the union bridge and were spray-painting purple fists on shirts as a line of people waited to have theirs done. Overhead, Billy saw a deep blue cloudless sky.

"Hey."

Billy turned around. It was someone from his dorm. He recognized the face.

"Look at this," he said, showing Billy a newspaper with a photograph of a young woman kneeling over a student. In the photo, the blood was flowing away from his body, making a dark pool on the concrete.

"You going to march?"

"I don't know," Billy said.

"Well, we ought to. Fucking National Guard could be here tonight, shooting *us*. Nobody is safe. Besides," he said, as he shot Billy a wolfish grin, "might be a good place to meet chicks." As he said this, he cocked his head toward a spot in front of him, where a pretty, braless coed stood, rocking gently to the acoustic guitars.

Billy thought for a few seconds. "OK."

The boy said, "My name's Jack Reynolds. I've seen you in the dorm. What's your name?"

"Billy McCord."

The new protesters shook hands seriously. A few minutes later, the march moved out, down the long hill, winding around to Straight Street, heading in the direction of downtown. The thousand protesters sang songs along the way; onlookers shouted obscenities at them. There were some speeches at the square downtown, and then the protesters moved back to campus.

The next day, a black and white photograph of the students ran in the morning paper, a snapshot taken from the vantage point of a hill overlooking the city. The photo included Billy and Jack in a group of about seventy-five other marchers. In the photo, Billy is looking off to the side, while Jack's eyes are locked onto a girl about ten feet directly in front of him. For some reason, Billy studied the photo closely. Most of the male students in the photograph had decided to grow their hair long about six months before; they were still combing it diagonally across their foreheads; and only a few had shoulder-length hair. Bushy sideburns inched down past the ears to the jawline, mustaches hung on the upper lips, and the standard 1960's black glasses and button-down shirts had not yet been exchanged for wire rims and T-shirts.

All of the girls had long, straight hair, parted in the middle, flowing past their shoulders. Two of them held up a banner that read, "Bring the troops home now." Billy remembered now, two years later, the serious look they had, and thought how it must have been a hundred years ago, before all of the dope bags, before his friends grew up, before the hospital.

"Hey, man."

Billy came back into the present. Jack was crouched in front of him.

"Hey. You all right?"

He was back in Jack's apartment again. The grimy room was thick with marijuana smoke.

"Yeah."

"What were you thinking about?"

"I was remembering the Kent State march. Seems like a long time ago."

"It *was* a long time ago. Two fucking years. And then we had all the other stuff in between. The other protests, the courthouse stuff, the march in D.C. last year."

"Sure," Billy said. "That was a big one."

"Of course, that was when we were going to *change the world*, remember? We were going to make a difference."

Jack took another pull off of the pipe.

"We drove all night to get there, remember? I brought that reel-to-reel tape deck we ran off the cigarette lighter. Man, there's nothing like driving over the Ohio into West Virginia listening to Crosby, Stills and Nash full blast at two in the morning. Remember?"

"Yeah, I do," Billy said, and went over to the refrigerator for a beer. "And I remember driving around Connecticut Avenue looking for a place to park, and then walking all the way to the Lincoln Monument."

"And the SDSers and the communists and the D.C. police, " Jack said.

Billy was warming up now.

"How about when they stopped us in Maryland at that checkpoint on Route 50? I can still smell that sweet, wet grass when we jumped out of the car at six am."

"That wasn't the only grass you were smelling, if I recall correctly," Jack said.

Billy came back to the couch and sat down. "You know what was funny? How the march gets organized and we're going along and everyone is saying the 'One, two, three, four, we don't want your fucking war,' and then this SDS guy is in front singing, '*Give me the new kind of freedom, give me the new kind of freedom, give me the new kind of freedom, it's good enough for me,*' like it was 'Give Me That Old-Time Religion.' And we're all singing and looking really purposeful, and then he changes the words. He starts singing, '*It was good for Chairman Mao, it was good for Chairman Mao, it was good for Chairman Mao and it's good enough for me.'* Did you notice how we all stopped singing?"

"I don't remember that," Jack said. He was busy refilling the root beer pipe.

"Oh yeah," Billy said. "I remember all the songs. I even remember some of the Weathermen or some other radicals singing about Kim Il Sung, the Korean premier. They were singing it to 'Maria,' that song from *West Side Story*. You know, *'Kim Il Sung, I'll never stop saying, Kim Il Sung.'* You don't remember that?"

"Jesus, man, that was two years ago. How am I supposed to remember? Do you know how many joints ago that was?"

Jack lit the pipe and the nasty-looking root beer bubbled through the Barq's bottle.

"Besides," he said, as he exhaled slowly and passed the bottle over to Billy, who waved it away, "that was the last protest march I'll ever do."

"Why?"

"Well, for one thing, we didn't find any girls."

"Oh, yeah," Billy said. "Like that's the reason we drove ten hours."

"Speak for yourself. As I recall, you were too high to drive."

"That," Billy said, "is a lie."

He took a long pull from his beer. Whenever he drank beer and smoked dope together, it made him depressed. "Listen, Jack," he said, as he picked up the pop-up Jethro Tull album. A paper cutout of the band sprang up when he opened the album cover, which prompted him to stand up himself. "I have an announcement to make."

"Yeah?"

"Yeah. Jack, I am at my nadir."

"Your what? Your Nader? Like Ralph Nader?"

"No, N-A-D-I-R. I'm serious. My nadir. The bottom. The end. Can't-get-any-worse time, bottomless free fall."

"That's just the weed talking," Jack suggested. "You'd better stop for now."

"No, it's not, Jack. I mean, here we are." Billy gestured around the room with the beer bottle. "All the marching, the songs, the protests, and nothing's changed. All we do is sit around and smoke dope, drink, watch old movies and play music."

"You and your old flicks. Well, nothing wrong with that."

"Nothing's wrong with that, if all you want is to be is a pothead," Billy said. "No, I mean it. There's got to be more than this. Like today. First I hear that Hopalong Cassidy died."

"Yeah, I know. I was there when Chuck Beck came in. I'll turn in my secret decoder ring tomorrow."

"Then that woman died on the table in Room 1. And she didn't need to. There was no reason for it. And you know what? At the same time, over in OB-GYN, a baby was being born. I know it."

"All part of the cycle of life, God's grand plan for us all, forever and ever, peace be with you, amen," Jack said, as he took another drag from the pipe. "I got the album somewhere—*Turn, Turn, Turn,* you know, the Byrds. I got that record somewhere around here.

Jack started to flip through the stack of records on the floor.

"You think too much. Anybody ever tell you that?"

"I know it," Billy said. "That's my problem. My mind's always running. It's hard to shut off."

He drained his beer and put the bottle down on the *Rolling Stone.* The condensation from the bottle left a dark ring on George McGovern's smiling face.

"I think we lost it."

"Wait a sec," Jack said. "I don't get that. Hang on." He tried to light the pipe again, but there was nothing but ashes in the bowl. "Be right back."

Jack came back in with a fresh bowl of dope and a bag of Fritos. He tossed the bag over to Billy and sat down by the stack of records again. "Is this all the food you've got?" Billy asked.

"What do you think this is, a grocery store? We can always go out for more later, when it gets dark."

"Hey, Jack, guess what. It's dark now."

He picked up the *Stone.*

"Look at this. Look at this headline from Hunter Thompson: 'McGovern Over The Hump.' Back then, even Thompson thought McGovern had a real chance to win."

"Maybe he does."

"You really think so? You're crazy."

"No, Billy, I think he can win."

"Then you've got seeds and stems for brains. He's not going to get in. You may as well accept it. Four more years. Four more years. It's Nixon and Agnew again. See, Jack, all that protesting and for nothing. The war's still going on."

Jack thought for a minute. "Well, I really believe we're going to get rid of Nixon."

"You think so?"

"Yeah, I do. I think old George has a good chance."

"That's right," Billy said. "About as much as Goldwater did. Nixon will kill McGovern in November. You've read what the polls say. McGovern has no chance."

"But everybody's going to vote for George. I'd vote for him."

"You aren't even registered."

"Well, I *would* vote for him. Anyway, there's a lot of freaks out there."

"So what?"

"So the freaks make up a lot of votes."

"No, they don't, Jack."

"Oh, yeah, I almost forgot," Jack said. "You're one of those half-empty instead of half-full guys. You look at a lid and say, 'Hey, that's only a lid.' Now I look at that same lid and say, 'Hey, man, don't worry, I got a key in the closet.' "

Flipping through the stack, Jack came across the Judy Collins album. "Aha," he said. "Here it is, your favorite." He crawled over to the amp and turned up the volume so that Judy Blue Eyes' beautiful soaring soprano could paint the room. It was one of Kathryn's records, one of the few that were tolerable to Billy and Jack.

The song was Leonard Cohen's *Suzanne*, and the words and hypnotic music never failed to take Billy along with it when he heard it.

Billy stopped fighting and let the beer and the grass wash over him. He closed his eyes as Collins' honey-smooth voice sent him gliding with her to the river.

Now Billy felt safe and did not have to think about the hospital or anything else. He let his body take over as he became conscious of the steady beating of his heart, his diaphragm rising and falling, the air going in and out of his lungs, even the small capillaries expanding and contracting, taking over now, with his mind shutting down. It was a comfort to feel the lungs working whether he wanted them to or not, and not thinking; not worrying; not dealing with anything. There was really nothing at all to worry about, nothing to be concerned over. *Just lie there,* all the parts of his body said. *Be still. Let the rest of us take over for awhile. We know what we're doing.*

And Billy let them.

*

When Billy woke up, the record was clicking on the turntable. Jack was over in the rattan chair, a copy of *Siddhartha* cradled in his lap.

Billy walked into the kitchen and flipped on the light switch. The floor and the countertops were a mass of cockroaches and silverfish, scattering in all directions. He was used to this. He could usually count up to thirty creatures on the table alone. It was the ones he couldn't really see that bothered him, the ones that hid in the cupboards. They would stick their antennas out and wave them derisively in a triumphant display of species superiority every time he came in and snapped on the light. He thought their arrogant behavior was a slap in the face to *homo sapiens* everywhere.

He knew that the roaches especially disgusted Kathryn from Nantucket, Jack's girlfriend, who had tried everything she could think of to exterminate them. She swept and treated the floor with D-con, emptied all the cabinets and moved the refrigerator out, and bought some powerful DDT spray from the hardware store, which made Jack green for a few hours because he refused to leave the apartment when she sprayed. The roaches were back the next day. She even paid $40 to have a Terminex man come; but the roaches only disappeared for a week and then returned.

The mice behind the pantry wall didn't behave like the roaches and silverfish; they saved their appearances for special occasions, like when Kathryn came in at three or four in the morning for a glass of water. Jack said you could hear her screams all the way down on Ludlow Avenue.

Now Billy stood in the kitchen and watched the waving roach antennas. Kathryn would be home at any minute, and he really wanted to leave before she showed up. Ever since she stopped doing drugs, she was convinced that Jack's friends were the main reason he was still smoking, which was obviously untrue, because Jack had been one of the biggest potheads in the Western Hemisphere long before he met Billy. She hated all of Jack's friends but for some reason, she hated Billy the most, probably because he was at the apartment almost every day.

A quick movement caught Billy's eye. It was a small brown mouse, feeling its way with its whiskers along the baseboard. He had an idea of catching it and putting it in a jar for Kathryn from Nantucket, but he was too slow. The mouse had already disappeared under the sink.

He really had to leave. Billy wanted to make sure that he was gone before she returned.

Then Billy heard her key click into the lock. He couldn't leave through the front door undetected, but he could go out through the back. Silently, Billy opened the back door and crept down the creaky wooden steps and around the old house to the street, into his car, and back to his apartment. He didn't have to stick around to figure out what was going to happen next.

Kathryn from Nantucket put her bag of groceries on the kitchen table and went into the darkened living room, the air lying heavy with the sickly sweet smell of marijuana. She walked over to the stereo and switched off the turntable, watching Jack sleep in the chair. She watched his chest rise and fall for a long time, studying his lips as they moved in the darkness.

Then she came over to him and gently touched his shoulder.

"Jack," she said. "Come on. It's time for bed."

Jack didn't move.

She rubbed his shoulder a little bit more. "Jack, honey."

He stirred a little.

"Jack. Come on. Get up, sweetheart," she said in her best kindergarten teacher voice. "You're stoned again."

After a few more seconds of prodding, Jack rolled over and looked at the Mickey Mouse clock. 9:12. He stretched out on the couch and stumbled to his feet.

"Hi, Kat."

"Hi yourself. Are you hungry, babe?"

"No."

"Let me help you to the bed then."

She put her arm around his shoulders and helped him into the bedroom and he dropped onto the double bed.

She took off his boots and began to unbuckle his belt.

"You know what happened today?" she said as she slid her hand down inside his jeans.

"No, what?"

"Sally lost her wallet at the grocery store and now she has to get a new driver's license."

Jack closed his eyes again and put his hand on her blouse. He began to unbutton it slowly.

"Who's Sally?"

"You know, Sally. My sister."

She massaged him a little longer, slipping her hand down under his shorts.

"Where's Westy?" she said in a low voice, caressing him. "Where's the general? We can't start without the general."

"Westmoreland? He's around here somewhere," Jack said.

"Maybe he's over in 'Nam reviewing the troops. I'm sure I can bring him back. Oh, wait a minute," she said with a smile. "*Here* he is. At attention."

Jack finished unbuttoning her blouse. He opened his eyes a little to see if she was wearing her black brassiere and smiled slightly, pleased that she was.

She stood up and unbuttoned her jeans and slid them down her thighs. He loved the way the black bikini panties hugged her hips. Then she went over to the curtains and closed them slowly.

Kathryn slid into bed. She felt him under the covers.

"Seems to me the general's on the parade grounds already."

"Come here," he said, squeezing her against him. "Time for your medal."

The rickety bed squeaked for a few minutes and then it was over.

Kathryn stood up and put on her bathrobe.

"I love you, Jack Reynolds," she said softly, but Jack was already asleep.

She looked at him for a long time. The root beer pipe was on the floor next to his hand, on top of a pile of dirty wash, a couple of plates, and an empty carton of beer bottles.

Then she went into the kitchen to put away the groceries before they went bad. "Omm," she whispered, as she picked up some frozen peaches. "Ommmmm . . . . "

*

That night, over in his apartment, Billy had a dream in color, which happened whenever he fell asleep stoned. He dreamed he was in a protest march, holding some bread, walking along, when a man on a white horse rode up to the front of the line. It was William Boyd, dressed up in his Hopalong Cassidy outfit. He was the march leader. Around him, Billy's fellow protestors were yelling, "One, two, three, four, we don't want your fucking war."

Hopalong flinched. The cowboy clearly didn't like the obscenity.

"Don't swear, children," he kept saying. "Don't swear. Please don't swear, oh my beautiful children."

Billy and the other marchers followed Hoppy down around a corner. Then Billy watched as Hopalong Cassidy and the marchers in front of him turned into a red brick wall that grew higher and higher. He could see the bodies changing into cracked bricks that climbed up to heaven.

He woke up sweating. Rolling over, he looked at the clock.

6:25.

Time for work.

CHAPTER 5

Arcola Brown had filled Billy's dance card with long, complicated cases that day, starting with the Whipple procedure, which could easily go four to six hours, since parts of the pancreas, the duodenum, the bile duct, the gallbladder, and in this particular case, a piece of the stomach are removed. This one ran the full six. Standing for six hours wasn't too hard, once your body became used to it. It was simply a matter of shifting weight from one foot to the other, although leaning on the patient was frowned on, since clots could develop.

After a few joints and a thoracotomy, Billy clocked out, lit a cigarette and walked through the OR lobby, past the family waiting room and the bank of elevators, down the stairs to the main hospital lobby. He liked looking at the six straggly ginkgo trees outside, their fan-shaped leaves waving against the car exhaust. Over his head, a sparrow was settling into her nest in the "Y" on the FREY MEMORIAL marble lettering while in the distance he could hear an ambulance making its way up the long snaky road to Pill Hill.

As he walked out to the parking lot, he noticed that although it was only mid-September, already some of the leaves were blowing around the lot, mixing in with the discarded newspaper sheets and collecting in small dirty piles against the chain-link fence. Now he could feel the first cold breath of fall in the air, bringing with it the coming threat of winter. The approach of fall was usually cheering to him, but not this year, not now.

He drove over to the west side and turned onto Harrison Avenue, then calumped the car over the double set of railroad tracks and down McDougald Street, right into the driveway at McDougald and Norman. He pulled behind the copper-colored

Cougar and snapped off his ignition. Good, he thought. Carol was home. The car ticked as the iron cooled down and Billy sat there for a minute. He took a deep breath and climbed out.

Billy was always surprised at how quickly someone at Carol's house came to the door when he rang the bell. It was never more than about five seconds, as if they were waiting in the alcove, peeping through the lace curtains, watching traffic go by, hoping that one of the cars would turn in to their driveway and someone would jump out and visit them.

Carol flung open the door and smiled without showing her teeth, which were a little crooked.

"Hi, Billy," she whispered, and gave him a peck on the ear.

"Ow. Hey, not so hard."

"Sorry. Did you eat yet?"

"No."

"Well, come in," she said.

Everything was quiet in the house because Carol's father worked third shift at the machine tool plant and slept for most of the day. Everyone was afraid to wake him up, so at meal times, the family spoke in soft tones around the table, passing the serving dishes noiselessly, and trying hard not to click the silverware on the plates. After the dinner meal was through, they switched on the TV and watched the news with the volume barely on, so low that Billy couldn't hear anything. He had to be content to watch Walter Cronkite mouth the words, the old newsman as serious as a mortician. Everything about the house was muffled; even when Billy and Carol made love up in the attic, they were as quiet as possible. She liked it best when they made love in her house; it gave her a secret thrill.

Billy sank into the broken-down flowered-pattern couch, as Carol went into the kitchen to set an extra plate and silverware. He watched her walk away and thought how much she had changed in the two years they had been together. He met her when she was a volunteer at Frey, the first month he was on the job. She worked part-time at the hospital, taking the book cart around and occasionally moving discharged patients out to their cars. Billy had noticed her immediately because she was so tall, kind of willowy-looking, with black hair and a pale complexion. When he first met her, she dressed as if she was still in high school, dark skirts, light colored blouses and penny loafers.

Billy considered it a triumph of some sort that she now wore bell-bottoms and T-shirts, although he couldn't get her to lose her bra on a permanent basis. And he was pleased that Carol's musical preferences had also evolved; especially since she now shared his taste for the women troubadours, Judy Collins, Buffy St. Marie, and a few new ones that she had just discovered, Carole King and Carly Simon.

Whatever shyness she had before was long gone. Now he always felt that she was chasing him somehow.

Carol came back and flounced down on the couch, banging into him as she kissed him on the cheek.

"So how's my darling Billy?"

"Good," he whispered back.

"How did it go at work this week?"

"Great. I got into trouble with one of the docs over a case, and now he's got it in for me."

"You look tired. You want a beer?"

"Sure."

She popped up and disappeared into the kitchen, coming back in a minute with a Tall Boy. She cupped her hand of the top of the can so that when she opened it, the can made a small sisssss.

"You know," he said, "you should try to be more quiet."

"I am being quiet."

"I was kidding."

"Listen, Billy, you know after supper we can take a walk. By the time we come back, everyone will be asleep. If you want, we can go upstairs."

"Why do we always have to make love here? We could go back to my apartment. It's hard to do it up there when you have to be so quiet."

"I don't want to go all the way back to Clifton. I was at school there all day. Besides, I like loving you here. I really do, especially when we have to be quiet. It excites me. It seems so . . . sinful."

She slid closer to him on the couch.

Billy took a long pull on the Schlitz.

"Maybe we could go out later," Carol said. "We could see a movie."

"Sure."

He turned so he could get a better look at her. She had filled out a little, still somewhat on the tall side, but nicely put together with long legs and small firm breasts, and that pale complexion which he always loved in women.

"I saw that the Alpha is showing *Five Easy Pieces*. Maybe we could go to that."

He knew that Carol had gone through the paper looking at movies, screening out the ones she thought he wouldn't like.

"Yeah?" She had his interest.

"We might make the nine-thirty show."

"I don't know. I'm tired."

"Well, if you want, we can just stay here," Carol said, and snuggled closer to him.

Carol's mother made her spaghetti every Friday. It was Billy's best meal of the week. Billy, Carol and her mother ate with very little noise and no conversation. All three watched Walter Cronkite as he mouthed the words. There was some footage from Vietnam, a few snippets of Nixon and McGovern smiling and waving, and a cruise ship being towed into port. After a short baseball story of some sort—Billy guessed it was because the pennant races were tightening up for the World Series next month—Cronkite stopped talking and the CBS eye appeared.

Carol went over and clicked off the TV.

"Did you get enough to eat, Billy?" her mother asked.

"Yes, thanks, Mrs. Fears."

He helped Carol clear off the table and wash the dishes. Her mother put the food back in the refrigerator, after carefully wrapping each item in Saran Wrap. She picked up a sponge and wiped off the kitchen table, washed her hands, and joined Billy and Carol on the front porch. They could speak in regular tones outside without disturbing Carol's father.

As always, Mrs. Fears frowned when Billy lit a cigarette.

"Does your mother know you smoke, Billy?"

"Yes."

"Well, I wish you wouldn't. It's a terrible habit."

"I know it is."

"Then why do you smoke?"

"I guess it helps me relax."

"I saw an article in *Time* magazine last week that said that each time you smoke a cigarette, you lose fourteen minutes of your life."

"Mrs. Fears, if that's true, I'm only going to live to twenty-eight."

"Billy, don't *say* that." Carol said.

"All right. That's an exaggeration. I'll probably crack thirty; thirty-five for sure."

The three of them watched the traffic filter past on Norman Avenue. A black Mustang convertible with no muffler rumbled past.

"Carol's brother Lenny wrote us a letter," Mrs. Fears said, and pulled a folded air mail envelope from her dress pocket.

"Really? Is he killing any gooks yet, Mrs. Fears?"

She ignored him.

"He's still at Quantico. Don't you want to hear what he has to say?"

"Sure."

Mrs. Fears unfolded the letter, which was printed in large block letters with a pencil. The paper was creased from having been read several times.

"Dear Family," Mrs. Fears read out loud, raising her voice over the traffic, "How are you? I am fine. The weather here is good. Do you miss me? I miss you all. Except for Dad. Ha Ha."

Mrs. Fears held the letter up closer to her eyes.

"Last week we had our first leave, and some of us drove down to Charlottesville and saw Jefferson's house. Monticello, that is. It was neat. Everyone at the camp has been doing maneuvers. I got a sharpshooter's medal last week. We are all excited about going over to Vietnam. Hope the war doesn't end before we get there.

"Tell Dad I'm sorry that I ran off and joined the Marines without telling him. I thought it was the best thing that I could do, and that he would be proud of me. Hope he can come down for the ceremonies next month when we get out of boot camp.

"How is Carol, my favorite sister? Well, I hear taps. It must be ten o'clock. We have a big day tomorrow. Write soon, Lenny.

"Oh, and P.S. Don't worry about me. I am doing fine."

Mrs. Fears folded the letter and put it in the pocket of her dress. She wiped away a stray tear and went back into the house, making sure the screen door didn't bang shut behind her.

Billy and Carol looked out at the traffic for a long time without saying anything.

"It wasn't right for you to say that, Billy," Carol said.

"What did I say?"

"About him killing Vietnamese."

"I didn't say Vietnamese. I said gooks."

"Well, that was rude. I'm sure you hurt Mother's feelings."

"I'm sure I didn't."

"You know, Billy, not everyone feels the same way you do about the war."

"Look, let's not get on that Ferris wheel again."

He took another drink.

"Anyway, your brother's just dumb enough to get killed over there."

"Don't say that about Lenny. You can't get down on him. He just wants to do what's right."

"All of us want to do what's right, " Billy said, and finished his beer.

Carol moved away from him on the glider.

"What are you mad about? Why are you so angry all of the time?"

"Not all of the time, sugar beet," Billy said. "Not when I'm stoned or drunk. I'm not angry then."

He clinked the empty beer can against the lawn chair leg.

"Hey, fish out another one of these for me, could you?"

"Why not wait awhile?"

"No, I feel like another beer now. I really feel like about six or twelve beers. It's eight o'clock on a Friday night."

Carol came back with another Schlitz. "Listen, Billy. Promise me, Billy, you won't act like you did the last Sunday."

"Was I acting? How did I act? I don't remember."

"You know, you tried to pick a fight with Dad."

"I like your dad, but he insulted my intelligence."

"How did he do that?"

"He said, 'Why would anyone be against the war?' "

"So? He's entitled to his opinion."

"Yeah, I guess so. Let's face it. He just doesn't like me."

"Do you think he knows about us?"

"Of course he doesn't know about us."

She snuggled up against him on the glider and slid her hand up under his shirt. She was always feeling sexy when Billy was thinking about something else.

Carol rubbed Billy's chest and then moved her hand down to his belt.

"Shouldn't you check and see what's going on inside first?"

She gave a mock sigh and went inside for a few minutes.

"It's all right. Mom's watching TV in her room. She won't come out until bedtime."

She took Billy's hand and led him up the first floor stairs to the second floor and then up the creaky wood stairway to the attic.

"I . . . want . . . you . . . to . . . come . . . over . . . here," she said, and pulled Billy closer. She unbuttoned his shirt and then slipped off her blouse.

"Hey, you took off your bra," Billy murmured.

"Oops. Now I wonder where it went," Carol said.

She unbuckled his belt and ran her hands inside his pants.

"Wait a minute. Shouldn't we, I mean, I have a rubber."

"I'm on the pill now, remember? It's OK."

They made love on the old couch, right next to the large painting of Jesus that used to hang in the dining room.

The couch squeaked and groaned.

"Shh. Not so loud, Billy."

Billy didn't hear her. He closed his eyes and let the sensations come over him.

Now he was there.

"Billy. Shh. Oh. Billy," she whispered.

They came together. Everything went away as he had the calm feeling of sailing through a sea of purple mountains and then it was over and he lifted himself off of her, rolling gently onto the floor.

After a few minutes, he stood up. She opened her eyes and smiled back at him.

"How are you doing?"

"Well, I'm fine. Just fine. Was it all right for you, Billy?"

"Yes."

"Do you know where my panties went?"

"I don't know, but they couldn't have gone too far. I'll tell you what," Billy said. He was feeling pretty good now. "We'll find them, track them down and kill them."

Carol stood up. Her body was pale in the strips of moonlight filtering in through the window slats. She reminded Billy of the ginkgos in front of Frey that always bent slightly in the wind.

She seemed to read his mind and began dancing slowing in the light, her body moving in and out of the shadows.

"Come back here," he said and tossed her down playfully on the bed.

"My Billy," she said, and pulled him against her body.

They fell asleep in each other's arms on the couch.

After awhile, Carol woke up. She placed her hand gently on his neck and rubbed his hair.

When he opened his eyes, she was smiling at him.

"Listen, Billy, we have to talk."

"I hate it when you use four-letter words."

She giggled.

"Anyway, what do you want to talk about?"

"Oh, things. Have you thought about it any?"

"Thought about what?"

"You know, about . . . about us."

"Sure. I think about us every hour of the day."

"Please don't be sarcastic, Billy."

"I'm not. I do."

"And?"

"Well, I . . ."

"Well, what?"

"I think we still have a ways to go."

She pushed him away a little bit and began getting dressed.

"What do you mean, 'a ways to go'?"

"A ways to go. Before we get serious."

"I thought we were serious. I'm serious."

"You're always serious. You were born serious."

"Well, I can't help it."

"You act as if you have some kind of timeline in your head. 'I want to married at twenty-three, have my kids by the time I'm thirty, and get a condominium when I'm sixty-five.' I can't think like that. I don't even know what I'm going to do next week."

"Well," Carol said as she finished getting dressed, "we've been going together for two years; you'd think you'd be able to make up your mind about it. And besides," she said firmly, "we do love each other, don't we?"

Billy hesitated for a moment.

"You do love me, don't you?" she persisted.

"Yes, Mother. But let's not talk about it right now. Let's not think about that."

"Why not?"

"I just get tired of making the effort."

"Oh, so now you're saying it's an effort when we're together?'

"Yeah, as a matter of fact, sometimes. It is for me. I can't speak for you."

"Well, that's a fine note. Here," she said, and threw him his T-shirt, "you better get dressed." She flounced away from him in a move he thought he'd seen in an old Bette Davis movie. "If that's how you feel, you can go home."

Billy finished dressing, catching his belt buckle so it wouldn't make any noise. He picked up his shoes, crept down the back stairs and let himself out.

It was 9:00 pm. The grass outside was all dewy and wet as he sat on the back porch and put his shoes on. He wondered what Jack was doing. He thought about driving all the way over to Jack's place, but he hated coming into a party when everyone else was already stoned and he'd have to play catch-up.

He sat on the back steps for a few minutes and listened to the crickets. He could see the fireflies fluttering in the soft pale glow of the moon, scattering their bodies above the grass, the males sending their special mating messages to the females laying low in the pine needles. Far off somewhere, he could hear an owl, or maybe a mourning dove, woo-wooing at something, while someone with no muffler accelerated down the hill.

The trouble with Carol Fears, he thought. Ah, what was the trouble? The trouble was that he didn't love her, or didn't care enough for her to go through a lifetime of marriage. He liked her enough, but only for a few hours at a time, and then she began to grind away at him, a welterweight working his body, trying to get in. *He* didn't even know what was inside of him, so how was someone else supposed to find out?

Just don't think about it. Don't think about the predictable two-lane as life meandered along, through marriage, children, old age and death. Thinking about it was a complete waste of time.

He looked at his watch.

9:20.

Whatever was happening over at Jack's apartment would be in full swing now. There would be beer, drugs, possibly some girls and most of all there would be no goddamn thinking. Now it was too late tonight. They would all be too far along to stop and notice his feeble attempts to catch up. He just couldn't do it.

Billy got into his car and sat with the windows open for a few minutes. The din of the crickets was deafening tonight. He lit one last cigarette and drove back down into the dirty, dark city, back to where he belonged.

CHAPTER 6

Billy didn't wake up until about eleven-thirty the next morning. He flipped on his radio and sat in his one good chair. The disk jockeys on his favorite FM station made an effort to match the music with the mood. Just now they were playing "Come Saturday Morning" from a movie called *The Sterile Cuckoo*. The music relaxed him as he shaved and put on his T-shirt and bell-bottoms. Billy made some coffee and poured it into an old thermos he'd bought at a garage sale. He stood at the doorway, trying to think if he needed anything else. Oh, yes. Breakfast. He reached into the refrigerator and grabbed half a loaf of bread. Jack Reynolds never had much food.

He parked on Jack's street and walked around back to the motorcycle. Two kicks, three kicks, and then the engine caught, idling roughly. Billy revved the bike for a few seconds until Jack appeared as usual, baseball bat in hand. He let Billy in and Billy saw that the apartment was trashed. There were beer and wine bottles all over the place, scattered marijuana roaches, alligator clips, empty baggies, records on the floor, turntable still spinning, and stale cigarette smoke hanging in the air, clinging to the cheap rattan furniture.

"Jesus, Jack. Some party."

"I didn't have a party last night."

"You mean all this crap is from you?"

"No."

"So what happened?"

"Don't rush me. It's not good to rush a man."

Jack settled back into his chair.

"Kat went out to look at a chair over on Bates Avenue. I'm just sitting here when three of the cute chicks—you know, Wendy, Nancy and Pam, the ones who work over in Division H, came by. They know I have weed. One thing leads to another and the next thing I know we're all four of us getting it on. Check it—first I'm putting the Hollies on the turntable, and the next thing I know I'm in a *menage a diez y siete.*"

"Really?"

"Yeah, no shit. It was a little weird. It reminded me of those art slides we saw at college. You know, the ones by Hieronymus Bosch, with the writhing bodies all around. Then the weirdest thing happens."

"Kathryn comes back?"

"No. I sell them a couple of lids—this really good shit I just got yesterday—and they get dressed and leave. Just like that."

"Just like that?"

"Just like that," Jack said, as he plugged in his electric guitar and snapped on the amplifier.

"What else?"

"That was pretty much it. Some thrills, some spills, and a bunch of pills."

Jack's face brightened up. He had already moved on. "Hey, listen to this record I bought. It's by the Hollies."

He dropped the needle on the record and accidentally skated it across the tracks, making a deep scratch in the grooves.

"Whoops. Sorry. Now listen. I almost got the guitar track down from this one cut, *Long Cool Woman in a Black Dress.*"

He began to play along with Tony Hicks, the Hollies' guitarist, but in a different key, a different tempo and different notes. The only thing the two had in common was that they were both plucking sounds out of a six-stringed amplified instrument. Picking the strings, singing along, rocking back and forth, Jack looked up to see if Billy had noticed how well he was playing.

Billy smiled back. If nothing else, he thought, you had to appreciate Jack's enthusiasm. In his own mind, Jack sounded better than Clapton, Hendrix and Jeff Beck put together.

Jack finished up the song at about the same time that the tune ended. He wasn't a very good guitarist.

"Great song, Jack. What's the name of the album?"

Jack was very pleased.

"*Distant Light.*"

"I'll have to check it out. Maybe I'll go over to the record store this weekend. I think they're having a sale right now."

"Yeah, but it's never on the new records. It's always on the Glenn Yarbrough and Mitch Miller stuff," Jack said.

"Hey, Jack, you want to see a movie tonight? Carol and I wanted to go yesterday, but it didn't happen. It's called *Five Easy Pieces.*

"No, I'll pass. I'd rather stay right here with my eight friends," Jack said, pointing over to the Little Kings.

Billy stood up and looked around.

"You never want to do anything anymore. All you want to do is sit around and get stoned or drunk."

"So what?"

"So, it's pretty damn boring, that's all."

Jack sat up and switched off the amp.

"Well, what do you want to do?"

"Anything. Anything at all."

"Want to rob a King Kwik?"

"Very funny, Jack. You're a funny man."

"OK, then. Let's hear what you got."

"That's the trouble. I don't have any ideas." Billy watched the dust moving around the room. "I need to get out of here. I need to go away for awhile."

"Why not?" Jack asked. "That's a good idea. Go far away. Go out west somewhere. Can you imagine us in Colorado? In the mountains? We could drink a little Coors, smoke some mellow weed, be high all the time."

"No."

"Why not?"

"It's too crowded there. Everybody will have the same idea we have."

"All right," Jack said, as he put his guitar down. "Just exactly what do you have in mind?"

"I'm thinking about it."

"Take your time."

Jack stood up and went into the kitchen for a beer.

"All I know is that it would have to be something far away from this dumpy town," Billy said, loud enough for Jack to hear in the other room.

"How about Dayton?"

"Funny guy. No, I'm serious, Jack."

"I can see that."

"I want to get away from here, from all the shit, far away, someplace where I can start all over again. I'm tired of this place, I'm tired of you, and most of all I'm tired of Billy McCord."

"I'm sick of him, too. What a dipshit."

They both thought for a few minutes.

"How about this?" Jack asked. "We could go to Alaska."

"What?"

"Think about it," Jack said, warming up to the idea. "You get a Norton to go along with my Triumph, we truck up there like Fonda and Hopper, looking for dope, screwing Eskimo women, shooting moose, building igloos."

"I never even thought about Alaska," Billy said, half to himself. "I wonder what it's like?"

"Hey, use your imagination. It's got to be a damn sight better than this town."

"Jack, that's a pretty good idea."

"You're goddamned right it is," Jack said. "I'm full of good ideas."

"I'll have to think about that," Billy said. "Alaska?"

"Alaska. That's right."

Billy stood up.

"Hey, where are you going?"

"Errands."

"You sure you don't want a beer?"

"Nope."

"Well, the hell with you," Jack said. "I don't need you. I don't need anybody—except for my little green friends here." He clinked the bottles together.

"I'll see you at the butcher shop on Monday," Billy said.

He went to the door and turned around.

"Alaska."

"Alaska," Jack answered.

*

The first hard rain of September came on Sunday morning. As the drops ran down the window, Billy made himself some toast and switched on his favorite Sunday morning entertainment, Ronnie G. Lord, the lacquer-haired evangelist who had been on TV as long as he could remember. Ronnie—his face was so familiar that Billy thought of him as a first-name acquaintance—was on every Sunday at 10:00 am, always talking about building Tomorrow's Palace of God, a great glass and stone structure in some field around Akron, a place Ronnie hoped would evolve into some cornfield Mecca. It was always amusing to listen to Ronnie, who shouted out Biblical parables and prophecies while never forgetting to weave in the impassioned request for everyone who was watching to send a small weekly contribution to the Tomorrow's Palace of God building fund. Billy suspected that these additions to the Palace were built during the day, and then Ronnie himself would sneak back to the site at night and knock the dried mortar out, pitching the bricks all around, so that the project would never be finished.

Sundays usually brought Billy the traditional kicked-in-the-face feeling that accompanies large amounts of beer intermingled with grass. The shock of waking up again, wondering for that millisecond exactly where he was, room spinning counter-clockwise slightly, swinging the legs over and gratefully finding the floor; lurching over to the refrigerator to see if there was anything decent to eat, fumbling for some instant coffee, rinsing out the mug and flopping on the couch, snapping on the TV in the same motion—these were part of his Sunday morning ritual. But this Sunday, as he watched Ronnie roll into the sermon of the week, was different. He felt more clear-headed than he had in months— Jack's idea about going to Alaska gave him some hope.

He liked mulling it over; the idea of going to Alaska seemed so pure and simple on its own that it needed no embellishment from his mind, although he couldn't help himself. He could become a new person, he could refinish his soul the way a woodworker would sand and stain a stubborn piece of wood; he could start over and leave the whole sad mess that was his life far, far, behind. There would be no more grass, no more beer, no more Carol, no more arrogant surgeons, and no more sick and dying patients.

It was funny, he thought. The night before he had no direction at all, but now he had his own compass, pointing to the northwest. He'd wait it out until the long, brutal winter was over and leave.

As he watched Ronnie G. Lord swing into the home stretch of the Sunday sermon, Billy smiled. He watched patiently until the preacher finished and then snapped off the television. The room filled with wonderful silence, and then Billy heard birds singing outside his window. It sounded like cardinals and blue jays. Even though it was still drizzling, Billy couldn't remember a more beautiful morning.

CHAPTER 7

Alaska.

The three syllables now became a mantra, pushing everything else out of his mind. He found that by saying it to himself, over and over, Billy could hear his boots crunching through permafrost somewhere above the Arctic Circle, or stepping over twigs in some primordial forest. He could see Eskimos, their leathery faces pulled taut by ten thousand years of sun and snow; he could see unnamed mountains silently marching off to the horizon and rivers flowing out from some hidden source.

Alaska. Billy repeated the word to himself all day throughout the different surgical procedures; he said it out loud once in the morning when he woke up and again at night as he lay in bed; he even thought it in the middle of conversations; he loved the way the word was always in his mind. He considered going to the library and finding out more about the land, but part of him felt that reading about it would somehow spoil the idea. Billy believed it was better to go and experience it, roll the dice and see what the spots showed.

Billy was afraid to tell anyone else about it, as if that would spoil it somehow. The only person he talked to about Alaska was Jack Reynolds, who had come up with the idea four months ago.

When Billy brought up the subject between puffs on a joint, Jack didn't hesitate. "Go to Alaska? Sure, why the hell not?"

He gave Billy a sloppy grin. "When do we pack the dogsled?"

"No, Jack, I'm serious. Don't you remember? The whole thing was your idea."

"My idea? Really?"

Jack paused for a moment, trying to focus. Then his face broke into a grin again.

"Oh, yeah. Alaska. I hear they grow great dope up there. I read something about it once. Did you know that the sun is out twenty-four hours a day in the summer? Can you imagine the THC content in those buds? It'd have to be goddamn incredible."

"No," Billy replied in a tone of exaggerated patience as if he were talking to a child. "We wouldn't be going up there for the dope."

"We wouldn't? Well, if not for the weed, then why? Why go there at all? Is there a boatload of horny Eskimo babes waiting for us near the Arctic Circle?"

"No," Billy said. He stood up.

"No twenty-foot high dope plants. No women. No gold. No reason except one: I have to go."

"Oh, now *that's* real deep," Jack said.

Billy reached for his jacket.

"See you around."

"Well, go ahead, then. Go up there and freeze your ass off. See if I care."

Billy and Jack never talked much after that. They saw each other in the locker room every day and sometimes they would be assigned to the same chest case or D & C, working together, gowned elbow to gowned elbow, but they stopped getting together after work.

Billy had opened up a savings account at his bank. He was clearing about $80 a week, but was able to put some away every paycheck by cutting down on the beer and cigarettes. He began a checklist in the back of his new bank account booklet, writing all of the clothes he would need.

The ironclad days passed by slowly. Billy dreaded Christmas, the third one since his sister Karen had died. He spent most of Christmas morning at the old house with his mother whose face was red and teary all of the time now. She didn't bother to get dressed and spent the time sitting at the kitchen table in her faded pink bathrobe, drinking coffee and looking out the window at the birch trees. At lunchtime, his mother made a couple of ham sandwiches and they ate them silently, Billy studiously avoiding looking at Karen's favorite kitchen chair.

He finished his sandwich and kissed his mother on the forehead.

"Merry Christmas, Mom."

"Yes, Merry Christmas," she said. She was gazing through the window at the trees.

"I like to look out at the woods. Do you know why?"

"No."

"Because that's where you and Karen used to play. I can still see you two with the Ouija board out there. Remember?"

"Sure I do."

She lit a cigarette. Neither one spoke for a few minutes.

"Billy boy, do you want to know where your father is?"

"Not particularly. Why?"

"I thought you might want to say hello."

"I've got nothing to say to him."

"You used to be close."

"Oh, yeah. We were close once, back when I was eleven. I bet my baseball glove is still upstairs. Maybe I could look him up and we could play catch. Just like the old days."

She began to cry and he was sorry as soon as he said it. He stood up.

"Look, I have to go now. Bye, Mom. I'll see you around."

"Bye, son. Take care of yourself. Your mother loves you."

"I know."

He felt vaguely sick to his stomach.

Billy kissed her on top of her forehead, gave her a hug and left.

December faded into January. Richard Nixon was sworn in, with inauguration ceremonies as pompous as an English king's coronation. Then on February 20, the same day that the baseball teams began spring training in Florida and Arizona, Billy saw a robin in one of the ginkgo trees. A few days later, the long winter gave up, the jet stream dipped from the south back to the north, trapping the cold air in Canada, and the first crocuses began pushing up through the hard ground. Then the jays and cardinals were back as well as all the other birds of spring, flying all around the sky with a maniacal energy. The buds of the ginkgo trees in front of Frey Memorial popped out suddenly on April 2; Billy noticed the date because he was counting down the days till his departure.

He had decided that April 7 would be his last day at the hospital. Billy cleaned out his apartment and gave away the few pieces of furniture he had. His list of things to do dropped from fourteen things to twelve to nine, seven, four, and two.

Then there was just one left—Carol Fears.

Billy had saved her for his last chore. He'd cross her off the list after his last shift at Frey.

Cutting sutures, holding retractors and clamps, taking patients to Recovery, kidding with the Central Supply women, Billy sleepwalked through the last five days, the long surgical procedures and short cases flying past him in a blur.

He realized there was only one person whom he would miss at Frey—Craig Maxwell. The retarded black man still came in every day at 6:50 am with Billy's medium scrubs, which were still hot from the big dryers down in CSR. Billy tossed him the mouthwash bottles, and Craig happily cracked open the plastic caps and chugged the yellow Cepacol down.

"Any word on the SATHO man, Craig?"

"Nope," Craig said, wiping his mouth. "I'm still looking."

"Me, too," Billy said.

And then it was Friday. At lunch, Billy pulled all his money from the bank, cleaned out his car, and smoked his last cigarette outside of the hospital gates, watching the ginkgo trees waving in the breeze. His gaze shifted from the trees up to the granite front entrance and the words FREY MEMORIAL HOSPITAL and he was pleased to see that the sparrows were all in the O's again, their nests looking better than ever.

Billy stubbed out his cigarette and crossed Burnet. He felt wonderful; everything was humming along, except that he hadn't counted on Jonny Barlow on Ward Two. He couldn't have seen that one coming.

The problem began that afternoon. Billy was sitting in the locker room, smoking on his break, when Arcola banged on the door. She stuck her head inside.

"You free for transport?"

"Sure," Billy said. He put out his cigarette and picked up the patient tag. "J. Barlow. Ward 2." Rolling out the gurney—it was the old one with the left front squeaking wheel—taking the elevator down to the wards, hot even in April, a thought occurred to him that this would be the last patient he would take to surgery.

Down at the station, the nurses were all watching *All My Children*, at least all of them except for Pat Mitchell. She was a good nurse, tall, thin and proper. Pat reminded Billy of the nun from the *Madeline* books.

When he arrived, Pat was standing alone at the station, looking over the charts.

"Hi, McCord." She always called everyone by his or her last name.

"Hi, Pat. Is the patient all ready?"

"Uh, well, he's pre-opped and everything, but he doesn't want to go."

"He doesn't want to go?"

"Nope," she said, and pulled the patient's chart, tossing it on the shelf under the gurney.

"Go on back. Second ward, third bed on the right. Good luck."

Billy wheeled the gurney back through the big double doors. The same old sour smell hit him as he passed the eight patients in the first room, all of them elderly men, conversation ceasing as he went by, their eyes now silently watching him as the gurney squeaked by.

Billy stopped at the third bed, right-hand side. He looked at the ID sticker pasted on the battered white crank bed, the only ones left in the hospital. He glanced up at the patient in the bed. The chart stated that Jonny Barlow was eighty-nine years old, but he looked at least ten years older than that. He was a gaunt little man, just over five feet tall and probably weighed 110 pounds at most, with a ring of white hair. His reddened eyes were focused on Billy, watching his every move.

The patient was crouched at the head of the bed, legs drawn up, and he was clutching what looked like a large leather belt.

"Hi, Mr. Barlow," Billy said kindly. "I'm here to take you."

"I ain't going. I told them. I ain't going. Not unless I take my money with me."

Jonny Barlow pulled himself up higher in the bed for emphasis. *"And you ain't taking me."*

"Look, you have to go to surgery," Billy said in a soft voice. "I've got to . . ."

"No. Not unless I take my goddamned money."

The last two words echoed off the walls through the rest of the ward, all the way down past the nurses' station, where Pat Mitchell was already on the phone to the OR. They bounced out to the main corridor, causing visitors, doctors, patients and security to stop and look back to where the shouting had come from.

Now Jonny Barlow was in the game, concentrating, crouched in his bed, focusing his efforts, fighting through the pre-op sedative, trying to keep his red-rimmed, bloodshot eyes on Billy, who now clearly saw that there was no way he would ever be able to keep the patient on the cart without restraints, which this old gurney did not have. He would have to find one from Division H, the psych ward, and there was no time for that now.

Billy walked back through the double doors to the station.

"I can't get him to go," he said to Pat Mitchell.

"I know. I heard. We all heard. I knew that at twelve forty-five, before we gave him the pre-op, which is probably going to wear off if it hasn't already."

She turned and slapped a chart into a hanging rack. "He doesn't want to leave his money belt here. He wants to take it with him, as you now know."

"Is anyone from his family here?"

"He has no family. But don't worry, McCord, the cavalry's coming. He should be here in a few minutes."

Billy didn't know what she meant, but he wanted to try one more time. He left the cart and walked back through the double doors to Jonny Barlow's bed. The patient had relaxed, but now that he saw Billy he tightened up again and scrambled up to the head of the bed away from the tech.

Billy put his hands out, palms up in supplication.

"Mr. Barlow, you know you have to have this surgery. Your money will be safe here. You'll get it right back when you come out of the Recovery Room."

"*No.*"

"I'm telling you, it will be all right," Billy said in a low, soothing voice.

"*I DON'T TRUST YOU. I DON'T TRUST ANYBODY. GET AWAY FROM ME.*"

"Look," Billy said, and took a five dollar bill from his own wallet. "Here's some of my money. Put it with yours and it will be safe together."

The old man licked his thin lips nervously as his little red eyes darted from the outstretched money to Billy's face and back to the bill again. His shoulders sagged a little, and he crabbed over the bed to Billy, never taking his eyes off the tech's face.

He was about to snatch the bill when the doors to the ward-
room burst open. It was Dr. Reimers, dressed out in scrubs, ready
for surgery. It was the first time that Billy had seen Reimers since
the bronchoscopy in Room Eight. The doctor was very angry,
that was clear. Billy could see it by the stiff way that he walked
as well as in his face.

"Hello, sir. My name's Dr. Reimers." He chose to ignore
Billy. "What's the problem, sir? Why did you bring me all the way
down to the wards?"

The old man retreated to the head of the bed, drew his bony
knees up to his chest, and clutched his money belt tightly.

"*I AIN'T GOING.*"

"Oh, yes you are," Reimers muttered. "Give me that money
belt. I'll take care of it."

"*NOBODY IS TOUCHING MY MONEY,*" the old man screamed.

"Give it to me. Right now," Reimers said in a slow, measured
tone, as if he were dealing with a petulant child.

"*No.*"

He made a grab for the belt, but the old man was quicker and
scratched the doctor's forearm with a yellowed fingernail.

Dr. Reimers looked at his arm. "Son of a bitch," he said. He
turned and walked stiffly back to the nurse's station.

"Get me 300 mg of pentothal. I'll knock this son of a bitch
out right here."

"He's already had his pre-op, Doctor," Pat said calmly.

"I don't give a damn what he's had, give me a syringe with
300 mg of pentothal, stat."

"I'm sorry. I can't do that."

"What's your name?" He looked at her badge. "Mitchell? I'm
going to make your life a living hell if you don't GET ME THAT
GODDAMNED SYRINGE."

"No."

Reimers stood in front of the station, clenching his fists. After
a few seconds, he turned and went back to the ward.

The doctor stood by the bed. Slowly, a crooked smile spread
across his face. "What's your name?" he asked Billy. Reimers had
forgotten that they had worked together in Room Eight.

"Billy McCord."

"OK," Dr. Reimers said. "OK. Listen, sir," he turned to the
patient. "Did Billy tell you about the safe we have in surgery?"

"*WHAT SAFE?*"

"The safe. The big black beautiful safe we have over there for all of our patients' valuables. Oh, it's something to see, that safe. It's a Mosler, you know, with two big black doors and a painting with red roses on the front. It must weigh two thousand pounds. This safe was especially designed for us. It was installed when the hospital was built. Other people want to put their valuables in there but we always tell them, no, no, no, it's for our surgical patients only. Oh, yes, it's a fine safe."

Jonny Barlow's arms relaxed slightly as he absorbed the doctor's words. "And you're saying that my money will be . . . "

"Your money will be totally secure in that big, big beautiful Mosler safe," Dr. Reimers said, as he moved slowly between Billy and the bed, holding the gurney. "I keep my own money in there myself. Now," he said brightly, "be a good boy and hop onto the cart. I'll show you the safe as soon as we get there."

Mr. Barlow thought about it for more than a minute. Then he slid his legs down from his chest and loosened his grip slightly on the money belt. Reimers locked the cart down so it wouldn't move when the patient was transferred from the bed.

At the same time, the words formed in Billy's brain, moved through the neurons into his larynx to his voice box. He took a breath and applied air and they came out of his mouth slowly and distinctly in a calm, measured tone:

"That," he said quietly, "is a lie."

"*WHAT?*" the patient shouted, agitated all over again.

"It's a lie, Mr. Barlow. There's no safe up in surgery."

The patient stopped moving down toward the cart, and quickly clambered back to the top of the bed, drawing up his knees in the process.

"Shut up," the surgeon hissed to Billy. "Shut UP."

"We don't have a safe, Mr. Barlow. There isn't a safe. There never *will be* a safe. It's a fairy tale. If I were you, I'd hang onto my money. You keep it."

"*YOU BET YOUR ASS I'LL KEEP IT,*" Mr. Barlow said with a victorious smile. "*I TOLD YOU THAT NOBODY WAS TOUCHING MY MONEY.*"

Dr. Reimers' face turned Betadyne-red. He looked at Billy. "What is your name?"

"It's Billy. Billy McCord. You asked me that once before. You should have remembered it."

"You're fired. I want you out of here immediately."

"No problem, doc. It's my last day anyway."

Billy turned and began to walk back through the ward. Then he stopped and said, "Hey, Mr. Barlow, I'd ask for a different doctor if I were you. This one's a Demerol junkie."

He heard Dr. Reimers running over to the nurses' station, screaming about police, but by the time the hospital security arrived in the ward, Billy had changed clothes and was down in Central Supply, looking for Craig.

Billy found the retarded man, sitting by a stack of purple obgyn sheets. "Goodbye, Craig. This is my last day."

Craig looked up, startled.

"Your last day? What do you mean?"

"I'm finished."

Craig sat there for a few moments. "Who'll get me my mouthwash every day?"

"I'm sure you can work out something with Antonio or one of the other techs. Anyway, Craig, so long."

They shook hands.

"Oh, before I forget. I know who the SATHO man is."

Craig's face broke into a smile.

"You do?"

"Yep. It's Dr. Margolis."

"Margolis? The hospital president?"

"It sure is."

"I knew it. I knew it," Craig said, and then, ""How did *you* find out?"

"I saw him writing on a supply cart last week," Billy lied. He hated himself for saying it.

Craig stood up and began to sing in a low voice:

"Now I know the SATHO man
The SATHO man, the SATHO man,
Now I know the SATHO man
His name is Dr. Mar-GO-lis."

Billy walked up the stairs to the OR suite. Arcola was standing talking to one of the new nurses.

"Well, Arcola, this is it."

She looked at Billy.

"It's a half hour early."

"I know. I didn't take lunch today."

"All right. Take it easy, Billy."

"I will."

Billy walked up the stairs and out the front door. He crossed the street and took one last look. He watched the sparrows for the last time and saw that there were eggs in the nests now by the way the female sparrows settled down in the straw and mud.

The sun warmed his back as he walked to his car. It felt good to be leaving the parking lot for the last time. He stopped for a second, looked at the hospital one last time and turned left onto Burnet Avenue.

*

Now to cross off the last item on his list. He hoped that it wouldn't be too bad, telling Carol Fears that he was leaving.

He drove through the grimy city, up the long hills to the western suburbs. Billy pulled into Carol's driveway, turned off the ignition, and sat for a moment while his hot engine made dull clicking noises as it cooled down.

Good. No one in the house had seen him yet. He took a deep breath, and let it out slowly.

Billy rang the bell and she answered the door, her pale face a little flushed from the heat of the stove, wiping her hands on her blue and white checkered apron. He could smell the garlic and onions from the spaghetti sauce.

"Hi, Billy. You're just in time for supper."

"Yeah. My timing's really good today."

She didn't give him his usual hug and kiss. Billy wondered why she seemed a little cold.

Carol picked up a wooden spoon and dumped the sauce into a hot pan of sautéed onions and garlic. The sauce sizzled as she mixed it with the other ingredients.

"That smells good."

"Does it? I hadn't noticed."

He moved closer to her and she pulled away.

"What's the matter, Carol?"

She didn't say anything and just kept stirring the steaming sauce.

"Come on. I know you too well. What is it?"

Neither one spoke for a few minutes.

"Billy, I've been thinking a lot. About us. And I don't think we should see each other any more."

This caught him by surprise. After all, he had come over to say goodbye to her.

"Why not?"

She stirred the sauce a little faster.

"Lots of reasons."

"Such as?"

"Well, for the last week, I thought I was late."

"What do you mean, late?"

"My period. I thought that we, that I was pregnant."

"Why didn't you tell me? Are you?"

"No. I don't think so."

"Well, that's a relief." He was watching the sauce, which was beginning to boil.

"So I thought a lot about it last week, about us, about where we're going. We want two different things. I don't know what you want, but I want to get married, have a family."

"Jesus, Carol, you're only twenty-one."

"Shhh. Not so loud."

"I know. You're dad's asleep. He's always asleep."

She began stirring the sauce a little faster.

"The more I thought about it, the more I realized that I couldn't see it happening with us. You're too . . . "

"I'm too what?"

She turned and faced him.

"Too distant for one thing. I mean, I'm talking to you right now and I don't know what's sinking in and what's not. And you're so different from me."

"You never said anything about this before."

"I never thought about it much. But now, the more I think about it, the more I know it is the right thing to do."

"Are you sure?"

The sauce was boiling now, splattering dime-sized dots onto the porcelain stovetop.

"Your sauce."

"What?"

"I said your sauce. You better turn it down. It's boiling."

She turned back to the stove. As she bent over to adjust the heat, a tear fell next to one of the red spots.

"Listen," she said. "Maybe you better go."

"Maybe I better."

She put down the spoon and began to throw her arms around his neck, but stopped short.

"I'm sorry it didn't work out."

"Me, too."

"Goodbye, Billy."

He saw a quick white flash of the times they had made love quietly up in the attic with the brown horses on the wallpaper.

"I'm going now."

He turned and didn't look back as he walked back through the living room. Her mother was reading the paper in the broken-down leather chair by the TV.

"Hi, Billy. Are you staying for supper?"

"No," he called over his shoulder, and without slowing down, walked out the door to his car. It was at least ten minutes before he realized that he wanted to break up with her. He had forgotten to tell her he was going to Alaska. It was just as well, he thought. A lot cleaner this way.

He drove back to his apartment and took off his clothes in the dark. He lay down in his bed and fell asleep in two minutes. One might have expected to dream about the hospital or Carol, but Billy slept the sleep of the unconcerned. Even in his subconscious, he had stopped worrying about patients, surgeons or a nagging girlfriend.

He had done it. He had finally disconnected his mind.

As Billy slept, eleven miles away Carol Fears looked out her little bedroom window, down to the small white ellipse that the streetlight had thrown onto the pavement. She looked at the light for a long time before she lay down and began crying softly so no one else would hear it.

The worst thing in the world, she thought, the absolute worst thing in the world right now would be to wake up her father.

CHAPTER 8

Billy had given up the idea of going to Alaska on a motorcycle for several reasons. Besides having no maps and not enough money for the trip, he couldn't afford to buy a decent bike, and since he already had a car, he decided to drive to Chicago and sell it there. But most of all, he wanted to get there, and he wasn't sure how long it would take to ride a bike all the way across the country and up the Alcan Highway. No, driving to Chicago, taking the train to Seattle and flying to Anchorage would be perfect.

Going through Indiana, he saw what he imagined was a preview of the western prairies, the landscape flat from horizon to horizon in some places, with a few abandoned cars scattered along the highway's shoulder. The farmland spread out before him, a yellow and black crazy quilt, still dotted with a few patches of dirty snow. Cornstalk stubs from last fall poked through the soil, and red-winged blackbirds perched on the rusted fence, cocking their heads as he passed by.

He sold his car to Straight-Shootin'Al Udovic's Used Cars of Chicagoland and one of the salesmen took him to Union Station, where he purchased a ticket for a sleeper on the Empire Builder, one of two trains that went from Chicago to Seattle. He loved that powerful-sounding name of the train—it brought up images of the nineteenth-century railroad barons.

Five minutes after he settled into his compartment, the train grunted out of Union Station and began its three-day push up to the northwest. Billy waited until the train crossed into Wisconsin before he pulled out a small brown paper bag. Inside was all that was left of his marijuana, about three-quarters of an ounce that Jack had sold him about two months ago. On his knees, he drizzled the dope into the toilet.

"No more," Billy said. "So long, Mary Jane. I'm through with you."

He flushed the toilet as the train lurched on the aging tracks. Swaying with the car, Billy stood up and folded the two chairs down together to make his bed, and lay down, cracking the window shade for one last look. It was his first night on a train, and Billy wanted to stay up, but his body wouldn't let him, and he fell asleep within a few minutes.

All night, the train pushed northwest, angling up through Minnesota. When Billy awoke, he folded the seats back and opened his shade. The only reading material he had with him was the Empire Builder's timetable, which he faithfully memorized as the old train rattled and clacked across the 2,200 miles to Seattle, swaying unsteadily on uneven portions of the old railroad beds and blasting through on the smooth ones, past large cities he didn't recognize and faceless towns so small they didn't appear on the schedule; grimy red-brick railroad stations that the Great Northern line had built eighty years ago, rusted-out pickup trucks abandoned along the right of way, weeds growing up through their missing hoods; rolling light khaki-colored hills under a mottled blue and white sky; 45 degree and 90 degree intersections with a line of stopped trucks and semis; the drivers resting their tanned forearms on the door sills, silently watching the train as it passed by them.

The Empire Builder blew by rusty water towers, mushroom-shaped against the ragged sky, grain elevators, cattail swamps, yards full of abandoned cars and refrigerators and then the train shrugged off the larger cities and arched up into North Dakota. Now the towns had strange-sounding names like Bemidji, Chinook and Fosston, chosen either from the immigrants' native land or the local Indian tribes. Billy wondered if two of the cities, Glasgow and Havre, were named after their European counterparts in the hopes that these small Montana settlements would grow to be the same size as the ones in Scotland and France. He watched as a dozen no-name burgs and junction towns moved from left to right across Billy's dirt-streaked window. Billy saw diners, grain silos, buildings that hadn't been

clean in fifty years; one-yield-sign towns with a single movie theater on Main Street, gamely holding out against the constant pressure from the surrounding prairie with cotton-white clouds
framing the scenes. Then the train rattled past the small towns,
breathing free as it drove into the deep embrace of the western
country, powering through the sandstone cliffs and fresh alfalfa
fields, following the Lewis and Clark route, up along the Missouri
and the Milk Rivers past the scrub brush, hemlock and fir trees
as the Bitterroot mountain range waited just over the horizon.

Deep into Montana, Billy was sitting in the dome car at sun-
set, watching the train chase its shadow through a curve, the fading sunlight flashing through the trees onto the silver-skinned
engine. The car was nearly deserted. At one end, three old men,
two of them in jeans and t-shirts and one in a brown suit with
a bolo tie, were playing gin rummy, while a girl wearing jeans,
a denim blouse and a tan cowboy hat sat in the corner, smoking and looking out the window at the countryside.

The card game broke up. Two of the men stretched their
arms, and went down the stairs, while the third walked down
the aisle next to Billy. He gestured at one of the big chairs.

"Mind if I sit down here, son?"

"No, go ahead."

"Thanks," the old man said, and, lining himself up with the
chair cushion, let go of every muscle and dropped into the seat.

He was a pinched-looking, wiry little man, his brown suit
worn through at the elbows, white shirt with silver tips on the
lapels, bolo tie, and broken-down white ten-gallon hat. His
lined face was the color of an old baseball glove, and the
crosshatched wrinkles showed a life working outdoors. A small
battered straw suitcase with a brown leather handle dangled from
his right hand while the other hand's gnarled fingers grasped a
cigarette. The whole package, the man and the suitcase, could-
n't have weighed more than 150 pounds.

Billy and the old man didn't say anything for several minutes,
as the train approached another small town along the line.

"Goddamn. Here we are in Shelby," the old man said.
"Shelby, Montana. That's where we are. You know about Shelby,
don't you? July 1923? The year the town went broke?"

"No."

"I expect you don't. You look like a flatlander to me. Say, what's your name?"

"Billy."

"Mine's Folkes. Hubert Folkes."

They shook hands.

"Anyway," Hubert continued, "I was just a kid, about your age, when the circus came to town. By the circus I mean there was a prize fight between Tommy Gibbons and Jack Dempsey. You know the Manassas Mauler, don't you?"

"I'm afraid not."

The old man shrugged and continued, "So, I got to Shelby the year before, in 1922. Worked in the oil fields there. Big strike that year, and it was something, I'll tell you. We were spending the money as fast as they could print it up. Then some bright guy had the idea of holding a prize fight here, the world heavyweight championship, and they got Dempsey and Gibbons together."

Hubert stopped talking and fished out a cigarette.

"You want one?"

"No, thanks."

"OK. So, anyway, the town ponies up three hundred grand for Dempsey to come. All of the banks kick in. Then the trouble started. Dempsey's manager was a shifty little horse thief named Doc Kearns, and he was one clever son of a bitch, and he fixed it so that he said Dempsey wouldn't fight. Then at the last minute he gives it the OK again. So instead of a huge crowd, only about seven thousand people showed up. Kearns takes the money and hops on the train. Three or four banks went under, I forget how many exactly. I don't think Dempsey saw any of it, and for sure Gibbons got nothing."

Hubert took another drag.

"I lost about five hundred bucks. That was big money back then. But I got it back that winter in Cut Bank. Had a poker game that lasted three days in a blizzard. Shut down the whole state. No food. Did nothing but drink and play cards, day and night."

"That must have been rough."

"Far from it. Happiest three days of my life, I'd say."

He looked at Billy.

"Where you from, son?"

"Cincinnati."

"Cin-cin-nata," Hubert said, rolling the word in his mouth, chewing on the syllables. "Cin-cin-na-ta, Oh-Hi-Yo. Well, you're a long way from home. Where you headed?"

Billy hesitated. He wasn't sure he wanted to tell a stranger about his plans.

"Well . . . I'm going to Alaska."

"Alaska. Now that's big country. Young man's country. Always wanted to go there, but never had the time or the do-re-mi. What are you gonna do up there?"

"I don't know."

"Oh. Well, that's OK. Sometimes best to just let things happen as they come."

Hubert reached into his hip pocket and pulled out a small silver flask as the train clacked over a dried-up riverbed. "Care for a snort? It's never too late."

"No, thanks."

"Sure?"

"No. Thanks all the same."

"OK. Suit yourself." Hubert raised the flask to his lips. "To happy times." he said, and rocked his head back. Then he carefully screwed the cap on and put the flask back in his pocket.

"Alaska, huh? Friend of mine went up there a few years ago. Welder from Bozeman. Waiting for the oil pipeline. That's where the real money's going to come from, this fellow said. He told me he could make more in three months than he could in three years down here. But he's still there waiting around, I guess. Maybe they'll never build the damn thing. Now I used to do a bit of wildcatting myself, in Shelby and other places. But look at this."

The old man held out both his hands. They both were shaking.

"Might be nerves, but the doc says maybe Parkinson's. Anyway, I don't have a trip like that in me anymore. I've about run my course."

He took a long drag.

"Now you, you're a young fellow. Plenty of time to see everything, drink it all in. That's my big regret in life. Never traveled much. Oh, I been to Spokane and Salt Lake and all the way to Moorhead, Minnesota once, but never been east of the Big Muddy, the mighty Mississip. Now, here," he said and swept his arms out wide, "we have the Rockies, the Cabinets, Bitterroots, the Sawgrass, mountains all the way to the Cascades. That's really all a man needs. But to some, it's not enough. It ain't Alaska. No, sir.

"Now me, lived here all my life. But a man gets itchy. He's got to go. Oh, I had the itch—just never scratched it. I listened to my wife, Lucy. She's long gone now, but she used to say, 'Hubert, your roaming days is over.' So we had a small farm, grew wheat, squeaked by, raised a couple of kids, they grew up, moved away. One boy's in Missoula, the other's in Denver. See 'em every now and then. By the way, where did you say you was going up there?"

"I thought I'd start in Anchorage and see what happens."

"Anchorage. That's good. From what my friend Donny tells me, that's a big town. But then again, he also says there's only two things to do up there—drinkin' and whorin.' They call them massage parlors up there, but they're really whorehouses. Plus, he says the state's full of people who think they're Wild Bill Hickok. Everybody's packin' up there. Some of them's even got Colt Peacemakers. Buy you a beer and then shoot you in the back, at least that's what Donny tells me."

"Thanks for the advice, but I can take care of myself."

"Imagine you can. But look out all the same. And take comfort every once in awhile. Now this," the old man said, as he fished out the flask again, "this here's my comfort. Southern Comfort. Warms me up at night. Makes my old bones feel good, 'specially on a long trip like this."

"Where do you get off?"

"Whitefish. Up the line. Pretty country. Gonna do some fishin' and huntin'."

Neither one spoke for a few minutes, lost in their own thoughts, listening to the squeaks and rattles of the Empire Builder as it ground along the old railbed. The artificial light thrown out by the fluorescent bulbs made the gathering dusk just outside the train's chromed walls close in on them.

"We'll be in the Rockies soon. Probably too dark to see 'em when we go through. Just my luck. You know, every time that I come through, I never see them. I've never seen the tops. My daddy told me that you never can see the tops of the Rockies because that's where your soul goes when you die, way up there in the clouds, and God doesn't want you to see that place."

Hubert looked at Billy.

"That's kind of a comfort, wouldn't you say? I always thought it was."

Hubert took one final drag, stood up and stubbed out his cigarette in one of the ashtrays.

"Well, I got to go back and catch me a nap before my stop. Nice meeting you, Billy."

"You too."

"Hope you find whatever it is you're looking for up there," the old man said, "as for me, I guess I'll just keep on laughin' and dancin'."

He picked up his straw suitcase and walked stiffly down the stairs. Billy watched him go, then sat back down and gave in to the rough rocking. He fell asleep.

The next thing he knew, it was dark outside and someone had sat down next to him.

It was the girl with the cowboy hat.

"Jesus, it's about time. You've been asleep for almost two hours. I've been sitting here all this while waiting for you to wake up."

"Where are we?" Billy asked. He looked around. There was no one else in the observation car.

"Just past Whitefish. Working our way over to the Idaho panhandle. Say, what's your name, anyway?"

"Billy. What's yours?"

"Oh, you don't need to know that. I'm just a girl on the train. It's not important."

She reached over and twirled Billy's hair in her fingers.

"You know, you're cute. I thought so as soon as I saw you. Where are you from?"

"Ohio. What about you?"

"Someplace east of here."

Billy turned and looked out the window.

"I know there are supposed to be mountains," he said. "I saw them on the map. I just can't see them now, that's all. All I can see are black shapes in the dark."

"Who cares about mountains?"

"I'd like to see them."

"Well, I don't," she said. "I couldn't care less. That's all I've ever seen my whole life. There's nothing out here but mountains and prairie, mountains and prairie. I'm sick of them."

"What do you want to see instead?"

"Water. Big water. Oceans," she said, as she placed her hand on the back of his neck, caressing him.

"Have you ever seen the ocean?"

"Once, when I was little," Billy said.

"Atlantic or Pacific?"

"Atlantic."

"You're ahead of me then," she said. "I want to see the Pacific. I heard it was the biggest, strongest ocean."

"It must be pretty big."

She rubbed his shoulders.

"You feel strong. I bet you have some big muscles, too."

He turned away from the window.

"Where did you say you were from?"

"Ohio. Back east."

"Back east. Tell me, Billy," she said in a husky voice, "do they have these back east?"

She unsnapped the mother of pearl buttons on her denim blouse. Then she took Billy's hand and placed it on one of her breasts. It was warm and firm and he could feel her heart fluttering.

"That's right," she breathed softly, and reached for Billy's belt.

"Hey, there may be people coming."

"I don't care."

She had Billy's belt undone and was slipping off her jeans and panties.

"Come on, Ohio. Let's see what a flatlander's got."

They made love on the uphill grade, their bodies moving slowly in rhythm to the train's beat. It was uncomfortable on the seats.

When they were finished, Billy looked over at her.

"I still don't know your name," he said, still breathing heavily.

"It doesn't matter. I told you that," she said as she got dressed. She stood up and kissed him on the lips.

He fumbled with his pants.

"So long, Billy. See you around."

"Hey, hang on. Wait a minute," Billy said, as he watched her walk the length of the dome car and go down the short spiral stairs. He finished dressing and started to go after her, but something made him change his mind. He sat back down and after a few minutes, fell into a deep sleep.

When he woke, it was light outside, and he knew that he had missed the mountains. He checked his watch against the schedule and figured out that the train had dipped down through Idaho and the mountains long ago and was now clattering across the Yakima Valley, blossoming apple trees scattered along the rail right of way, all of the country green and fresh and new under the high dome of the blue sky. Now he began to feel excited all over again, just as when he boarded the train three days ago in Chicago. He could feel it now, the power of Alaska, a kind of palpable magnetic force, pulling him north.

When the Empire Builder throttled down and idled into Seattle's train station, Billy was not prepared for the crowd of Boy Scouts, farmers, tourists, and businessmen who surged around him after he left the platform and entered the high-ceilinged station room. Now he stood in the center of the big station, collecting himself, back in the world again. Billy retrieved his two suitcases, found the taxi stand, and took a cab to the Sea-Tac airport, wishing all the way that there was a train from Seattle to Anchorage. He had thought of taking a ferry up the Inside Passage, but decided against it, as he couldn't wait any longer.

The 737 flew high over the Canadian Rockies, peaks so sharp and beautiful it hurt you to look at them, rough, black and white mountains, lifted directly from an Ansel Adams photograph. During the flight, he saw an animal far below, perhaps a wolf or moose, making its way across a snow-filled valley, a small black figure striking out against the white background.

Then the plane landed in Anchorage. From the airport, the city looked the same as any other, except for the rather large mountains perched at the edge of town. These were the Chugach Mountains, big and broad-shouldered, but not as impressive as the Rockies. The Chugachs weren't pointed with dipped snow caps; they appeared to have hunkered down right outside the Anchorage city limits, as if God had surreptitiously strewn them there the day before yesterday. Gray-green and rough-faced, the mountains were so close and alive Billy felt he could reach right out and touch them.

Even the airport was different-looking. Although the terminal structure was standard utilitarian issue, built perhaps twenty years ago, its plastic seats and tinny sound system indistinguishable from others, it was what was inside that struck Billy. He'd never been in an airport that had a stuffed wolf, moose, and polar bear right next to the Ambassadors Lounge, nor one that offered flights to Hawaii and Nome. Every few minutes, the PA system would crackle with strange-sounding names: Barrow, Soldotna, Unalakleet, Nome, Sitka and Ketchikan. The clumps of people draped over chairs or sleeping on the floor told him that some flights had been delayed for a long time, some even a few days. The people all looked so different to him. He could pick out fishermen, prospectors with wide-brimmed hats and rubber boots, Indians and very few women, scattered around the handful of businessmen in three-piece suits, who looked hopelessly out of place. They seemed uneasy, and were constantly looking around at all the other men in flannel shirts, jeans and boots. Billy guessed that the business types were probably connected with the oil pipeline.

He picked up his suitcases from baggage and scanned the list of hotels from a board by the door. Billy selected the Roosevelt, because it was the only one he saw that offered a free ride from the airport. The small hotel on H Street was about ten minutes from the airport, just off the main downtown area of Anchorage.

He walked into the dusty lobby and several pairs of eyes looked up at him. Nine men, smoking or dipping snuff, stared at him for a few seconds as he walked over to the front desk, where an old man had his face buried in the *Anchorage Times*.

"Hi. Got any rooms?"

"Yeah," the man said, and put the paper down. "Eighty-five dollars a day. In advance."

Billy had known that the cost of living was high in Alaska, but the price still came as a shock. He took out his wallet and counted out three one hundred-dollar bills.

"For three days. Hey, what are those Indians waiting for over there?"

"They aren't Indians. They're Eskimos. Fairbanks is socked in. Been that way for almost a week. They're all over town like that."

The old man looked Billy up and down. "Come up for the pipeline?"

"No."

"Good," the old man said. "If you was, you'd be about two years early. Lot of people up here waiting for the pipeline to start. Seems like every roughneck driller and Cat driver in the world is hanging around A-town and Fairbanks, waiting. They're all gonna get rich, if they don't shoot or stab each other first."

He reached back and pulled out a key on a golden plastic fob. "Here you are. Oh, and watch out for them goddamn Aleuts. They'll steal the fillings right out of your teeth."

Billy carried his suitcases up to his room. Suddenly he felt very tired, as if he hadn't slept since he left Ohio. He kicked off his shoes and fell diagonally across the bed. He slept a dreamless sleep, and when he woke up, the sun was hanging low in the sky. Disoriented, he didn't know where he was, and that frightened him.

He made himself calm down. That's right, he thought. That's right. Alaska.

Billy picked up his room key and walked over a few blocks to Fourth Avenue, the main street in Anchorage. A Depression-era post office anchored the left side of the street, with a companion movie theater and its brightly-lit marquee on the other side. Flanking the theater were a couple of bars, one of which had a sign: "Beer—still only $1.00 a glass." Now Billy had to be careful to step over the Natives who were sprawled in front of the bar. In the first two blocks of his walk, he counted seven of them sleeping on the sidewalk, their knees pulled up to their chests as if they had been wadded up and thrown away. Most of the bars and liquor stores up and down the street were doing a brisk business.

He walked slowly along Fourth and took it all in. Hubert's friend appeared to be right. The main street of the largest town in Alaska was a mix of broken-windowed, iron-gated businesses, pawnshops, bars, massage parlors, and liquor stores on both sides of the street. Billy continued down the wide street, walking past the Army-Navy store, the Klondike Bar, Furs! Furs! Furs!, and a couple of rundown hotels. He stopped and looked into the window of one of them, the Palace Hotel. The two-story building was a shotgun-flat setup with a half-dozen broken-down leather chairs scattered around the lobby. Each chair held an old man who sat staring at the black and white TV in the corner, waiting for the test pattern to disappear. The lobby's walls had yellowed photographs of hunting and fishing scenes that looked as if they were a hundred years old. A small stuffed black bear about three feet high stood in the corner, the fur rubbed down to its skull from years of people walking by and touching it. The bear's round little brown glass eyes were sunk deep into its skull, and its mouth was open to show a fierce array of yellowed, broken teeth.

Billy stopped and bought an *Anchorage Times* from a machine inside the door. The hot musty smell of mildew and sweat made him catch his breath as he pumped the change into the machine. No one moved; some of the old men were sleeping in the worn-out leather chairs as if they had been born in that particular spot. Billy had a quick memory of the second-floor wards at Frey Memorial as he folded the paper under his arm and walked back out into the dull sunlight on Fourth Avenue.

CHAPTER 9

Billy became more familiar with Anchorage as another week passed. He walked down Knik Arm and over to Earthquake Park, where the damage from the 1964 quake was still visible. After he became tired of that route, he developed another walking loop, from the park over to the seaplane base at Lake Hood, along Park Row where the Glacier Pilots, a minor league baseball team, had their games, and back over to the Palace Hotel on Fourth. Billy decided that there was nothing to this town, no substance to speak of, only the scraggly set of seedy businesses jammed along Third and Fourth Avenues, with clusters of drab government buildings scattered around the city's core. Tourists came in from the airport, eager to take pictures of something, but Billy never saw them raise their cameras from around their necks. There was nothing in Anchorage that was worth any film, except perhaps the odd, mustard-colored Captain Cook Hotel. In fact, Billy thought, the only things that separated this city from those he knew in Ohio were the rough-looking Chugachs, their tops covered with powdered sugar-looking snow. More than anything else, Billy wanted to climb those mountains, to lose himself on the trails around them. The thought of it made him ache inside, but he knew he couldn't do it—at least for now. He thought of the mountains as a reward for when he became settled in the town with a job and an apartment.

The Natives were everywhere in jeans and ragged T-shirts, clutching their bottles in torn brown bags, their filthy, starling-black hair parted down the middle, begging for quarters on Fourth, lying on the street, urinating on themselves. You couldn't ignore them; in some parts of downtown, you had to step over their bodies as they lay sprawled out on the sidewalk. At first he gave them a dollar when they asked; then a couple of quarters, until after a few more days he stopped giving them any money.

Billy knew he couldn't afford the Roosevelt Hotel and left there when his three nights were up. The Aleuts who seemed to be permanently parked in the hotel lobby, waiting for the weather to clear somewhere, sat with their arms folded across their chests and barely looked up as he lugged his heavy suitcases out onto H Street. He walked around town, dozing off in the library and on the steps of the Fourth Avenue post office.

He drifted over to Fireweed Books. The owner of the bookstore, a short, squinty-eyed man named Sam Kashivaroff, let Billy sleep on a couch for a few days, but then the customers began to complain about the smell.

"Hey kid, wake up. You got to go. The customers don't like you here anymore. Kid," Sam said again. "Wake up."

He shook Billy's shoulder gently.

"I said wake up."

Billy stirred.

"You can't sleep here anymore."

Reflexively, Billy grabbed for his suitcases.

"Hey, take it easy. Nobody's stealing your stuff. Here." Sam wrote down something on a scrap of paper.

"It's the Palace Hotel, over on Fourth. I'm sure they got a room for you."

Billy stood up.

"I know where it is. Thanks for letting me kill some time at your place."

"Sure. Good luck, kid."

Billy walked over to the hotel. It was the same one where he had bought a paper his first day in town, but he didn't remember all the dust and dirt.

The check-in area was a battered school desk protected by a wire screen. An old man was drinking out of a bottle of Geritol and didn't care whether Billy saw him or not. The man finished his drink and banged the bottle down on a paper napkin.

"I need a . . . "

"Fifty-five. Fifty-five a night. In advance cash payable each morning at ten."

Billy pulled his last three fifty dollar bills out. "That's for two nights."

"I can add," the man said.

He slid a small pile of bills back to Billy.

"Room Seven. Second floor. No cooking in the rooms. And no girls." He took a small breath. "Bathroom down the hall. We run a clean place here."

"I can see that," Billy said.

He walked up a half-flight of stairs and down a long shotgun hall with even-numbered black doors 2 through 12 on the right and odd-numbered rooms 1 through 11 on the left. The brightly-painted red hallway with matching crimson shag carpeting reeked of stale urine and sweat. Each room had gold numbers on shiny red doors.

The top nail in the room number 7 was long gone; now the number hung upside down and resembled an italic L. The doorknob had been hit with a heavy hammer at one point; the door had also been jimmied open, as there were pry marks all over the jamb. Billy could count at least three different drilled holes for keys, and once a padlock system had replaced the doorknob and key. There were scuffs on it and a bootprint about three feet up from the floor.

He tried the key. It didn't work. He checked the number and gently pushed the key into the lock. The key bent a little, but still wouldn't turn.

Billy worked on the lock a few more times, then went back to the front desk.

"This key's no good."

"What room?"

"Seven. You just gave it to me."

"Oh yeah. Seven. That's the *old* key for Seven." The old man turned and fished around in a drawer. "Here."

He gave Billy a key marked "New 7" and watched him go back to the stairs.

"Hey, kid. Did you leave your suitcases in the hall?"

"Yes."

"Don't ever do that. They grow legs."

Billy jumped up the short stairs and back into the hallway. The door to room 12 was open and a tall thin man was stroking his chin, looking at the suitcases.

"Those are mine," Billy said.

The tall man said nothing.

Billy tried the lock, feeling the man staring at the back of his head. The key worked and he dragged the heavy suitcases in, slamming the door shut and locking it with the slide bolt.

The room had nothing in it except for two tired black metal bed frames. Each one had an iron box spring and a thin army cot mattress thrown on top of the big springs. When he lay down on one mattress, he could feel the sharp ends of the springs working their way through the cloth to his back. A puff of dust rose up when Billy tossed the mattress onto the floor.

He dragged the other mattress off the bed and put it on top. He could hardly tell the difference, but it would have to do.

He stood up and left his room. Number 12 was still in the doorway, watching. He hadn't moved since Billy opened the door ten minutes ago.

Billy walked back out to the lobby, where the men in the broken-down leather chairs were watching a baseball game. A woman was singing the National Anthem.

"Hey, I know this game," Billy said. "It was Opening Day, about a week ago."

"Shut up. We don't want to know the score. We're watching it."

"But that game's at least a week old."

"So what? Just shut up or get the hell out."

"Sorry," Billy said, and walked out the lobby onto Fourth Avenue.

He bought an *Anchorage Daily News* and scanned the want ads. There wasn't much, outside of some dishwasher jobs. Providence Hospital was looking for a surgical technician, but Billy was not interested. It depressed him to think that he would even contemplate the same job he had back home. He thought that he might have a better chance beyond the mountains, away from the big city; maybe somewhere in the interior of the state.

Now the town had grown old and stale to him. There was no place he hadn't walked to and no sight he hadn't seen. And as his money flowed out of his pockets, so too did his spirits, sinking right into Ship Creek.

He could see it.

Billy was stuck. Again.

He walked over to the Klondike Bar on A Street. The heavy-set man on the stool next to him had on a dirty yellow Cat hat and a red and black checked flannel shirt and wrinkled jeans.

The man put a quarter and a nickel on the bar.

"Looky, kid, are you a betting man?"

"No," Billy said. The man didn't hear him.

"Here's how it works," he said. "I'll bet you a beer that there's thirty-five cents on the bar. If I'm wrong, you buy me a beer."

Billy looked at the coins.

"OK," Billy said. "It's a bet. A quarter and a nickel are thirty cents. Pay up."

"No, you didn't listen," the man said. "I said, 'If I'm wrong, you buy me a beer.' I'm wrong. So buy me a beer."

The bartender laughed. "Got another one, huh, Ike?"

The Cat hat man grinned. "Works every time."

Billy motioned to the bartender. "Another Oly for him."

"Hey, no hard feelings, kid. What's your name? You look like a cheechako."

"A what?"

"A cheechako, a new kid, a tenderfoot."

"Well, my name's Billy."

"Works for me. Mine's Ike. Ike Morgan. You here for the pipeline?"

"No."

"Me too," Ike said. He took a drink.

"Only we're too early. Maybe six months, maybe two years. Hard to tell. But I'm ready. I'm a 'neck—a roughneck. Driven D9's all over Oklahoma and Texas, laid pipe, you name it. If it burns oil, I can drive it. There isn't any kind of work I can't do. You ever hear of Red Adair? The oil well capper? He's my cousin. Look at this."

He showed Billy his hands. The fingers were rough, callused and curved with cracked yellow nails. There were scabs on the back of the man's hands.

"They tell me that a man might make a hundred grand a year once the work starts. And that's just for openers. I'd like that. I could live with that. It would make the waiting worth it, don't you think? I hate spending the cash to live up here, but like the fellow says, it takes money to make money."

"I'm not interested in the pipeline," Billy said.

"You're not?" Ike looked Billy up and down. "Well, you sure don't strike me as no gold bug."

He took a pull from his Oly and ran his stubby fingers through his greasy black hair.

"Well then, hell, what *are* you doing up here?"

"Just looking around. I want to see the country."

"Oh lordy, another one of those. Man, you're in the wrong place. There ain't no *country* here. This place is a bank, a big bank, that's all, waiting to be cracked wide open. And I'm going to be here when the doors open at 9:00 am Monday, whenever Monday's gonna be. If you're smart, you'll stick around until then."

The bartender was putting glasses away.

"It could be years," the bartender said. "There's a lot of jerks in the Lower 48 that don't want this thing built."

"Well, Frank," Ike said, "you know what I say about that? It's like the sign in a window I saw last week: *LET THE BASTARDS FREEZE IN THE DARK*. The goddamn oil is for them, too, after all. If they don't want it, let 'em freeze in the dark down there. I don't care. But it's coming. Sooner or later, it's coming. And nobody can stop it. I just want to be here when it comes, making the long green, along with everyone else, driving my Cat, doing my thing. Now you," Ike said to Billy, "you're a young buck. You'll get it too if you stay up here long enough. You'll get it. Everybody gets it. That's the deal here. Everybody can come out of here rich if they're smart. And if the goddamn Eskimos and Aleuts and whoever the hell else they are can get it with all the claims and oil rights they file, why shouldn't we? We're as entitled to it as they are—maybe more so."

"I know about that," the bartender said. "Those crazy Indians. Every goddamned one of them is going to be rich."

"That's right. But first we got to build the pipeline," Ike said as he drained his beer. "It all starts with that."

He turned and looked at Billy. "So tell old Ike. What are you doing up here? You got a trade?"

"No, I said I came up to see the country."

"Well," Ike said and motioned the bartender for a refill, "you ain't going to get rich like that. Tell you what. You do your thing and I'll do mine. I'll see you in ten years. You'll know me by my gold Rolls-Royce."

The bartender brought two more Olys over.

"Where are you working, kid?"

"Noplace. I've been here about two weeks, just looking around."

"There's no work in A-town, except for fifty-cent jobs and such," the bartender said. "Maybe you ought to go out aways. I got a friend that's a foreman in a cannery out in the gulf. They're into tanners right now."

"Tanners?"

"Tanner crab. His name's Joe Picoro, Joe Pike, and he could always use a cheechako like you."

"Here," the bartender said, as he wrote something on a cocktail napkin. "Joe Pike on the *Aleutian Queen*. It's a cannery in Kodiak town. That's out in the gulf. You can't hitchhike there; you got to take a bus and the ferry. Call him up. Tell him Frank Gibbons said to call. There's a pay phone in the back, if you're interested."

Billy thought for a second.

"OK. Give me some change."

He slid two one-dollar bills over the thick oak bar and received eight quarters back. The operator gave him the number of the *Aleutian Queen*.

"Hello, the *Queen*," a voice answered.

"Is Joe Pike there?"

"Sure, he's down on the floor, I'll get him."

After about a minute, Billy heard someone pick up the phone.

"Picoro." The voice sounded rough and gravelly.

"Hey, my name's Billy McCord, I'm calling you from Anchorage and . . . "

"Looking for work?"

"Yeah."

"You ever been on the line before?"

"Yes," Billy lied.

"You're hired. Try to get here soon as you can."

The phone went dead.

Billy walked back up to the bar.

"That was fast," the bartender said. "Did you mention my name?"

"I didn't get that far. They want me there tomorrow," Billy said, and finished his beer.

"Best way to go is to take a bus to Seward and then the *Tusty* across to Kodiak. You know where the bus station is?"

"Sure."

Billy put a five-dollar bill on the bar.

He turned to Ike Morgan.

"I hope you find what you're looking for."

"Oh, I will. You better believe it. Remember, look for my gold Rolls."

They shook hands.

Billy walked out, blinking in the dull sunlight. He spent his last night in the Palace but he was too excited to sleep very much.

The 6:00 am bus to Seward rumbled past the shabby outskirts of Anchorage and followed the rutted road along Turnagain Arm, Portage Glacier, and the Hope Cutoff, deep into the Chugach National Forest. After Portage, the road meandered on for a few more miles, leaving tidewater now for the long climb through Moose Pass.

Billy took everything in. His eyes scanned the combination gas station-liquor store-souvenir shops along the highway, trying to see past them into the forest, but it was impenetrable, layer after layer of fir trees twenty or thirty feet deep, keeping all of the country's secrets from him. He strained to catch a glimpse of any wildlife at all but there was nothing except for a few ground squirrels darting across the road in front of the bus, and three ravens perched on top of a Sitka spruce tree down by Ptarmigan Lake.

The bus made it into Seward with about an hour to spare before the ferry left for Kodiak, giving Billy enough time to eat some breakfast at a small restaurant in the harbor.

By 9:00 am, the blue and white *Tustumena* was heading down Resurrection Bay toward the Gulf of Alaska. Billy stood on the top deck, feeling the cold air coming off the snowy mountains across the bay, watching the wake boil off the stern as Seward shrank behind him. One of the deckhands stood next to him, wearing a full set of Carhartt overalls and a blue watch cap, leaning over the railing with a Styrofoam coffee cup.

"Well, here come the rollers. Feel 'em, cheechako?"

"You mean the waves?"

"That's right." The deckhand took another drink of coffee and looked Billy up and down. He turned and planted his elbows back on the railing. "Ever been through the gulf before?"

"No."

"Hope you didn't have a big breakfast. Probably see it again in a few."

The deck hand dropped the cup in a garbage can and went below.

The *Tustumena* cleared Resurrection Bay, and now Billy could see the green breakers marching toward the ship from the southwest. The wide black mountains that ringed the bay slowly disappeared off the stern, and the bow began a rhythmic rising and falling, pausing at the top of its arc for a split second and then slamming back down into the sea. The salt spray stung his face, the sheet of needles hitting him as he fought for a few more minutes, legs spread, braced against the sea and the wind, until he couldn't stand it any longer and went below.

Looking around, Billy decided that the ship was almost deserted—either that or everyone else was in their cabins breaking out the Dramamine. Billy set himself up in a folding chair that looked out the big windows over the bow. He could hear someone retching from somewhere behind him.

He watched the bow whipping up and down. Thirteen hours to go. He fished a dog-eared paperback, *Sourdough Sagas,* out of one of his suitcases and read an account of the Klondike gold rushers coming up in 1898.

"All of us had a mortal fear of seasickness," a man named Lynn Smith had written. "Jim told me in a seance just before leaving Indiana, 'Just sit down with your back up against a wall and keep your hands clasped over your head and look out over the water and the feeling will soon pass away.' Well, the feeling passed away, but only after they carried me to my room and I had been on land for six days."

Billy laughed to himself. He didn't feel seasick at all. There was nothing to this sea travel, really; it was actually amusing to feel the ship move to the ocean's cadences while watching the handful of passengers on his level as they scurried, bent over, from the deck chairs to the bathrooms, back to their places, sit down, stand up a few moments later and repeat their crazy walk-run across the heaving deck through the other chairs to the sinks and toilets, some of them making it, others, well, almost. A few of them simply gave up and took their books and magazines into the bathrooms with them.

Poor bastards, he thought. It gave him a sense of superiority to know that he could handle the rough water on his first trip across the gulf—a simple mind-over-matter decision. Perhaps he had finally learned to put himself into the kind of Zen-like trance that David Schneider always used to talk about; just block out the rolling sensation and fix your eyes on the horizon. Picturing himself, not the ship, plowing through the white-caps, his arms flung out away from his body, Billy paid no attention to what his middle ear was telling his brain.

Then, flying over the waves to the *Tustumena* and right into his head, were the first seeds of doubt, along with a sense of queasiness. The lines of the book he was reading began to move slowly in front of his eyes. He took the book off his lap and put it on the deck, pages up, closed his eyes, and waited a moment.

That was when he heard the voice.

"You're going to be sick now," the voice said. "You're going to be sick as you've never been sick before."

Billy tried to focus on the horizon, which now had become a curving line as the waves whipped over the bow.

The voice was louder and adamant. "Get up. Get up now."

He opened and closed his eyes. It was worse.

Billy rose, and carefully placed his book on his chair.

"Leave the book," said the voice. "Go. Go."

Billy did make it to the bathroom, twenty-five feet away, before he lost everything—Rice Krispies, toast, orange juice, coffee, and even the gum he had swallowed back in Resurrection Bay.

The builders of the *Tustumena* certainly knew what they were doing. The toilet stalls were spaced so that a man of average size could brace himself against the pale green bulkheads with his elbows as he threw up. Each bathroom on the deck level had four stalls, so there was plenty of room.

He vomited until there was nothing left, and then he retched for ten more minutes, until his ribs were so sore it hurt to breathe. He felt grateful for the smallest of things—that there was no one else in the bathroom to witness this; that he had not eaten the huge "Sourdough Breakfast" in Seward; that he hadn't hit his clothes, and that he was finished.

At least he thought he was. For as soon as he returned to his chair and picked up his book, the nausea swept over him again, and then a third time. Finally, after forty-five more minutes in the bathroom, he was sure he was done.

But he was wrong. Five minutes later, he was back in his special stall, studying the rivets in the walls; glad again that no one else was there. He looked at his watch. Eleven o'clock. The schedule showed docking in Kodiak at 11:00 pm. Only twelve more hours to go. The waters in the gulf were getting rougher, with large angry whitecaps pounding the *Tusty*'s bow as the big ferry surged up and down.

There was something wrong with his watch. A minute finally passed. Then three minutes. After what seemed forever, he glanced at his watch again.

11:36.

It was pointless, trying to imagine another eleven and one-half hours on the ship. He knew he couldn't endure it, but what other choice did he have? Death was preferable to this, he thought. At least it would be quick. He could throw himself overboard, and last maybe five or ten minutes before he lost consciousness and drowned. At the bookstore in Anchorage, he had read a book about how horses coming up for the Klondike gold rush had been driven mad by the incessant rocking and had jumped overboard.

Billy looked around, moving his aching head from side to side in a slow effort to placate his torn-up guts. Everyone else was gone. Were they all hidden away somewhere, his brothers in seasickness, throwing up neatly into their private toilets or were they off on another deck, eating and drinking, laughing and having a good time? He didn't want to find out; he didn't even want to think about it. As far as he was concerned, his world had shrunk to the twenty-five foot trip from his chair to the bathroom.

He ached all over. His insides hurt, and he had a splitting headache. Worse, he was hungry, but he knew he couldn't eat. There was nothing to do but repeat the cycle, and try not to steal a look at his watch.

Billy couldn't help it. He had to look.

12:42—about eight hours to go.

He tried to sleep, he tried to think, he even tried some of his old operating room tricks such as letting his mind freewheel about baseball, women, Jack Nicholson movies—anything to make the hands on the watch move, but nothing worked.

Billy wasn't sure how it happened, but somehow the time passed. When the sunlight had disappeared, he looked over the bow and could make out a few red lights, flickering far away in the darkness, appearing and disappearing with the ship's movements.

The *Tustumena's* engines changed their pitch. They were slowing down. The ferry was taking a real pounding from the waves now, much more than before. Billy fought off the nausea and focused on what he saw off the bow. There were more lights now, not just red ones. These lights weren't blinking.

The ferry cut her speed down to a few knots. He could see lights clustered together now, and noticed it was rain and not spray that was pelting the bow windows.

Then the captain turned on the overhead lights. The ship's engines were barely idling now. Billy looked out and saw a long dock appear, sliding by on the starboard side. There were some men with bright yellow slickers and black rain pants, moving slowly in the rain, shielding their eyes, trying to catch the docking ropes. They reminded Billy of shiny wet bumblebees. Someone threw a line, then two, then a third, which the dockworkers caught and cinched tight around log pilings. As the ship maneuvered into position, Billy shouldered his backpack, picked up his two suitcases and made his way down to the narrow gangplank, trying hard not to fall on the slippery deck.

The cold rain hit him hard as the suitcases banged his legs. He stumbled and nearly fell.

"Hey, watch it," a man shouted behind him.

The gangplank went on and on. How much farther was it? He couldn't see.

Then his feet touched the dock planking and he put his suitcases down. Billy looked around, trying to figure out where he should go.

One of the bumblebees walked past him. The man's black hood was shiny and reflected the dull yellow lights of the ferry.

"Yeah, yeah," the man said. "Welcome to Kodiak. Now get the fuck off my dock."

CHAPTER 10

Billy spent his first night on Kodiak Island under a refrigerated Sea-Land truck, lying on top of his suitcases and watching the rain splatter off the black rocks. He wondered when the sun would ever come up and kept watch, looking eastward for any signs. After a while he stood up next to the ferry dock, wiping the moisture off his skin, until finally he saw the first shafts of light bending over the tops of the dark mountains and arcing across the harbor. Picking up his suitcases, he walked down toward the boat harbor, as he guessed that the canneries would be close to the water. He passed a few bars and some stores in the center of the town and turned left on Shelikof Street, past the floating docks where the fishing boats were moored.

Billy read the names of the fishing boats as he walked by: *Invincible, Verona, Lin J, John and Olaf, Jody Ann*—these were the ones that he could make out in the foggy light. Most of their hulls were battered and dirty, but the *Jody Ann* looked clean and new, with what Billy guessed were crab pots stacked eight feet high on its deck.

A man leaned against the wheelhouse, smoking a cigarette, watching Billy.

"Hi," Billy said.

The man reached for a coffee cup. He drank slowly from the cup, never taking his eyes off Billy, watching the suitcases swing back and forth. As he walked by, Billy could feel the man's eyes on him but when he turned to look again, the man was on deck, repairing some nets.

Billy passed the harbor and approached some low gray and white buildings, some of which were joined to large boats. He was right; they were the canneries; most of them were converted boats, drydocked long ago. Billy walked by the *Skookum Jim*, *Roxanne, Pacific Pearl*, and the B & B canneries, and then at the end of Shelikof he came to a red hand-lettered sign on a two-by-twelve:

ALEUTIAN QUEEN SEAFOODS

The cannery was actually a converted ship of some kind, attached to a barge in front. As he walked across the small gravel lot past a few cars and down a narrow gangplank, Billy saw a small door with a second hand-lettered sign: ENTRANCE. He used his suitcases as a battering ram and punched into the cannery.

The noise knocked Billy back a step and he stumbled against the doorway. The roaring from the heavy equipment mixed with the whine of several winches banged off the concrete walls and echoed throughout the barge as clouds of steam blasted up from the big retorts. Workers were running back and forth, shouting obscenities at one another, shooting water from white pressure hoses along the floor, and moving big white tubs full of brown crabs. The *CH-CH* sound of steam released from the machinery and the chuffs and whines of the crane motors just outside the barge mixed in with the low RPMs of some other machine that Billy couldn't see. At the other end of the barge, through a cloud of steam, Billy could just make out a small arched gangplank that led from the barge to the *Aleutian Queen* herself.

No one noticed Billy standing there with his suitcases in hand. After about a minute he put them down and walked over to a small man who was feeding crab legs into a machine.

"Hey," Billy shouted. "Where's the foreman?"

The man gave no response, but kept his eyes focused down on the crab legs.

"HEY. WHERE'S THE FOREMAN?"

The man turned his head slowly from where the noise was coming from, and looked blankly at Billy. He still did not answer.

"HE DON'T SPEAK ENGLISH," a man in yellow raingear and a bright red hardhat yelled back. "WHAT DO YOU WANT?"

"THE FOREMAN," Billy shouted. "I NEED TO SEE THE FOREMAN."

The man pointed over to a small man across the barge with a blue watch cap on.

"THAT'S HIM. JOE PIKE."

Billy wound his way around pieces of equipment, water spray and steam until he found the small man in the blue cap.

"JOE PIKE?"

The man turned. He was stuffing a wad of Red Man into his mouth. The front of his plaid shirt was stained brown with tobacco juice.

"DON'T EVER CALL ME THAT. NOBODY CALLS ME JOE PIKE."

The man with the red hardhat grinned.

"Kid," he said to Billy, "everybody calls him Joe Pike."

"IT'S PICORO. JOE PICORO."

"I CALLED YOU YESTERDAY ABOUT A JOB."

"YEAH."

The foreman looked Billy up and down.

"WELL, GREENGRASS, GO THROUGH THAT DOOR TO THE OFFICE. MILT WILL SET YOU UP. THEN COME BACK HERE."

"OK."

Billy grabbed his suitcases and made his way up over the small gangplank through a plastic door and into the *Aleutian Queen*. The noise stopped once he closed the door. He stepped down a small corridor into a small room marked OFFICE.

A ruddy-cheeked man with thin white hair was working an adding machine. He never took his eyes off the numbers as Billy came in.

"Are you Milt?"

"N-n-n-n-no, I'm Kate Smith. N-n-n-n-new hire?"

"Yeah."

The man's eyes stayed on his column of figures for a few more seconds.

"Shoe s-s-s-s-s-s-size?"

"Nine and a half."

The man reached behind him in a closet and dug through a box of rubber boots until he found the right size.

"Here. You can leave those suitcases by the d-d-d-d-door."

He handed an application form to Billy along with the rubber boots.

"Fill th-th-th-that out."

Billy filled out the form and handed it back to Milt.

"Another god-d-d-d-d-damned hippie," he said. "Where do they all come from?"

He put the form in a file cabinet. "Well, hippie, we pay three twenty-five an hour. You can start right n-n-n-n-now. The boots will be deducted from your first paycheck."

He waited until Billy put on the boots, and then led him through the inside of the *Aleutian Queen*, empty except for four big roller machines, each one covered with heavy plastic sheeting. Behind the machinery toward the bow of the old ship was a small room with hooks full of yellow raingear.

"Find some gloves, a rainjacket, and p-p-p-p-pants that fit and go back out to Joe Pike."

Billy pawed through the thick yellow raingear and fished out a jacket and a set of pants with suspenders that fit fairly well. The gloves were another matter, since all of them were either too small or size XXL.

He finally found a decent pair and stumbled out through the *Aleutian Queen*, over the gangplank and onto the cannery floor.

Joe Pike had a big crescent wrench in his hand.

"SON OF A BITCH," he yelled. "SON OF A BITCH. GOD DAMN IT. I TOLD YOU FLIP SONS OF BITCHES NOT TO OVERLOAD THE GRINDER. NOW WHAT ARE WE GONNA DO WITH ALL THESE GODDAMNED SHELLS?"

The other workers looked at the foreman and shrugged their shoulders.

"Don't worry about him, kid," said the man in the red hard-hat. "He'll be fine when he's back on the White Horse."

"White horse?" Billy said.

"Yeah, you know. White Horse." the man said, and tilted his thumb toward his mouth. "Scotch," he said.

Pike turned around.

"OK, GREENGRASS. GO OVER THERE TO THE BUTCHERS."

Billy followed where the foreman had pointed. Two men in raingear stood next to a large steel table that was piled high with upside-down brown crabs, the crustaceans' lined undersides showing dull white in the fluorescent lights. As he watched, one of the men snatched a crab from the table and held it against his stomach, flat side out. The man moved behind a machete welded onto a stand, parallel to the floor, about three feet high. Holding all of the crab's legs in his hands, the man ran the blade quickly through the underside of the crab as the animal's guts, shit, and fluids gushed out. In the same motion, the butcher ripped both sets of legs and claws off, expertly flipping the crab's shell into the grinder's mouth. He took both sets of legs and ran them over a hacksaw blade mounted next to the machete, dropping the cut legs into two buckets on either side of the blade. The whole procedure took perhaps six seconds, and then the man reached for another upside-down crab.

The other butcher had also finished a crab and tossed the shell in the direction of the grinder. It missed the grinder mouth and bounced off the floor, through an open door, and into the harbor.

Billy walked over to the butcher closest to him. He was surprised by the bright red scar running under the small man's chin.

"They told me to come over here," Billy said.

"No shit? You ever butcher before?"

"No."

"Ever work in a cannery before?"

"No."

"Ever done *any* work? Boy, they sure can pick 'em. Well, I'll start from the top."

The man picked up a brown crab. Billy could see its eyes on stubby stalks, almost opaque-looking.

"This," the man said, "is a crab. Snow crab. Tanner crab. Queen crab. All the same kind. Now look at this."

Billy watched as the man ran the crab onto the dull machete blade, ripped off the legs and claws, sawed them open, and then threw the crab shell toward the grinder.

"See? Now you try it."

Billy gingerly picked up a crab from the steel table and held it close against his stomach. He could feel the pebbly roughness of the shell through his gloves.

"No!" the butcher shouted. "You got it backwards. Turn it around."

Billy obeyed him, and held the crab with its shell against him.

"That's right. Now run him."

He slid the dull blade into the crab, and felt its guts run down his raingear pants.

"Pull the legs and claws off."

He gripped both sets in each hand and pulled down, ripping off all the appendages at once.

"Now saw the legs open on the stand."

Billy grasped the legs and claws and cut them across the hack-saw blade. The ends fell away, exposing the uncooked meat.

"Drop the legs in the bucket. The claws go over here."

He did as he was told. The legs and claws clattered into the steel buckets on both sides of him.

"Not bad," the butcher said. "At this rate, we'll be done by next Christmas. Now pick up the pace."

Billy nodded. He grabbed another crab and felt the dull machete blade drive through the crab into his own stomach. And then another, and another.

He watched the other butchers. They worked with no wasted motion. They were doing about two or three crabs to his one. He tried to speed up, but missed cutting open a pair of legs. He started to drop them in the buckets.

"DO IT AGAIN. YOU'RE NOT CUTTING THE LEGS RIGHT."

Joe Pike was right behind Billy.

Billy repeated the motions.

"DON'T MISS ANY OF THOSE LEGS. I NEED EVERY SINGLE GODDAMN ONE. DON'T CHEAT ME OUT OF ANY OF 'EM," Joe Pike shouted as he walked past the grinder.

Billy stole a glance at the big white clock. Seven minutes had gone by since he started. He grabbed another crab from the pile, ran it onto the dull blade and cut the body away from the legs and claws. As he filled up the metal buckets by his feet with claws and legs, a small dark-skinned woman would slip in and exchange the full ones with empty containers.

He watched his other two fellow butchers. They were raingeared robots, each one selecting a crab without looking, placing it in front of them, then quickly killing it and tossing the shell toward the grinder opening, simultaneously reaching for the next crab on the table. The Aleut next to him had a face that could have been carved from a mountain: chiseled nose and broad forehead, with black hair and thin, tight lips. Despite the exertion, his impassive face looked calm. The small white man with the red scar had a black rain jacket on and wore a hard-hat back on his head, exposing a clump of sweaty brown hair.

Ten crabs. Thirty-two crabs. Forty crabs. Billy lost count as his hands began to ache, especially the tips of his fingers. At the hospital, he had learned not to look at clocks, not to trust clocks, but he couldn't help himself. He stole another glance.

Only thirty-two minutes had passed since he started. What was it with this slow Alaska time? Just as when he was on the *Tustumena*, he thought that the clock must be broken because the minute hand ran so slowly.

Then Billy began to see spots where the brightly-polished table was showing through the hundreds of crooked legs waving slowly in the air. Now the table was almost clean except for a handful of tanners, most of which were already dead. Just as Billy thought that the butchers would get a break, a big white tub was winched over their heads until it dangled above the table. Joe Pike came over and tipped the container over, spilling out another few hundred crabs.

The other workers never changed their tempo as they shifted the stack of fresh crab within reach, moving their hands and arms in a kind of rhythmic dance. Billy tried to copy their motions, but everything he did was clumsy and uncertain. The muscles in his shoulders and forearms were throbbing, his fingers hurt, and he shook his head to keep the sweat from running into his eyes.

"HEY!"

He jerked his head back. It was Joe Pike.

"YOU GOT TO GO FASTER! I TOLD YOU TO LOOK AT THE OTHER GUYS. NOW YOU LOOK AT 'EM."

The two butchers were finished; their eyes fixed on Billy. He worked faster, and the pile in front of him grew smaller, until the crabs were all finished and the table shone in the fluorescent lights.

"OK," Joe Pike said. "YOU GUYS TAKE YOUR BREAK."

Billy followed the other two butchers over the arched gangplank into the *Aleutian Queen*. They walked through the machinery to the raingear room near the bow of the old ship. At the bow were a bench and a small set of stairs. The butchers climbed up the steps and the Aleut pushed open a thick metal door, which opened out onto the *Queen*'s bow.

The misty cold air felt wonderful. Billy could see that the fog was rising, revealing a half-ring of snow-capped black mountains across the water. Another mountain seemed to grow right out of the road at the base of the cannery. Through the mist, he could begin to make out the low buildings behind the harbor, the town of Kodiak pressed hard against the mountain on one side with a narrow channel and cluster of islands on the other.

Both butchers lit cigarettes. The small white man offered Billy one. He took it and felt the smoke ease into his lungs.

"That'll be a buck."

Billy stared at him.

"Ha ha. Just kidding. Nice view, isn't it?" the small man said. "See that mountain way over there? That's Barometer Mountain. Know why it's called that? Because if you can't see Barometer, it's raining. If you *can* see it, then it's going to rain. Say, you're awful quiet. What's your name, cheechako?"

"Billy."

"Billy? What the hell kind of name is that for a man? That sounds kind of hilljack to me. Mine name's Tal. Tal Malinovsky."

The little man jerked his thumb at the Aleut. "His name's John Charlie. He don't talk much. Fact is, John can go a month of shifts without talking. Not even to his wife. Right, Johnny boy?"

The Aleut said nothing.

"Oh, yeah, he's a real Tonto, that one."

John Charlie turned to Tal. Slowly, he unsnapped his rain jacket and pulled a Buck knife from its sheath. The blade flashed dully in the pale light.

"Cut you."

"Come on. You want to try it?" Tal gestured with his hands. "Come on. I've been waiting for you. I'll tear your goddamned head off. I swear to Christ I will."

John Charlie held the knife blade out in front of him, con-tem- plating his next move. He wasn't a very tall man, only about 5'8", but he had very strong arms and hands. Billy could see that, even through John's bulky rain suit.

The Aleut looked from Tal down to the knife blade and back up to Tal.

The scene was frozen in time, the three men in a small cir-cle no less than ten feet across, standing on the bright blue bow of the *Queen*.

Then Joe Pike stuck his head out.

"BREAK'S OVER. GET BACK TO WORK."

He didn't notice the knife blade.

John Charlie waited a few more "don't fuck with me" seconds and slowly slid the Buck back into its sheath. The Aleut walked past Billy and Tal through the door. They heard his boots clomping down the steps and across the floor toward the barge.

Billy realized that he had been holding his breath.

Tal shrugged. "See, *that's* how you treat them goddamned Aleuts. Show 'em who's boss. Don't cut them any slack or they'll stick a shiv in you quick as hell. Just like the Filipinos. Only difference is the Flips wait until you're asleep."

Tal turned and walked down the steps.

Billy looked around and tried to calm himself down. His heart was hammering away. He heard some seagulls screeching overhead as they wheeled over the cannery, hovering, searching for bits of crab that had fallen into the water while far above them, a bald eagle punched its way above the boat anchorage as it flew toward one of the harbor islands.

He buttoned up his stiff yellow rainjacket and followed Tal back to the butchers' table, trying to forget about the pain in his back and arms. Now he could hear the grinder revs drop as it crunched another shell, and he knew that John Charlie had already begun working through the pile of tanners on the table.

CHAPTER 11

While it is a fact that two and one-half hours breaks down into 150 minutes, or 9,000 seconds, the cannery seemed to be operating on some different method of time measurement. It was something that Billy had never seen before, not even on the ferry. No heart case in surgery, no seven-hour Whipple procedure had prepared Billy for this total suspension of time that he was experiencing. Each second passed as a minute and each minute stretched into an hour and an hour was impossible to comprehend, and then when the butchers had finally worked their way down through the pile to the shiny steel, along came another tubful of tanners, dumped onto the table, the upside-down crabs clattering across the flat aluminum surface right to the edge, their claws waving in the air.

The three butchers worked without stopping for another two and one-half hours until twelve-thirty, when they pushed through their last white tub. Tal and John straightened up, took off their gloves, placed them on the saw blades, and walked down the line to the gangplank into the *Queen*. Behind them, the next cannery station fed the crab legs through an extractor that squeezed the meat out, while the claws were cut halfway through and tossed into a three-foot-high iron basket. The cookers slammed the baskets shut, lowering them into the steaming water. Past the cook area were the canning machines, where the workers packed the steaming red meat into cans of different sizes ranging from tuna fish-size six-ouncers to five-pound ones, separating the legs and claws. The cans went on big pallets that were winched outside and loaded into a refrigerated Sea-Land trailer. When the trailer was full, a truck came and hauled it to the city dock, where it was loaded on a ship for the long trip down to Seattle.

At lunch, Billy was too tired to eat any of the donuts that were put out for the workers. He took off his rain gear in the break room and stepped out onto the bow again. He sat down on the *Aleutian Queen*'s capstan, flexing his fingers, and looked out over the bow toward the B & B cannery. They were pulling halibut, black on one side and white on the other, out of a Boston Whaler moored to the pilings about twenty feet below. A fisherman in the skiff, wearing black hip boots, was dragging the fish into a basket while a dozen gulls circled overhead, watching and waiting. The beep-beep of a forklift backing up cut through the other sounds as the little Cat took the halibut into the cannery.

It felt good to sit down. The noises from the cannery next door faded as Billy fell asleep. When he woke, he knew he was late; he struggled into his raingear and ran back through the *Queen* to the processing barge. Joe Pike was working at his spot, the crabs flying off his fingers. Billy stood by him for a minute, until the foreman finished a few more crabs.

"IF YOU'RE LATE AGAIN, YOU'RE FIRED."

As Billy moved past the foreman and reached for a crab, Joe stopped him.

"NOT SO FAST. I GOT ANOTHER JOB FOR YOU."

He pointed under the butcher table. There were a handful of legs and claws that had fallen off the table.

"PICK THOSE UP."

Billy dropped down to hands and knees. The floor was six inches deep in yellow crab shit, gills, and bits of brown shell. The noise from the cannery became tinny, and Billy felt as if he was going to pass out.

"THAT'S IT. THAT'S IT." Joe Pike rubbed his hands together. "I NEED 'EM. I NEED 'EM ALL. DON'T MISS A ONE. CRAWL FOR THAT MONEY, BOY."

Billy took several deep breaths as he picked up all the scattered crab legs and claws and butchered them on his stand. He dropped the cut-open legs into the bucket and trudged past the other cannery workers, still finishing up the last batch of crabmeat. He could barely work his fingers; they had become stiff, and the tips were covered with pinhead-sized blisters. They were so sore that he had to use his teeth to unsnap the top button of his rainjacket. After he finished his shift, Billy hung up the jacket and pants on a hook with the others, placed his hardhat on a stack, and clocked out.

His suitcases were in still in Milt's office, just where he had left them. He picked them up and shuffled out of the barge onto Shelikof Street. There was already a procession of unloaders and butchers from other plants walking down the street toward town and Billy fell in among them. He saw a sign for a Travelodge flush against the mountain and walked up onto the main road to the hotel. He didn't have enough money for one night, but didn't want to sleep under a truck again, so he went in and registered. He'd figure out a way to pay it off until he found a more permanent place.

Billy dropped his suitcases in his room and walked over to the window. He was unable to shut out the light because he couldn't close his hands around the cord—his fingers were bent in the butcher position, the exact diameter of a crab leg, but it didn't matter; he could have fallen asleep under an arc light. Billy fell across the double bed and slept for twelve straight hours. It was a dead sleep, and when he awoke, his arms began moving in the rhythm of the butchers.

He stretched and looked at his hands. The small white blisters were hard now and he could barely move his fingers. He rubbed his eyes with the back of his hand and walked over to the window.

The fog had lifted, but the sky was still overcast and gray. He could see snowy mountains ringing the harbor as wide as they were tall, green with white tops. The water now was a choppy greenish color, with whitecaps popping up here and there. Billy could see a couple of boats going out, rising and falling against the swells, their decks piled high with rectangular steel crab pots, while overhead, a red and white floatplane had just taken off and was climbing lazily toward the mountains.

He dressed and walked down the hill to cannery row. The floor of the *Aleutian Queen* was shiny and fresh-looking. He clocked in, picked out his raingear, and stepped into the cold yellow rubber pants. He hitched the suspenders over his shoulders and slipped the raincoat on. His gloves were right where he had left them.

"Hey, cheechako," a man with a red-and-blue checked flannel shirt said. "Let me see your hands."

Billy took his gloves off.

"Jesus Christ. Didn't they give you liners? You have to have liners. Here," the man said, and fished out a pair of cotton gloves from a cardboard box.

"You put *these* on first so you don't wind up with *those*. Those blisters. See?"

The man flexed his fingers.

"You can go for twelve hours now. No problem."

"Thanks."

"Did you just come into town? Where'd you stay last night?"

"Travelodge."

"Are you nuts? That's eighty bucks a night. Here." The man reached into his jeans and pulled out a piece of paper and a pencil nub.

"Unless you're a highliner, you can't stay there. Go to Jan Day's boarding house. She's an old whore from down the Panhandle, around Ketchikan way. Big purple and white house, up on Rezanof. It'll cost you fifty dollars a week."

"Thanks. What do you do here?"

"I'm an unloader, and I got a feeling that unless you pick it up soon, we'll be working together. I've been watching you, boy. You're slow. Real slow. Worst butcher I ever saw."

"Anyway, thanks for telling me about the boarding house . . ."

"Ray. Ray Griebling."

"I'm Billy."

They shook hands.

"Well, Billy, try to pick up some speed today."

Billy nodded and followed Ray back over the gangplank into the cannery barge. John and Tal were already working on the pile, the bucket at their feet nearly filled with tanner legs.

He tried to keep up, but it was useless. The other butchers worked with a dazzling efficiency. Billy wanted to stop working just to watch how smoothly they selected a crab, ran it onto the knife, tore off the legs and claws, dropped them in the buckets while simultaneously reaching for the next crab. There was no wasted motion. By the time Billy grabbed a crab to the moment he reached for his next one, John and Tal had butchered two or three each. He caught a glimpse of Joe Pike watching him, and he tried to speed up, but he wound up botching the whole thing, cutting the legs and claws sloppily so that the meat became hung up in the shells.

"HERE," Pike shouted over the grinder noise. "LET ME SHOW YOU AGAIN, GREENGRASS."

He picked a crab off the stack, lined it up, and butchered it expertly, turning to the hacksaw blade and neatly outside onto the short bow deck.

After work, he walked over to the motel. He picked up his suitcases and slipped out past the front desk, promising himself that he would pay off the bill later.

As he made his way into town, his suitcases banging against his legs, Billy saw that there were three streets coming off Center Avenue: Mill Bay, Rezanof and Mission Road.

Billy climbed up the short hill to 212 Rezanof.

The house was painted in a gaudy purple color with white trim and had three floors, with plenty of windows overlooking the wide bay. The front of the house had been covered with an enclosed porch that held snow shovels, rubber boots, raingear, rope, fishing rods and a five-foot long steel gaff.

Billy dropped his suitcases on the porch and knocked on the door.

"One," a woman said.

"Three," a man said.

"One," Billy heard the woman say again.

"Three."

Billy knocked again. After about a minute, he heard a chair creak and the door opened a crack.

The man who answered was about 6'3" and weighed maybe 150 pounds, a flannel-shirted Ichabod Crane. His straggly black hair—what there was of it—was combed across his head in a careful weave, and his clothes looked rumpled and slept-in.

"What do you want?"

"I need a place to . . . "

"Wait a sec."

The man closed the door on Billy, and he heard some discussion taking place. Ichabod came back and motioned Billy inside.

An enormous woman sat in the corner in an oversized easy chair. She must have weighed more than 450 pounds and was wearing a faded flower print housedress. The woman didn't look up at Billy at all, but instead was staring at a black and white TV that had on some slick-haired, smiling game show host. Billy saw that it was Monty Hall and *Let's Make a Deal.*

"Sit down," the fat woman said, without moving her eyes from the screen.

Billy sat down on a broken-down davenport.

"You working?"

"Yeah."

"Which cannery?" She reached for a glass.

"*Aleutian Queen.*"

"Who's the foreman there now?"

"Joe Picoro."

"Joe Pike? That old cock still around? I thought they would have fired his ass long time ago. He drinks too much."

A ripple of applause burst from the TV.

"Well, here's how I work it. It's fifty a week, payable in advance. With kitchen privileges. I have nine cats here: Captain, Betsy, Paula, Big Boy, Patch, Chief, Little Bit, and, uh . . . Burt and Sheba. All of them will get treated better than you. They'll eat better than you, they'll sleep better than you, they get to sit in my easy chairs and you don't, and they'll sure enough screw more than you. You can sit in the kitchen and on that couch. That's it. You can't sit anywhere else. If I see you do anything to my cats, I'll throw you out myself. Don't think I can't, either. I can whip three of you, no problem. Used to do it once a week in Ketchikan on a regular basis. Ain't that right, Jimmy?"

Jimmy didn't answer. He was watching the TV intently.

"I don't have the money right now," Billy said.

"What a surprise. Tell you what," Jan said as she leaned forward, the easy chair making a loud creak, "Give me a little each week from your paychecks. We'll work off that, starting next week. You'll be caught up soon enough. OK?"

"Sure," Billy said.

"Jimmy, show him the room upstairs. The second one on the right."

Jimmy shuffled up the stairs. There were four rooms off the stairs, each with three single beds.

"Here's your room. You can put your suitcases under the bed." Billy slid the heavy bags under the mattress.

"I'll show you the kitchen."

The kitchen was filthy, and the refrigerator was dark inside, the light bulb obscured by all of the paper bags and plastic-wrapped food. A small butcher-block table stood in the center of the room, it's top marred by hundreds of knife cuts.

"Food goes in the fridge."

Jimmy walked over to the living room and fell back into his easy chair.

"Who won?"

"The blonde," Jan said, reaching for a jar of Sunny Jim peanut butter. "Door number fucking one. Monty likes blondes. That's why they always win. Blondes always win on this show."

She stuck her finger in the peanut butter and looked over at Billy. "The show's rigged, of course. All of them are."

"Quiet, Jan," Jimmy said. "Let's hear what she won."

The three of them listened to the announcer read off the list of prizes as the blonde jumped up and down and hugged Monty Hall.

"Well, so long," Billy said, and when neither one answered, walked back out into the bright gray light. Even though it was about eight o'clock, the sun was still high in the sky. He went back toward Center Street and walked past the Orpheum movie theater, Kraft's General Store, a used car lot, the Island Maid bakery, a small post office, and a few apartment buildings.

Billy turned around and went back down Center to the dock where he had landed on the *Tustumena* just the day before yesterday. A couple of kids with hand-lines were fishing off the wood pilings.

"Any luck?" Billy asked the older one.

"Naw. Just a few bullhead and a flounder."

"What do you use for bait?"

"Oh, we use salmon eggs and jig for 'em."

He watched the boys fish for a while, and then turned back and walked across Center to The Mall, a square with three sides, the fourth side open and facing the bay. He bought a hamburger and a Coke at the J & J Restaurant with his last $10.

Back at the boarding house, Jan Day and Jimmy were watching *Jeopardy*. Two cats were sleeping in Jan's lap.

Billy took his boots off, went upstairs, and fell across his bed.

The pain in his hands woke him up several hours later and he couldn't go back to sleep after that, so he put his boots on. The other two beds in his room were filled with both occupants fully-dressed, sleeping on top of their sheets and snoring loudly.

Billy cut across a vacant lot and crossed Center Street. The town was quiet, with kind of a deserted feel to it. It was about 5:00 am and he was the only person moving, across the parking lot by Kraft's, down between the buildings to Shelikof Street, and along cannery row to the *Aleutian Queen*.

Down the road about half a mile, he could already hear the grinders fired up and running, the *tchock* of the steel blades slicing through the halibut heads, the short chuffs of steam blasting out of the canneries and the whine of an unloading crane as its boom moved in and out of a docked boat's lights.

He walked down the gangplank to the *Queen*. The inside barge was gleaming and wet, waiting for the workers. Billy clocked in and put on his raingear, flexing his hands inside the two sets of gloves. He walked over to his spot by the butcher table and found Joe Pike standing there, waiting for him.

"I'VE BEEN WATCHING YOU. YOU'RE STILL TOO GOD-DAMNED SLOW," Pike said. "YOU ARE NOT GETTING ANY FASTER." Even when there was no machinery running he still felt the need to shout.

"SOMEBODY ELSE IS GONNA BUTCHER IN YOUR SPOT TODAY. YOU ARE NOW AN UNLOADER. GO TOPSIDE. THERE'S A FLATBED TRUCK OUT FRONT. LOOK FOR RAY."

Billy turned to go out.

"WAIT. GIMME YOUR RAINGEAR. YOU WON'T NEED IT TODAY."

Billy took off the gear, handed it to Pike, and walked back up the gangplank.

A yellow Ford flatbed with six 4X4 white tubs sat in the gravel parking lot next to a small crane. Ray was sitting in the truck, wearing a brown Robin Hood hunting hat, casually smoking a cigarette.

"I knew you'd wind up out here. Let's go."

Billy climbed into the flatbed and Ray drove down Shelikof about a hundred yards to the *Roxanne* cannery.

"OK, here we go," Ray said, and pulled the flatbed up to the cannery entrance. He flicked the gearshift into reverse and backed down a long drive with about five inches of clearance on each side of the truck.

At the end of the drive was the *Roxanne*'s dock. Billy hopped down from the flatbed and climbed over to one of two big, rusty rectangular iron tanks, about fifteen by twenty feet, each filled with water. Five feet down were all the tanner crabs in the world, swimming around and fighting each other with their claws.

Ray grabbed a knife-shaped lever and strained to lift it. The veins in his neck stood out as he pulled up on the lever, releasing the dump valves and sending the water gushing out of the live tanks, down to the bay thirty feet below. Now Billy could see the crabs more clearly, as the water level dropped, exposing their wet brown shells, the droplets of water sliding off onto the rusty floor of the live tank.

As Billy watched, Ray lowered himself gently into the tank and motioned to the craneman for the bucket. The craneman swung the heavy steel container down to the bottom of the tank just as Ray tossed in the first cluster of crabs. He threw in a few more armloads and then straightened up.

"You want a fancy invitation, kid? Get your ass in here."

Billy climbed up the side of the tank and down the three inside steps, landing on several crabs. He heard the shells crack from his weight as he walked over to Ray.

"No, no, no," Ray said calmly. "Don't walk around like that. That kills 'em. Breaks their shells. Stay in one spot. Work toward the corners, and try to do it without any wasted motion."

As he spoke, Ray had pitched about ten or fifteen more crabs, which now covered the bottom of the bucket.

Billy bent down and tried to collect the crabs as Ray had, but he only came up with two or three at a time. Their pincers were long and pointed and he was afraid of losing a finger.

"Hey. Stop for a minute," Ray said. "Look. You got to gather them, see? Think about scooping leaves into a bushel basket. Work the pile down until you get a hole to stand in, then reach up and pull them down."

Billy tried to follow Ray's directions, but he was still clumsy.

"I got to say this. You have all the makings of being the sorriest-ass damn unloader I ever seen. Tell me true—why'd your daddy run you off?"

"What?"

"I said," Ray said, not unkindly, as he tossed some more crabs into the bucket, "why'd your daddy run you off? You run away from home?"

"No."

"Well," Ray said, "I don't know much, but I can tell when a man's been run off from somewhere, and I think you got run off. Anyway, don't just stand there; pitch them bastards."

Billy bent down and began picking up the crabs.

"Hey. Always toss them upside down—legs up. They don't crawl off the top that way. And no females. No female crabs."

"How can you tell if they're females?"

"How can you tell? Easy. The females have tits."

Ray tossed a few more crabs into the hopper.

"The crew's supposed to weed them out, but we still get a few. Like this one. See? Here's how you know. She's full of eggs. We got to let them have their babies."

"OK."

The bucket was almost filled.

"Keep working," Ray said, then took the female crab and climbed out of the live tank. He tossed the crab into the water and walked over to the flatbed with the six empty white tubs and climbed up on the truck's cab, facing the bed. The craneman lifted the bucket out of the tank and swung it out over the water to where Ray was standing. Ray peered at the scale over the tank and shouted the weight—775—then flipped both left and right latches and pushed the bucket over as the crabs tumbled into the first two white tubs. Ray pulled the bucket back to himself, set the two latches, and began to climb down from the cab as the craneman winched the bucket back over to the tank.

Billy picked up a crab. He could feel it open its right claw and begin to squeeze Billy's finger. He felt the pressure through his thick rubber gloves; tighter and tighter, until the crab must have realized that it had little effect, for Billy felt the pressure slowly lessening on his finger, and the crab released its grip.

In a response that surprised him, he broke the crab's claw off without even thinking about it, and tossed it into the bucket, which was still moving down toward him.

"Bastard," he said under his breath.

"Attaway," Ray said. He had climbed back into the tank. "Make the fuckers pay for it."

The bucket floated down between them and settled onto the tank floor. The two men worked mechanically and had the container filled again in a few minutes.

"Now it's your turn to go up on the truck," Ray said.

Billy climbed out of the tank, walked down the dock to the truck and up onto the cab. He felt slightly dizzy, standing high on the roof, kicking his rubber boots against the slick metal, trying to grab a toehold as the bucket moved out to him. He turned and looked back for the container. It was right by his face. He reached over for the latch on the left side and nearly fell into the tubs. He regained his balance as the craneman brought the bucket in again. Billy reached again for the bucket, caught it, and began to fumble for the latch.

"What's the weight?" the craneman yelled.

Billy watched the arm stop.

"Seven fifteen this time."

"Seven fifteen."

The craneman wrote the number down on a clipboard.

Billy caught the latch and released the left side. He spun the bucket around, freed the right side, and dumped the load into the white tubs. Then he grabbed the bucket back and flipped over the latches.

Climbing back into the tank, Ray said, "That was OK. But you know how close you came to going into the water? Always be balanced when you're waiting for the bucket. Wait till you try dropping the bucket when it's ten degrees and there's ice on the cab. Or if that crazy shithead Soltana is the craneman. He's always drunk or hung over and that's when he starts bouncing and jitterbugging the bucket around. Don't reach. Never reach for it. Let them bring it to you. Otherwise, you'll fall in for sure. Remember, ten minutes. That's the magic number. That's about all the time you got in that water before hypothermia comes. Same as going to sleep, the SAR guys out at the Coast Guard base told me. The only difference is that you wake up dead. And they say that even the ones who fall into the water and get rescued—they never get warm again. They spend the rest of their lives bundled up with quilts and hot water bottles in a rocking chair."

"I'll remember that."

"You'd better. Oh, yeah, I forgot to tell you. When you call out the weights, always round down. That's the cannery owner's orders. The boats want us to round up, but we always round down. So, if it's 663, say 660. Say, where you from?"

"Ohio."

"A flatlander, huh? Well, this is Alaska, and there's about sixty-five things waiting to kill you each day. Go into the woods, there's bears, fall in the water, there's the cold. Go out of town to Pasagshak in the winter and have your car break down—that's it. This country will kill you quick and easy or long and slow if it wants it that way; it seeps into your goddamned brain and just when you stop thinking about it, it kills you. Or maybe it won't come that way. Maybe you'll get distracted for a second and get mixed up in a piece of machinery so you'll just lose a finger or an arm. Happens every day. It's not you; it's the country. It kills. Don't forget that."

"I won't."

"See that you don't," Ray said.

The bucket came down.

"Oh, yeah. And here's one more rule. Don't stand under the bucket. It's hard to pitch crabs after it smashes down on you and you wind up a foot and a half high."

Sweat poured off the two men as they bent to their work. After two more buckets the white tubs on the truck were filled, and Billy climbed out and rode back with Ray to the *Queen*, where another craneman lifted the tubs onto the forklift.

"One more trip, then lunch," Ray said. "Let's see if you learned anything."

Billy had picked up some speed, but he wasn't near as fast as Ray. They wiped out the live tank as he lost track of how many buckets they filled, but then another boat came in and they worked through lunchtime until two o'clock, and then he could begin to see the rusty floor of the live tank through the bubbling, oxygen-starved crabs. Finally, Billy and Ray filled the last bucket and all that remained were a few dead crab bodies on the bottom of the tank.

"OK. Lunchtime," Ray said. "The *Challenger* will be ready for us this afternoon. We'll take what we can right from its hold and winch the rest into the live tanks."

They drove the flatbed back over to the *Queen* and watched the crane as it picked the white tubs full of crabs from the truck. When the last tub came off, Ray parked off to the side while Billy walked back to the break room and clocked them both out for lunch.

Ray came in and pulled out a lunchbox from a locker.

"Bring your lunch?"

"I'm not hungry."

"Bullshit. Here," Ray said, and tossed over a bag of carrots. "A man's got to eat something."

Billy ate as the lunchroom began to fill with cannery workers. The two butchers, John and Tal, walked right past him without saying anything, through the door onto the bow of the *Queen*. A half dozen women chattered away in a corner, while two bearded men played chess. From what he could tell, a few of the women looked like college girls, while the older ones were Filipinos or Aleuts.

"I can read your mind," Ray said. "You're thinking about those girls over in the corner. Well, forget it. Don't think about it. You got as much a chance of getting laid here as finding a gold watch pinned to one of these crabs. The men outnumber the women six to one, maybe eight to one on the Rock, so the girls can pick and choose who they want, and they sure don't want you. It's not worth thinking about, it really isn't.

"Now me, I got it made. Got a wife over at the Coast Guard base, worships the ground I walk on, waits for me to come home every day with a can of Lucky cracked open, and why? Because I got two jobs, one as a base carpenter and this one. I am making the serious money, son."

"Tal said that the fishermen make lots of money. You want to go out on one of the crab boats?" Billy asked.

"Hell, no," Ray said, as he ate his sandwich. "Not me. Sure, those guys can get rich, but they can also get dead. And the ones that don't get killed get banged up, lose a finger or hand. Go down to Tony's and see for yourself. See all the fishermen with their index fingers missing, caught it in the power block when they pulled up a pot, or look at what a halibut gaff can do to a man's hands.

"See," Ray continued, as he took a sip of coffee, "it's like this. These guys come up here for a whole bunch of reasons. Some come to get away from a bad marriage, a bad business, everything bad. They come Inside and this is it—their last chance. So they start at the canneries at $3.25 an hour, like you, but their eyes are on those Bender wheelhouse beauties in the harbor.

"So they work their way on up, from the small purse seiners and Boston Whalers to the really big boats, the ones from Washington with those high Bender wheelhouses. And all they're thinking about is the handful of highliners—the real great fishermen here, like George Reiter, the ones who bring in fifty, sixty, or a hundred grand during the season. But they never think about the bodies lying at the bottom of the ocean. Because the ocean don't care if you're George Reiter or Jon Jensen or Kai Wendling or where you came from. It'll pluck you off the boat just as smooth as can be and the next thing you know you're bobbing up and down in the gray water and it's so cold you can't catch your breath. You feel your raingear and boots filling up and they throw you a life preserver and you have only one chance to catch it."

"So why do they do it then?"

"Why does anyone do anything? For the money. Man, you're not the brightest bulb in the socket, are you?"

Ray took another drink of coffee.

"Tell the truth now. You can tell old Ray. Why'd your daddy run you off?"

"Nobody ran me off," Billy said.

"Then why are you up here?"

"I wanted to see the country."

"Now that's bullshit right there," Ray said. "Yes sir, that is 99 and 44/100 percent pure bullshit. Nobody comes up here to 'see the country.' Everybody knows there's only two reasons to go to Alaska: to get away from something or to make money. Now you ain't a pipeline guy, I can see you wouldn't know where to sit on a D9 Cat, and you ain't a fisherman, and we know you sure as hell ain't a cannery hand, and you ain't never been a placer miner, so I am asking you again: why are you here?"

A line from *Casablanca*, one of Billy's favorite movies, popped into his head:

"I came for the waters."

"Waters? What the shit kind of answer is that?" Ray asked. "Well, you and I are going to be spending a lot of time together in the tanks; I'll find out sooner or later."

Ray's face brightened.

"Got a girl in trouble?"

A quick flash of Carol's face passed across his mind.

"No."

"Well, it's something. I know it is. Ol' Ray will figure it out sooner or later."

They clocked in and walked back through the plant to the flatbed. The six white tubs had been emptied and replaced. Ray started the truck up—there was no key, only a can opener dangling from a string—and the bright-yellow Ford rumbled down the gravel road back to the *Roxanne*. Ray backed down the long dock to the live tanks and parked the truck.

The craneman winched them over to the *Challenger* and they began working out of the hold, unloading the crabs from the boat right to their truck. Billy and Ray worked past five, six, seven pm without a break, trying to empty the hold for their last shift. Finally, they loaded the last bucket about half-full. Billy clambered out of the tank and up the side of the flatbed to the cab roof.

"Two ninety-five," he called out to the craneman, and dumped the crabs neatly into the front two tubs on the flatbed. Billy and Ray drove back to the *Queen*, parked the truck and clocked out.

"See you tomorrow, kid, if you don't quit first," Ray Griebling said. He walked across the small gravel parking lot to a black and white Bronco.

Billy walked back down Shelikof Street. The bars along cannery row were full with pickup trucks jammed every which-way on the gravel lots. He could hear the country music guitars twanging through the windows with some high-pitched hoots and shrieks of laughter riding out above the jukebox. Past the Anchor Bar, he heard the sound of breaking glass, while across Shelikof the boats bobbed gently in the black water.

He was tired and hungry as he trudged up the hill to Jan Day's boarding house. Before he reached the door, he could hear Jan and Jimmy's voices.

"Two," Jan Day said.

"Door number three," Jimmy said. "Hey, greenhorn. Take off your goddamn boots on the porch. This ain't no hotel."

Billy had forgotten to remove them, so he did as he was told and put the rubber cannery boots in a line with half a dozen other pairs. He closed the screen door carefully and padded upstairs to his room. The other two beds were filled; he could hear his roommates snoring from the stairway. Billy took off his shirt and pants and climbed into bed in his long johns. He was hungry but fell asleep anyway after a few minutes.

*

The rest of April was a blur—eighteen- to twenty-hour days spent unloading tanner crabs and putting in extra time for cleanup. Until he began receiving his paychecks, Billy lived on the donuts the cannery bought from the Island Maid each morning. He squared his rent with Jan Day and paid his bill at the Travelodge. He still had a few dollars left over to open an account at the First Bank of Alaska on Center Street, which he picked over the only other bank in town because of the enormous stuffed brown bear in its lobby. He had become faster at unloading; now he was almost as quick as Ray Griebling and because Billy was about fifteen years younger, he could easily outlast Ray.

Every day was the same routine. Roll out of the bed, get dressed, walk through the darkened town at 5:00 am, work until ten or eleven at night, then trudge back down Shelikof to Jan Day's.

For some reason, each morning as he was getting dressed, Billy thought of the words from an old Fred Astaire movie, *Top Hat*, except he was putting on cannery gear instead of a tuxedo. After awhile, the routine was something he didn't even think about.

First he put on the long john top and bottom for the cold mornings. You could strip off your flannel shirt and work in the long john top by afternoon. Then came the Frisco jeans, two pairs of thick socks and then the steel-toed rubber boots. He had a special set of yellow Helly Hansen rainjacket and pants stowed away at the *Queen* in case the weather turned.

He always dressed in a hurry, because Billy was quick to understand that speed meant money; more crabs unloaded meant more crabs processed and more crabs sent to Seattle. The *Queen*'s long shift could run through several thousand pounds without breaking a sweat, but by late April two boats would come in simultaneously. He'd lean on his mop at cleanup and watch them both tie up to the *Roxanne* and fight over who should be unloaded first. That meant double shifts for everyone on the cannery payroll.

There was no time for anything except working, a few meals and sleeping. The rest of the world just slipped off somewhere. Outside of the Armed Forces Radio Network station transmitting from the Coast Guard base there was no source of news. The town's one TV station carried the news and TV programs from the previous week. The two newspapers from Anchorage—the *Daily News* and the *Times*—were flown in each day unless the weather was bad, which Billy estimated at about once or twice a week. Kodiak did have a small paper of its own, the *Daily Mirror*, which was full of stories about a possible strike for the upcoming shrimp season.

The Orpheum showed movies that were anywhere from two to fifteen years old, mainly Clint Eastwood and Charles Bronson films, but it wasn't unusual for *Cinderella* or *Dumbo* to appear on the bill. The film cans sat in the window, so Billy could see what was playing by reading what was on the cans each day. One of the biggest cinematic events that spring was when the movie theater owner, a mousy little blonde-haired man with a droopy mustache named Bob Douglas, scored a triumph of sorts when he located a scratched-up copy of *Love Story*. Even though the movie was now two years old, every woman in town over the age of thirteen had to see it, and each day for three straight weeks, the line stretched down the block. Wodlinger's Drugstore ran out of Kleenex, and *Love Story* became an island phenomenon as women from as far away as Karluk caught the mail plane into town to see it. The story even made the *Mirror*'s society box, right next to an ad about the seal-skinning contest.

The boats came in every few days from the Bering Sea, their holds filled up to the wooden covers, first with tanner crabs, then Dungeness. The money ebbed and flowed through the city, a dirty green river swirling around the bars and strip joints, the grocery stores and the two banks in town.

"You have to remember," Eddie Walsh, an unloader from Sand Point, told Billy, "this town is all about money. Forget about this 'love of the sea' shit. You ever hear that poem, 'I must go down to the sea in ships?' What a lie, the biggest of all time. It's money. That's all it's ever been about here."

Billy didn't spend too much money, but when he needed anything, like everyone else on the island, he went to Kraft's, the combination supermarket and general store that sold everything from peanut butter to tuxedo shirts.

Around the corner from Kraft's was Tony's, which was a combination steak house, Chinese restaurant and strip joint. Each of the four waitresses was a topless dancer. They were in their early twenties, and not bad looking, but Billy thought that their eyes had a kind of soft sadness to them. Each woman would take orders and bring food out until it was her turn, and then she'd walk over to the jukebox and put a quarter in for her two songs, which were almost always *Tie A Yellow Ribbon 'Round the Old Oak Tree*, or Sammy Davis, Jr.'s *The Candy Man*, tunes so saccharinely sweet that they made Billy's teeth hurt.

Then the waitress would slowly peel off her shirt and gyrate around, the place becoming quiet except for Tony Orlando or Sammy while the ten or twelve flannel-shirted men seated around the little card tables munched on their steaks or chop suey and stared at the woman's fishbelly-white breasts. Most of the crewmen had just come in from three days at sea and they had what Billy came to recognize as the Bering Sea Stare—eyes glazed, mouth open, several days' growth of beard, black watch caps still on their heads, spittle in the corners of their open mouths, quietly watching, not speaking, barely breathing, their eyes focusing on some skinny girl from Tacoma or Portland as she gyrated around the small plywood stage.

The two jukebox tunes lasted about five minutes; then the dancer would step down from the stage, pick up her top where she had dropped it and walk between the tables to the kitchen for her order pickup. Billy had to admire the efficiency of the operation; the dancers served the food, the fishermen ate without much conversation, then stood up and left, walking past a clump of men who were standing on the sidewalk outside, trying to get a free look as the door swung open.

The whole scene seemed so strange to Billy, that the crewmen who just ten to twenty hours ago were wrestling pots onto the deck would now be back in port, watching strippers. It was a kind of victory celebration, he thought, since the fishermen had rolled the dice with the ocean and won. They hadn't died; they hadn't lost a finger or an arm. Tony's was the reward for making it back, chugging up through Shelikof Strait with a hold full of crabs.

*

By the time the steady Kodiak rains had washed the last part of April away, Billy had learned how to be a good cannery hand. His efficiency as an unloader had increased, and since he had been there for a while from the beginning of the season, the crews on the different crabbers knew him by name. Several times Billy did all of the work himself, when Ray Griebling couldn't get away from his carpentry job at the base. Billy would back the truck down the long dock, fill the buckets and winch them over to the white tubs on the flatbed. Even when Ray was there, it seemed like the faster Billy became, the more Ray slowed down. And now Billy occasionally worked alongside Tal Malinovsky and John Charlie, when the two butchers were overloaded. He was much quicker, almost as fast as Tal now, but he still couldn't catch John, the Aleut who was the fastest butcher on the island. He had won a medal at last year's Crab Festival to prove it and often wore it pinned to his raingear.

The man with the red hardhat from Billy's first day had been right about Joe Pike. It didn't take more than two weeks before the foreman had climbed up on the White Horse again. The more boats came in, the more times Joe would duck behind the retort with his silver hip flask. He no longer shouted at the butchers to move faster; in fact he became invisible as every day the boats docked, their holds filled with tanners, the crabs swimming and fighting with each other down in the shimmering darkness.

CHAPTER 12

Everyone who stayed in Kodiak for more than a few days had to pick out his favorite bar. The decision might take some time, but it was a choice that simply had to be made.

Where one drank depended on the caste system in town, Billy discovered. At the bottom of the ladder, the natives—Eskimos or Aleuts who either came from somewhere else in the Interior or way down along the Chain—preferred one of the two downtown bars, the Breakers or the Ships. There were fights almost every night beginning around ten in the Breakers, battles so loud that Billy thought he could hear the shouts and glass shattering all the way up at Jan Day's boarding house. Longtime Kodiak residents stayed away from the Breakers and the Ships and took their business to Solly's Office or the Mecca, while boat captains, cannery owners, town businessmen, and other members of Kodiak high society never drank in town with the cannery riffraff, but would instead drive twenty to thirty miles out the Chiniak Road to the Rendezvous Bar in Middle Bay or the Kalsin Bay Inn.

The Coast Guard base had two bars, one for officers and one for enlisted men, but these were off limits to civilians, and so cannery hands really had just two choices, and luckily for them, they were right across the street. These were the Anchor Bar and the Crab Pot.

The Pot, as the regulars called it, was a one-story, lime-green building whose name came from two ten-foot-high stacks of tanner crab pots, ropes still coiled inside, flanking the bar's front door. The fishing gear was the property of the *Madre Delarosa*, a fifty-foot crabber that sank with all hands several years before, and the pots had never been moved. In fact, a black watch cap that had belonged to the boat's skipper sat on a dusty bottle of Johnnie Walker Red, waiting for its owner.

It was Ray Griebling who took Billy to the Pot for the first time.

They had just finished their third week working together as unloaders, and by the time they had cleaned up and clocked out, the place was noisy with other unloaders from the *Roxanne*, B & B, *Pacific Pearl*, Alaska Packers and the *Aleutian Queen*.

"Everybody," Ray said as he pushed his way to the bar, "I want you to meet the greenest kid on the Rock. His name is Billy. Now I've been working with him for three weeks, and he *still* won't tell me why his daddy ran him off. Here, Billy, that's Harry, Butch, Alex, Bert way over in the corner there, and Bob the bartender."

"Where you from, cheechako?" Bob asked.

"Ohio."

"Christ. Another flatlander. That's all we need."

"Oh, he's not so bad," Ray said. "For a flatlander. Of course, he's not a real sourdough."

"That's right," Bob said. "To be a real sourdough, you have to drink an iceworm cocktail."

"What's that?" Billy asked.

"Well, kid, it's a mix of pure glacier water, Everclear, and of course the iceworm itself," Butch Edwards said. "See, the iceworm is a thin white animal with red eyes that lives inside a glacier. And not just any glacier. It can only be found in one: the Mendenhall, down by Juneau. These iceworms grow to about twelve or fourteen inches long. To be a real Alaskan, a sourdough, you have to drink a big iceworm cocktail. You up for that?"

"Sure," Billy said.

Bob disappeared in the back and came out with a large glass filled to the top with ice. The glass had "Sourdough" written across it in script. He unscrewed the cap from a bottle of Everclear liquor and poured it into the glass.

Then he fished out the iceworm from a jar under the bar.

"Here it is," the bartender said. "Get a good look. One genuine iceworm."

Billy's stomach flipped. The iceworm was pale white and about a foot long, a quarter of an inch in diameter and as far as Billy could tell, was looking right at him with its bright red eyes.

Bob placed the iceworm on top of the liquid and then stirred it into the drink.

"OK, kid. To happy days."

Billy took a drink. The Everclear was 200 proof—pure alcohol—and made him gasp. He had three or four drinks before his lips touched the iceworm. Then he stopped and held the drink out in front of him.

The worm was moving slowly in the glass.

"Come on, chug it," Butch urged.

Billy closed his eyes, and lifted the glass up. He drank a little bit more and now he could feel the iceworm in his throat, all slithery, and then he swallowed the rest, barely keeping it down until he slammed the glass back onto the bar.

Everyone cheered.

"OK. OK," Ray said. "So he's a sourdough now."

"Should we tell him?" Butch asked.

"Might as well," Bob said.

"There's no such thing as an iceworm. That was a piece of spaghetti with red ink spots for eyes," Ray said. "But don't worry. You're still a sourdough."

"I thought you were a sourdough if you stayed in Alaska for a full year," Alex said.

"No, Ray's right. He's a sourdough now," Butch said. "Don't let no one tell you different, kid. Say, did you ever hear the story about the guy who came to Alaska and he wanted to become a REAL sourdough?"

"Oh, God, no, Butch. Not that one," Harry said.

"Have you heard it?"

"Only about a thousand times. Don't you remember how many times you've told it?"

"Well, it's a good story. And it's true, too. Bob," Butch said to the bartender, "drinks all around."

Bob clanged a ship's bell and set about serving everyone in the place a drink.

"Now there was this cheechako who comes into the Pot one day about two years ago and gets to talking, and one of the regulars says, 'I can see you're new to Alaska. If you want to be a sour-dough, a real Alaskan, there are three things you got to do:

piss in the Yukon, wrestle a Kodiak bear and make love to an Eskimo woman.' So the guy runs out of the bar and comes back about a month later.

" 'I did it,' this guy says, " 'I pissed in the Yukon. One down, two to go.' Then he goes away again.

"Well, we don't see him for about a year. Tell the truth, we've forgotten all about him. I know I did. But then here he comes back. Man, he is one goddamn mess. Clothes all muddy and torn, bloodstains everywhere, face all scratched up, eyes black, and he says, 'Now, where's that Eskimo woman you want me to wrestle?'"

Everyone laughed except Bert.

"Hey, it's four-thirty. Time for the dance," Alex said.

All of them moved over to the windows and looked up Shelikof, and now Billy could see lines of workers coming out of all the canneries, walking slowly down the street. The butchers were first, clenching and unclenching their hands as they walked, their rubber boots swishing. After the butchers came the gillers, leg cutters and roller feeders. Next came the pickbelt women, some still wearing their stiff plastic aprons, their dark skin making them look somewhat tarnished in the gray light. Some of the Filipino women wore green or purple sweatshirts from other canneries out on the Chain, with drawings of king crabs stretched across the front.

The packers followed, swinging their arms as they walked, a mix of Filipinos and Aleuts. Then came the caseup crews, responsible for stacking the frozen boxes in the Sea-Land refrigerated trailers behind the canneries. When a trailer was full, they would haul it over to the city dock and put the load on an enormous ship bound for Seattle. Finally, the cleanup men walked down Shelikof, tired from their long shift.

"Well, shit. Just as I thought. Maybe a couple of college girls. A couple of new ones. But all in all, not a good-looking woman in the bunch," Harry said.

"What'd you expect? Miss America? This is Kodiak, for Christ's sake. They're just cannery girls. Now if you want a real woman, go over to Sally Perdido's."

"Yeah, Butch, but there were a couple of college girls here and there . . ."

"I saw some college girls, too, Harry. Maybe they came up for the season," Ray said.

"What do you care, Ray?" Butch said. "You're married."

"Never hurts to look. But as far as any action in this town, you just have to give it up," Ray continued. "If you don't want to go to Sally's, you're going to have to go to A-town to get laid. May as well shell out and hop on the afternoon plane tomorrow. Otherwise, you can always go back to that blind spot behind the shrimp rollers. Nobody will see you there."

"Go fuck yourself, Ray."

"Can't. I tried. It's anatomically impossible."

A man wearing an orange hunting cap came in.

"CC and water, Bob," the man said.

He looked around the bar. "Hey, did you guys hear about what happened last night with the *Miss Juneau*?"

"No, what, Danny?" Bob said as he poured a shot of Canadian Club.

"It went down off False Pass with a load of grass on board. Tommy Iverson at Solly's told me there was a half a ton of pot and hashish going out to Dutch Harbor."

"Who was the skipper?"

"Gil Hinckle. A CG 130 dropped a raft for them. They're all OK."

"Well, there'll be a lot of stoned pollack down there tonight," Ray said.

"You know, this conversation's very interesting, but it is not getting me laid," Harry said.

"Harry," Ray said, "you couldn't get laid if you were airdropped into a girl's dorm on homecoming night."

"You know what I really like about a woman?" Butch asked. "I like to see them sitting on a barstool with their legs crossed, in a short skirt, wearing high heels, with one shoe dangling. What a tease. One time, I was Outside, oh, about ten years ago, sitting at the bar at the Fairmont Hotel in 'Frisco, and this smart little chick came in, dressed all in red. Red skirt, red blouse, red high heels and a little red hat, with a pouty red-lipstick mouth. She sat at the bar and gave me The Look."

"The Look?

"Yeah, Ray. The Look. Remember way back, before you got married?" Butch took another drink.

"Anyway, she moves over a stool and asks me to buy her a drink. She's got her right shoe off and it's just dangling. We talked for two or three hours about this and that. Then her husband shows up. So she puts on this act about how she's so pissed at him for being late."

"Was he?" Ray asked.

"How the hell do I know? Anyway, he storms out, but now get this. Before she leaves she slips me a matchbook with her phone number on it. I pay my bill and go out and it's raining like hell and the rain washes out the last digit of her number. I went to a pay phone and tried all of the numbers from zero to nine but it was no good. Ever since then I can still see it like yesterday—the girl in the bar of the Fairmont, her pretty little foot with that bright red high heel dangling from it."

"I like a smart girl who's also good-looking," Alex said. "None of them dumb ones."

"You're out of luck, then, Al, " Butch said. "Trying to find a good-looking woman with brains in this town is like trying to find a garbage can that doesn't stink."

"The one thing all of us should remember," Alex said, as he drained his Oly, "is that none of this talk is getting us laid. That's the most important point here."

"Alex, I tell you something," said Swede Johansen, a big ruddy-faced man whose fingers were gnarled from years of pulling up halibut. "Better to forget them up here. There is always six of us and one of them. Are they gonna pick you over five other guys? No, I don't think so. So I tell you to forget about women when you are Inside. They make you go crazy, like Bert over there."

"Bert didn't go crazy over girls, Swede," Butch said. "Bert's always been crazy."

Bert sat in the corner, staring at some imaginary thing.

"I try not to think about 'em," Butch continued, motioning for another beer. "After all this time, I can take 'em or leave 'em. Really, I can. Been married twice. Wonderful women. The big mistake was that I married them. They wanted to get married. I didn't."

Butch stared out the window.

"Look at those drops of rain on the glass. You see how they work their way down to the bottom? You can't tell what they're going to do. They could go left or right. They could run straight down. Or they could just hang there."

He took another drink.

"Same with women. You don't know what they're going to do. Just like with my wives. Both native girls. Nothing wrong with siwashing it, going native. The first one was from Unalakleet and my second wife was from Nulato. Loved 'em both, loved the shit out of 'em, but they both left me. That Nulato girl was something. Small, but she could lift a hundred and fifty pounds straight over her head. Never complained; sewed hides a mile a minute, hunted and broke trail, and those nights when it was forty below, snuggling under that bearskin robe . . . "

Butch smiled and took another drink, remembering.

"Her father was a prick, though. He hated me. He used to make his snares, sitting cross-legged on the floor, talking to himself, and my name coming up every tenth word or so. That's the only part of what he said that I understood. I didn't know what he was saying, but I didn't need to. He hated my guts. Oh, the women were crazy about me, but I chased them away.

"I kind of got run out of Nulato and before that, Unakaleet. Nothing to do but play cards all night long in U-town. That and drink. And well, let's just say that I had to leave Unalakleet for a number of reasons, which I really don't care to discuss at the present time.

"Come to Kodiak a few years ago, I see all these boats in the harbor, and I said, 'If there's as many women as boats here, I'm set.' But there weren't. Oh yeah, women are always crazy about me, but I can take 'em or leave 'em."

Butch raised his scotch and stood up.

"What the hell. A toast, then, gentlemen.

"Here's to heat,
Not the kind that brings down shanties,
But the kind that brings down panties.
Here's to heat."

Everyone took a drink except for Bert.
"You too, Bert, drink up."

Bert said nothing. He was staring at his beer bottle.

"What's the matter, Bert boy? You out of beer? Bob, get Bert another Lucky."

The barkeep took another beer to Bert.

"Have a drink, Bert," Butch said. "On me."

Bert slowly raised his eyes from the bottle and stared at Butch. "No."

"I said have a drink."

Bert stood up. There was a Schrade knife in his hand.

Everyone stopped talking. The only sound was the click-click of the overhead fan blade. Billy saw Bob cupping a hand over a phone receiver.

"Nobody," Bert said in a slow voice, "tells me what to do."

"Bert," Ray said. "Nobody is telling you to do nothing. Just sit down."

"You want to give it a go, Bertie boy?" Butch said. "Let's go." He had a Bowie knife out. "Come on. Come on, you sick son of a bitch."

Bert shoved a chair out of the way.

The two men moved toward the center of the room where the small wooden dance floor was, away from the tables, and began to circle each other.

Now it felt dangerous in the bar to Billy.

"Hey, Butch," he said, "it's not worth it."

"Shut up, iceworm. This isn't your fight."

The two men continued to move in a circle around the dance floor, watching each other.

Bob tried to flip the light switch, but he accidentally turned on the metal globe instead, and the bar was bathed in blue and yellow dance lights as the men moved around.

Then Bert saw his opening. He lunged at Butch just as Terry Todd, one of the city police officers, came in with his .44 service revolver drawn. Terry brought the gun barrel down hard on Bert's hand just as the knife touched Butch's shirt.

The Schrade clattered into a corner, and Billy exhaled. He had been holding his breath the entire time.

Todd had Bert by the arm.

"Come on," Todd said as he put the handcuffs on Bert. "I'm running you in."

"And you," he said, gesturing to Butch, "you better get over to the clinic. He got you."

Butch lifted his shirt. His long underwear top was red.

"Son of a bitch. That square-head bastard."

Billy saw the blood coming out right under Butch's ribs.

"You better go to the clinic," Todd repeated.

"Son of a bitch got me. I can't hardly believe this shit."

"You want a ride?" Alex said.

"No," Butch said. "I'm OK. I can walk."

"I'll go with you," Billy said.

"Suit yourself."

The clinic was a new building on Mill Bay up the street from Jan Day's boarding house. The physician on call, Dr. Alvarado, was reading a copy of *Outdoor Life* when Billy and Butch came in.

"Need some help," Billy said.

"I can see that," the doctor said mildly. He put down his magazine, careful not to lose his place.

"Gun or knife?"

"Knife," Billy said.

"Filipino or Aleut?"

"What difference does it make?" Billy said.

"None, I suppose, except the Aleuts usually prefer longer knives. Well, hop up on the table here and let's see the damage. Lift up his shirt for me, please."

Billy helped Butch up and lifted the wounded man's shirt. The checkered weave in Butch's undershirt was red and sticky.

"You caught a break there. It's not too deep," the doctor said, and pulled some saline solution, lidocaine and epinephrine from the shelf. "You'll live, but I wouldn't get into any more fights this weekend. You've lost some blood."

He injected the lidocaine and epi around the wound.

"No kidding," Butch said. He forced a dry laugh.

The doctor washed his hands and snapped on a pair of gloves.

"Hand me a pack of sutures over there please. They're sterile inside, so you can open them and I'll fish out the sutures myself."

"Chromic?" Billy asked.

"No, non-dissolving will be fine. I think I can take care of this pretty quickly. It's more lateral than deep. I'll also need some . . ."

"Pickups?"

"Yes. You sound like you know what you're doing," Alvarado said as he dabbed at the wound. "Are you a doctor?"

"No," Billy said, "but I worked as an OR tech for a couple of years. I know my way around a sterile field."

"Good, then you can help me. It'll go faster. Put on some gloves from the rack over there."

Billy found a pair of 8's, ripped open the envelope, and smelled the old familiar talcum powder. It felt comforting.

He took up his assistant's position opposite the doctor.

The doctor was fast and sloppy.

"I like long tails. Please leave the tails a little longer than that," Dr. Alvarado said as Billy cut the sutures.

The two men worked in silence for a few minutes.

"Say twenty-two stitches total. People say I'm old-fashioned, but you know why I prefer these black closures instead of staples? They remind me of the color of my first wife's hair. Black as octopus ink. Now son, you're a lucky man," the doctor said, as he dabbed at the wound again, looking for any bleeders. "A little bit deeper and there'd be real trouble."

"I know it," Butch said. His red hair was drenched with sweat.

Dr. Alvarado threw in the last stitch, and Billy followed with a neat cut.

"Good," the doctor said, as he taped a gauze bandage over the wound and then sat down at a small desk. He tossed his gloves into a wastebasket and filled out a couple of papers.

"Here's a prescription for some codeine. You're going to need it tomorrow. Go over to Wodlinger's and get it filled. They open at nine."

Dr. Alvarado rinsed off the instruments and put them in the autoclave. "Come back in a week. We'll take those stitches out, and I'll have a bill for you then."

"Thanks, Doc." Butch grabbed at the paper with his thick fingers as the pain came in waves. The scotch had about worn off.

"Thanks for your help," Dr. Alvarado said to Billy. "Get him home and let him sleep it off. He'll probably wake up tomorrow and wonder what happened."

"Like hell I will," Butch said.

Billy helped him off the gurney and the big man's knees buckled.

"Take it easy, Butch." Billy said as he guided him out the door.

Butch lived in a trailer park out on Benson. It took half an hour to walk there and the hard Kodiak rain had drenched them by the time they made it to his place.

The door was unlocked. Billy helped Butch into his bed. The big man fell down hard on the bed and was asleep in a few seconds.

Billy took Butch's boots off and covered him with a blanket.

"See you later, Butch," Billy said, but the man didn't move.

Billy closed the trailer door softly and walked back into town, watching the raindrops as they made small craters on the gravel road.

CHAPTER 13

It was a week before Billy saw Butch Edwards again in the Crab Pot.

"Hey, iceworm. What was your name again?"

"Billy."

"That's right. Billy. Thanks for last week. Hey, let me buy you a drink."

Bob was already there with an Oly.

"Well, Billy," Butch said, as he raised his glass, "*honi soit qui mal y pense.*"

He threw back a shot of scotch.

"What's that mean?" Billy asked.

" 'Shamed be he who thinks evil of it.' It's French," Butch said. "I read about it in a magazine. The whores from the fifteenth century used to wear it on their garters. There were even some guys who called themselves the Knights of the Garter. Gives me a little class, wouldn't you say?"

"*I* wouldn't," Ray Griebling said. "You're not a Knight of the Garter or any other kind of knight, unless you're Sir Booze-a-lot."

"Always got to be a wiseass, don't you, Ray? Say, Bob, bring Ray another Lucky. Try to mellow him out."

Bob came back with the drinks.

"So, Bob, what's going on with the canneries?"

Bob drew a beer for himself and sat down on a three-legged stool behind the bar.

"Well, I heard there's going to be a strike before the shrimp season starts in July. It's going to be bad. From what Tiny Holmes on the *Invincible* says, the canneries will only pay a dollar-ten a pound and the fishermen want a dollar twenty-five."

"How about halibut?"

"Halibut? Sure, you can always make a little money looking for barn doors, but it's not like a good shrimp season," Bob said. "You still trying to get on a boat, Butch?"

"Yeah, I've been banging on wheelhouses for two months now, but I don't want just any boat. I'm tired of these penny-ante ones where you hump your ass off for fifteen hundred bucks at the end of the season, those little piss-ant twenty-five footers, like the ones they run down in the ABC's."

"ABCs?" Billy asked, puzzled.

"The ABC Islands—Admiralty, Baranof, and Chichagof Islands, down in the Panhandle. Anyway," Butch continued, "I'm holding out for one of those highliners. Meantime, I still got enough cash stashed away in the mattress for a few more months. I can ride it out. Low tide, high tide, makes no difference."

"It's always about the money, isn't it, Butch?"

"Here we go again," Bob said. "The conversation with no beginning and no end."

"Yeah, Ray. It is. I mean, that's why we're here. What else is there?

"Just checking to make sure, Butch."

"You're a fine one to talk. Last time I heard, Ray, you had two jobs."

"Yeah, but that's different. I need two jobs to make it. And the way I work it, I don't have to worry about getting killed each time I wake up in the morning. Who cares about what you have in the bank when you're a hundred fathoms down?"

"None of that's going to matter when the strike comes," Bob said.

"Let it come. This town will do what it always does. Get drunk," Butch said.

"That'll be real good for me," the bartender said. His eyes lit up as he walked the length of the bar. He stopped at the end, gave a short wave to someone who had just come into the Pot. Then he rang the ship's bell.

"Drinks on the house," Bob shouted. "From Jon."

Everyone raised his bottle to Jon Jensen, the big, blond-haired skipper of the *Chief.*

"Yeah, yeah, well, goddamned good for you," Butch muttered into his shot glass.

"Let the good times roll," Jon yelled as Bob handed out bottles of beer all around.

Billy drained his beer quickly.

"See you, Butch. I have to go."

"Where to? Jesus Christ, it's Friday night."

"I'm beat. Humped two crabbers today. I need to get some sleep."

"How old are you, seventy-five? There will be plenty of time to sleep if there's a strike. I've seen that before. This town will be dead for sixteen hours a day. But until then, it's apple blossom time."

Butch drained his Scotch. Bob was right there with another one.

"Tell you what," Butch said. "When you gonna be off next?"

"Well, the *Jody Ann* and the *Lin J* should be back soon. Probably end of next week."

"You know how to fish? I mean, you ever go after sheephead or bass, or whatever kind of shit fish they have Outside?"

"I've fished a few times," Billy said.

"Come back to the Pot if there's a strike. I'll show you around."

"OK."

After a few days, Billy had forgotten about Butch's offer as the cannery kept processing. The crab boats were lined up all the way to the Bering Sea, each one's hold brimming with tanner. Billy lost track of what day it was, what week it was. Sixteen hours on, eighteen hours, twenty hours, then back to the boarding house where he could barely get his rubber boots off before he was asleep.

Wake up again at 4 am, stumble into the boots, then down the hill and across Center Street, past the darkened Orpheum movie theater, Kraft's general store, where the night shift was restocking the shelves, then down dark Shelikof Street to cannery row, watching the lights from the docked boats as the black and red hulls bobbed gently with the harbor currents, the black mass of Pillar Mountain to his right and behind that Three Sisters Mountain, quiet and peaceful as he heard the foremen switch on the crane motors one by one along Cannery Row.

He tried to remember all of the strange events that happened each day. One time Ray opened up the hatch on the *Ocean Challenger* and they saw that someone had spray-painted some of the crabs white and arranged them into the words, "Fuck You." Another time one of the butchers, Tal Malinovsky, went around the plant singing *Strangers in the Night* to each of the women. Then there were the knifings, like clockwork every Friday; the handful of unmarried women in town who had made up laminated index cards that read "Get Lost." They used the cards to save themselves the effort of rejecting advances from all males in town who were over the age of 14. There were the endless bets in the Crab Pot on everything from which foot the next man would use to enter the Pot to whether he was left-handed or right-handed. The Pot had dart tournaments, quarter pitching and all of the red- and green-chili-eating contests, anything to kill the time until the next boat came in.

The town danced right along to the tanner crab tune, and then it was the end of June, the last boats brought in their loads, the crab season ended, and the canneries began the transition from crabs to shrimp. Strike or no strike, it still took time to change over from one season to the next one. The skippers pulled the round crab pots they'd been using for tanner and Dungeness and stored the gear over in Bells Flats. At the canneries up and down Shelikof Street, the crab equipment had to be stowed away under thick plastic sheeting, while the shrimp gear was uncovered, the peelers oiled and test-fired. The cannery hands living on board were kept busy moving the machinery into place, painting and chipping away rust, stacking the small six-ounce cans and big five-pounders.

Then after a few more days, Billy was laid off with all of the other workers who didn't live on board the *Queen*. He went to the accounting office for his last paycheck.

"You turned out to be a pretty good cannery hand, kid," Joe Pike, the foreman, said. "You don't know how close I came to firing your ass that first week. Come back around when we're in the shrimp."

But there wasn't any shrimp. The strike started the following week, and Butch Edwards was absolutely right. The town shut up tight, except for the bars. The canneries dug in; they would only pay one dollar and fifteen cents a pound and the shrimpers wanted one dollar twenty-five. Then right after that, the news came over the sideband radios that the Sea-Land ships bringing goods up from Seattle were delayed due to a strike; the town ran out of all perishables—bread, eggs and milk. The two gas stations in town were almost out of gas until someone had the bright idea of adding some water to the underground tanks to stretch the amount, which now had every internal combustion engine in town pinging.

Everyone was waiting, waiting for the strike to settle, waiting for the Sea-Land ships to dock; busying themselves by sharpening their knives, going to Ruby's Hairport or Curl Up and Dye for trims they didn't need; and looking out the window at the cloud cover to see if the afternoon plane was going to make it in from Seattle.

The shrimp strike was eight days old when Billy saw Butch at the Pot.

"I've been looking for you," Butch said as he sat down next to Billy.

"What for?"

"Well, remember I said I'd take you fishing, but you didn't have time? Bet you have time now."

"Oh, yeah," Billy said. "I have nothing but time."

"Let's go then. I'll take you out to the Flats. I got some rods, salmon eggs, spoons, Krocs and such. Ray's coming, too. Horse around on the Buskin; maybe hit the Russian River. The way the light is now, we can stay out to eleven, maybe eleven-thirty."

"Sure," Billy said. "What else is there to do?"

CHAPTER 14

Butch finished his drink and slammed the shot glass down.

"We should get going," he said, tossing a ten-dollar bill on the bar. "Probably get caught in the rain anyway. The clouds today are going up and down like a whore's drawers."

After Butch picked up some cheap wine and a six-pack of Oly, they were on the road out to the Coast Guard base, fishing rods clacking together in the truck bed.

"We're going to meet Ray at Bridge Number 2. There are seven bridges on the Buskin River Road from the bay up to the lake. Now," Butch said as he drove with his elbow on the doorsill, two fingers on the wheel, "you are a lucky shit. You really are, because you happen to be in the presence of the world's greatest fisherman. I know where the fish are, and how to get 'em. I tell you, the smartest lunker in the world in the deepest pool can't escape one of my spoons."

Spruce trees lined the two-lane highway as it wound past the East Point and the *Galactica* canneries toward the Buskin River. Every once in awhile the road would double back and Billy could see the town of Kodiak in the distance.

"Beautiful, isn't it?" Butch asked.

"Yes."

"Well, this is good country, no doubt about it. The whole island's not very big, say about a hundred miles long and a little over fifty miles across, but there's a lot of things going on all the time. You've got three to four thousand-foot mountains, dark green conifer with sphagnum and especially here in the northeastern part of Kodiak, spruce trees, alder thickets and devil's club. That's the plant with all the sharp needles in it. You have to watch out for that one when you're in the woods."

Billy looked back and he couldn't see the town anymore.

"The forest floor is covered with pine needles and moss, but if you were to dig down about twelve inches, you'd come across about a foot of ash. That's from the big Mount Katmai eruption of 1912. Covered the whole island. Eruptions, tidal waves—the Rock has seen it all. I wasn't here in '64 but some Coast Guard guy told me that right before the tidal wave hit, all of the water went out of the harbor and he could see fish flapping around right before the wall of water came back.

"Of course, the Natives were first. They called themselves Koniags and they did all right until the Russians came a couple of hundred years ago. The Russians were after the fur—otter, seal and fox. Then we bought Alaska from the Russians, and it was so long, fur trade. That was about the time the fishing industry got started. Guys like George Reiter and Jon Jensen are the last of the great fishermen. They're called highliners.

"See that base over there? It's Coast Guard now, but it used to be Navy. It was called Kodiak Naval Air Station," Butch said. "If you look around, you can still see some World War II stuff. There are pillboxes, machine-gun placements and landing ramps for PBY float planes all over Womens Bay.

"Now look over there," Butch said as he pointed toward a sharp peak. "That's Pyramid Mountain. Know why it's called Pyramid? Because it looks like an Egyptian pyramid was stuck on top. Of course, that's Barometer in front of us."

Straight ahead was the big, wide mountain, deep green in color.

"Know why they call it Barometer?"

"Sure," Billy said. "If you can't see it, it's raining; if you *can* see it, it's about to rain."

"Huh," Butch grunted. "Maybe you aren't as cheechako as you look."

Butch pulled off the road by Bridge Number Two. "They say Barometer's only about twenty-five hundred feet, but it sits right on Womens Bay, so it looks about five times taller than it is. In the summer, you can walk up the side of it, and there's a log up there for people who have climbed it. My name's on it. I did it about five years ago. Liked to have killed me."

"Hello, sweethearts."

It was Ray Griebling.

"Ray-ban. Right on time."

"Hey, I'm always on time. You're the one who's always late. Say, Butch, tell me again why we're on the Buskin. There are no humpies in yet. The run won't start for maybe another week or so."

"Well, we don't know that for sure, do we? There might be and there might not be. Besides, there'll be plenty of Dolly Varden."

"Dolly Varden?" Billy asked.

"Yeah, " Ray said. "Dolly Varden. Arctic char, Spotted trout, Alaskan carp—it's all the same. I think it's too soon for humpies, but the World's Greatest Fisherman here disagrees. He thinks the salmon might have started their run already."

Butch picked the fishing rods and a tackle box out of the truck bed.

"Always keep your fishing gear with you. You never know what you'll see when you're out on one of these rivers. A silver will jump right in front of you and your rod's behind the door back home. What do you do then?"

"Go home and get it?"

"No, Ray," Butch said. "You're missing the point, as usual."

Billy followed Ray and Butch into a clump of alder.

"MAKE A LOT OF NOISE," Butch shouted. "LOTS OF BEAR AROUND HERE. SIMPLE EQUATION. WATER PLUS FISH EQUALS BEARS."

Billy didn't need to be told twice.

"OK," he yelled back. "YOU SAY THERE'S A LOT OF BEARS AROUND HERE?"

"BEAR. THAT'S RIGHT. MAKE SURE THEY KNOW WE'RE HERE."

They fought through the alder to the edge of the river. The gray water ran past them on its way to Chiniak Bay, leaping over horse-size rocks as it moved under the bridge.

"Like I said, there are seven bridges that cross over the Buskin," Butch said, as he reached in the tackle box. "Fish it long enough and you'll get to know the pools by each bridge, where the big trout live, the overhangs on the banks, and the deep cuts where the salmon stop to rest as they go upstream. See, the river never stays exactly the same; it's always changing. And you have to read it. If there's no action here, try ten or fifteen casts and move up, or go down to the mouth by the base and try that.

"Fishing," Butch continued as he snapped a Pixie onto his line, "is like trying to get laid. Same exact thing. You stand on a street corner waiting for girls but they don't come by. Should you keep standing there if there's no action? Hell, no. You have to go to another street corner and try your luck again. Same thing with fishing. You try a spot for a while. Nothing doing? Move along."

"Billy, now tell the truth. Doesn't it give you a little thrill to be fishing with such an expert?" Ray asked.

Butch ignored him and handed Billy a black and yellow Mepps spinner.

"That one never fails," Butch said. He watched as Billy snapped the lure on the swivel.

"What do you have on, Ray?"

"Krokodile."

"Gold or silver?"

"Gold. Half ounce," Ray said. "Oh, and Billy, you better buy a license. Only thing more common than the no-see-ums and mosquitoes up here are the ADF and G—the Fish and Game boys. They're slick sons of bitches. They hide in the bushes, behind the bridge abutments and then they'll amble on up to you and ask what kind of luck you're having. They catch you and they make you pay—twenty-five dollars a fish or a hundred dollar flat fine, whichever is greater and . . ."

"Jumper," Ray interrupted himself. "Right in that pool over there to the left. Did you see it?"

Billy shook his head.

Butch picked out a Mepps, a Kroc and a Daredevil and stuck them in his baseball cap.

"Well, good luck," he said to Billy, and gave a half wave with his pole. "No sense in us standing here right next to each other. I like to move around anyway, so I think I'll try down here."

"I'll try upstream," Ray said, "Hey, remember when I asked you why you came Inside?"

"No," Billy said.

"We were in one of the live tanks when we first started working together. I told you I knew that your daddy ran you off. I forget what kind of bullshit answer you gave me, but I'll tell you—this is the reason you came. Take a look around."

Ray waved his fishing pole at the river in the shadow of Barometer. Then he began working his way upstream from Billy around one of the bends in the river, casting as he went.

Billy watched the river as it glistened in the gray light. The current was fast but made only a soft sound, not rushing, and as the flow swirled down, the bridge pilings broke the river into small eddies that appeared and disappeared as the clear water moved toward the bay. After studying the water for a long time, Billy could begin to see shadows darting among the speckled rocks that lined the riverbed. He couldn't see the fish themselves—he didn't want to see them; in fact, he would have been disappointed to see them. Sitting on the riverbank, he thought that everything would be spoiled if he saw the Dolly Varden. But he knew they were there, all right. The World's Greatest Fisherman had said so.

The shoreline was dense with alder, jagged rocks, and a few wayward spruce and hemlock trees. Clouds of bugs hung in the air, hovering no more than thirty feet from Billy, the humming of their wings pleasant and soft. On the side of Barometer he saw an old World War II observation tower about forty feet high, its rickety wooden legs bleached white by years of sun and wind, now in the shadow of the dark green mountainside.

He sat on the bank and watched the river, looking at the light as it arced over Barometer and broke over the peak into a hundred shards, flowing past the big mountain, a river in the sky of itself, flashing prisms, bouncing off the spray from the big rocks. Billy decided that he could never move from that spot, it was that perfect. Fishing was impossible at that moment; it would have ruined it for him. He wanted to build a cabin right there and spend the rest of his life watching the river and the mountain. It was a deep satisfaction that he had never felt before, a major chord that resonated through his bones, and for that one moment, he was happy beyond com-prehension. He knew that he could never tell anyone about this one moment, because talking about it meant that it wouldn't be his any longer.

Billy stopped thinking about everything and closed his eyes, listening to the current as the water moved over the rocks. He was half-asleep when he heard, or thought he heard, a strange kind of shuffling sound. Billy opened his eyes and saw an enormous bear, just twenty feet away, pawing at the cooler that

Butch had left next to the tackle box. The bear was chocolate brown in color and about five feet high at the shoulder on all fours, with claws as long as Billy's fingers.

Billy stood up. He couldn't run. He couldn't breathe.

The bear nonchalantly bit into the cooler, lifted it to about shoulder level and shook it. Cans of beer flew out, along with ice, a jar of mustard and some sandwiches. The bear was in no hurry; it nosed around and decided to try the beer first. Its long yellow teeth punctured the cans and the Oly ran into its mouth and down its chest. The bear lapped around the cans for a few minutes, and then ate the sandwiches, baggies and all, accidentally knocking the mustard jar into the river.

Then it stood up on its haunches, maybe nine feet high, snout up, quizzically sniffing a strange smell.

The smell was Billy.

The bear cocked its head, looking straight at him. Then it dropped down on all fours. It took one step forward, then another one, making a woofing sound as it moved. The bear's snout was much longer and more pointed than Billy imagined it would be, and the small brown eyes were set far back into the enormous flat head. Saliva dripped from the bear's mouth onto the rocks.

Billy was frozen to the spot.

The bear was about eight feet away when a gunshot rang out. The animal jerked its head in the direction of the noise.

Butch fired again. The bear ran up the hill into the alders.

"Jesus Christ, man, what the hell are you doing? You scared the shit out of me. I didn't see you right away because of the alders," Butch said. "I thought he already got you and was going back again."

Billy couldn't talk for a few seconds. He stood by the river, glumly looking at the rocks.

Ray came around the bend. "What happened?"

"Bear. What were you doing, Billy? Why didn't you shout?"

"I must have fallen asleep. I don't remember."

Ray spat some tobacco juice onto the rocks.

"Listen, kid, didn't you remember what I told you? Don't ever turn your back on this country. It'll kill you before breakfast. Anytime, anyplace. One of these bears . . . well, shit."

Ray reached down for one of the beer cans that were scattered on the ground. "Let me tell you a little story about bears," he said as he popped open the can. "Few years ago, back when this was a naval base, a sailor decided to go hunting. He gets dropped off somewhere around Uyak Bay. No guide. All by his lonesome. Took a backpack and a Springfield 30.06 with him. After a few hours, he sees this bear and shoots him. Bang, right in the chest. But he doesn't kill him. The bear gets up and runs into the bushes.

"So the guy looks and looks and he just can't find him. All he sees is some bloody spoor on the spruce trees. It starts to get dark, so the sailor finds a place, unrolls his sleeping bag and falls asleep."

Ray took a long drink.

"It took about a week for the search party to find his body, or what was left of it. He'd been bitten almost in half and then the other animals had a turn at him. The search party said they could hardly recognize that it was a human being, except that one of his arms was still there, along with a few pieces of his clothing."

"I'll say it again—don't ever turn your back on this country."

"What about if you have a big gun?" Billy asked.

"That won't help you much. Didn't help that sailor, did it?"

"This one would, " Butch said, patting his hip. "They don't grow 'em like this in the Midwest. It's a .44 Magnum, compliments of Mr. Smith and Mr. Wesson."

"That's great," Ray said. "Of course, Butch, you better make sure to file the sight off the end of that barrel. That way, if you do see a bear, it won't hurt so much when he sticks it up your ass."

"Shut up, Ray."

Ray looked at the shoreline. "I don't see any Dollies around here."

"No, I didn't even get the line wet," Billy said.

"Well, Raymond, it's clear that he's no Grits Gresham. I can see that. But I can teach him. That much I know. I *can* teach him. With this strike, there'll be plenty of daylight to burn. We got the salmon. If they aren't here they'll be here soon—reds, humpies, then silvers in September, and maybe even some halibut too if I can get a boat together."

"I think I've had enough excitement for one day," Ray said. "May as well pack it up. Hey, my wife's got some chili on the back burner if you want to come over."

"Sure, Ray," Butch said. "Be great. How about it, Billy?"

"That sounds a lot better than spaghetti from a can."

The three men gathered up their gear and packed it back to their trucks. Billy turned and looked back at Barometer's peak covered in fog. He wanted to capture the scene in his brain, so he could look at it whenever he chose: the river flashing silver in the light; gulls wheeling overhead, a young bald eagle perched in a spruce tree with no white head and tail feathers showing yet; clusters of insects hanging over the water; the lush green valley and the decaying World War II outbuildings and observation towers.

The air was cold as it came off the bay. Billy felt a raw, fresh feeling wash over him and then he knew.

This was where he was supposed to be.

*

Billy, Ray and Butch spent most of their daylight hours during the shrimp strike fishing. It might be something as simple as jigging for flounder off the city dock, or hitching a ride on the mail plane to fish the Karluk or Ayatulik rivers. Butch really knew the country. He knew to carry tidal charts for Kodiak. He knew all about the inlets and bays, from Monashka to Anton Larsen; he knew about the road to Pasagshak, forty miles of bumpy two-lane, leading to Narrow Cape, where the humpies and silvers would be running before long. Most importantly, Butch knew about the hiding places around Kodiak when you needed a break from the town.

Billy was a fast learner. He picked right up on watching the river, reading the river, looking for pools to cast in. Every once in a while, Butch would nick Billy's line while he wasn't paying attention and then laugh crazily when Billy's lure would sail twenty-five or fifty yards out. "A Guinness world record cast," Butch would say, and Billy would be so proud until he reeled back in to find nothing on the end of his line.

He would look over at Butch's choirboy face.

"I know you did that. You don't fool me, Butch."

But it still felt good. Even losing his lucky gold Kroc lure was-
n't bad. Every day they went out Billy became better and better, until he was catching more fish than Butch.

Standing at the mouth of the Buskin or the Pasagshak, Billy
would get a strike and see the big trout, a silver dollar spinning
and twisting through the clear waters.

"Now this isn't right," Butch would say. "It's not right that you
should catch more fish than me. No way should I get skunked
like this."

Of course, Butch didn't have his line in the water as much
as Billy; he was more fond of the cheap wine he always insisted
on taking along with them, like Cold Duck, Thunder-bird and
Annie Greensprings. He had a piece of a 2 X 12 plank that he
carried with him for the bottles so he could arrange them like
a miniature bar. Pine Ridge, Butch called it. Many times, he
wouldn't fish at all but would sit on the bank and watch Billy.

"You go ahead," Butch said. "I think I'll be on Pine Ridge
this afternoon."

"You know, you'd catch more Dollies if you didn't spend so
much time on Pine Ridge," Billy said.

"The fish will always be there, and when else can I spend
time with my dear sweetheart, Annie Greensprings?"

Every day during the shrimp strike, Billy would roll out of
bed, tiptoe past Jan and Jimmy, still asleep in their chairs with
the test pattern on the TV, slip into his cannery boots and walk
down Rezanof Street. He could look across the bay at Barometer, at least on good-weather days, which wasn't too often, but
when it was clear he could see the green peak pushing up into
the sky and he thought about the Dollies, holding themselves
steady in the deep pools and around the bridge pilings, working their fins over the pea gravel of the riverbed, darting
upstream and down, looking for whatever bug or salmon egg
might have fallen into the water.

Each night brought the promise of more fishing, and he could
hardly wait for the next morning when they would go out
again. Then one day after Butch dropped him off at the boarding house, a short ruddy-faced man in a red and black macki-
naw stubbed out his cigarette and walked over to Billy.

"You're Billy McCord, right? Off the *Aleutian Queen?*"

"That's right."

"Said I'd find you here. My name's Roy Brumfield. I'm the new foreman. Put on your boots. I've been rounding up the cannery hands all over town. The strike's settled, and we need you back." He reached into his back pocket for a package of Red Man and placed an enormous chaw in his mouth.

"What happened to Joe Pike?"

"Well, see, it's like this. Joe Pike went and got himself a little problem. Got a little careless. He dipped his wick where it should not have been dipped. No siree. Got caught in bed with Bonner's oldest girl, Betsy."

"Bonner Lynch? The *Queen*'s owner?" Billy asked.

"Yep. Right in the old man's house and everything. I think old Joe went Outside, down Bremerton or Everett way. Could be selling cars or something, for all I know. Anyway, we better be ready. Sideband says the first boats from Dutch are due in any minute. You all set?"

"Yeah. Let's go," Billy said, keeping his eyes on the clouds shadowing Barometer.

CHAPTER 15

Now it was the middle of July, and the pinks were coming in, running up the wide bays and into the rock-strewn rivers and streams on Kodiak. Four kinds of salmon made their runs during the summer and fall: pink, chum, silver and king, and the July fish were the pink salmon, the "humpies," so called because at the end of their lives the males grew large humps on their backs and their jaws became hooked in a horrible grimace. The humpies were in all the rivers; one of the fishing guides at Kraft's told Billy they had been in the Ayatulik for two weeks. Closer to the city, Billy could see jumpers out at Monashka Bay. He knew the fish were pushing the Dolly Vardens out of the way in the Buskin and the American River out past Bells Flats. Now every fisherman on the island was carrying the tide charts in his back pocket.

On these long summer days—the sun rose around 3:00 AM and didn't set until after 11:00 pm—Butch and Billy would clock out and head for Butch's truck. Sometimes Ray would join them, driving ahead on the two-lane gravel road, while Billy could hear the rods clattering away in the back of the Bronco. Once they arrived at the Buskin, it became a competition: who could bait up first, who could make the first cast, who could land the first fish, who could catch the largest and at the end of the day, who had the most keepers. The Buskin was too close to town for Billy's tastes, because you wound up fishing cheek by jowl with all of the Coast Guard boys. Butch called it combat fishing. It wasn't nearly as pleasurable as going to Monashka or Anton Larsen Bay or even Pasagshak, wading out into the cold, blue-black water so you could get real distance on the casts, feeling the water level rise over your crotch and noticing Butch's grin at the look on your face, having the whole bay to yourselves and clicking on your favorite Kroc and firing a cast out there. Cast after cast and nothing except perhaps a shred of kelp, perhaps a bullhead, a waste of time to reel in the scavenger fish and take it off the hook; a snag or a "tree fish," as Butch called it.

Then a large fish would strike and everything would change. The rod would bend toward the water and Billy could feel its body, the power of the fish as the sensation moved down the line and into his hands. Billy would rock back, digging his rubber boot heels into the sand, setting the hook the way Butch had taught him, keeping the line taut, careful not to reef the fish. His senses were switched on as he watched the deep C bend of the rod, the line as tight as piano wire at the rod tip, droplets of water hanging in a row down to the reel. Then, disconnected to him somehow, a fish, his fish, jumped thirty yards out.

The salmon, leaping again, now spinning crazily on all three axes, then hitting the water flat with a big splash; Billy taking up the slack line on the jump, glad for how well his Mitchell 300 reel was working; walking backwards to the black sandy beach, rod held high, pumping and reeling all the time. Feeling the water drip from him as he backed up onto the beach, the salmon fighting at the other end, pulling hard. And then beaching the fish, the slab-sided silver beauty heaving in the dull sunlight.

If they were lucky, they had enough for a shore dinner. Sometimes they would go three for three—three salmon for the three of them. They would build a bonfire on the shore as the sun finally sank, with Butch playing three-chord songs on his banged-up guitar and then they would snap open the Olys in response to the popping firewood. Two or three o'clock and sometimes longer than that, watching the wood as it burned down to nothing and then climbing into Butch's pickup for the misty ride into town and over to the *Queen* for the morning shift, with fifteen minutes to spare before clocking back in; working hard unloading the shrimp with a pitchfork, feeling good for an hour until the fatigue came in and squatted on your head all day, a good secret feeling, and then that night, falling asleep as soon as your head hit the pillow.

On these days, nothing could ever touch him.

The crews worked eighteen hours on, six hours off, sometimes twenty and four. Then sixteen and a blessed eight, six of
which were spent sleeping; Tilt-A-Whirl days mixed with
Krokodile nights when the humpies were in all over the island.
Billy had dreams about salmon, big as battleships, leaping over
his bed, and when he clocked out, Ray and Butch were waiting
for him by the pickup or the Ford flatbed that they borrowed
from the cannery.

One time, they were at Monashka Bay, and Billy tied into a
big one on his first cast, possibly a king or a jack salmon.

"That fish is gonna run all the way to Afognak, Billy," Butch
said. "Set your drag."

The line eeeed off his spool. Far away, almost across the bay,
he saw a fish jump.

"Thar she blows," Ray said.

Billy noticed the cold water was now about chest high. The
tide was coming in.

"Nice one, iceworm," Butch said. "Tighten that drag."

Billy tried and felt a clunk. "Feels like it's broken."

Butch and Ray were walking backwards toward shore, their
lures dangling off the ends of the rod.

"Well, you better hurry up. The tide's coming in. It's gonna
be up to your eyeballs in a minute."

Billy reeled and pumped, reeled and pumped, but this fish
had plenty of fight left. It was a little closer now, and jumped
again. The fish was just coming in from the ocean, and wasn't
one of those spent upstream salmon. But now the tide was coming faster, and the water was above his armpits.

"Give it up. Cut the line, man," Ray shouted from shore.

"No," Billy yelled over his shoulder. "He's too close now. I've
almost got him."

The fish was much closer now. Another jump, about fifteen
feet away and Billy could see him in the water, just beneath the
black surface. He worked the fish until it was close. Reaching
down, he saw that he had hooked it in the tail. Billy pulled
needlenose pliers from his chest pocket and held the fish with
one hand as he tried to remove the hook. He worked the hook
out and gently let the fish go. It disappeared in an instant,
down into the dark water, which was now up to Billy's chin.

He could hear the laughter from Butch and Ray bouncing off the pine trees. Drenched and cold, he waded back to shore.

"Fin boy. Fin boy." Butch laughed. "All that work for a finner. Wait till the guys at the Pot hear this one."

Ray was more concerned.

"Hey, Butch, come on. The man's shivering. We got to get him warmed up."

"Got just the thing for him in town—hot buttered rum," Butch said. "Fix a man right up. We'll go over to the Pot directly."

"Feel a little cold, Billy?" Ray asked.

"Y-y-yeah."

"Well, kid, that was a true salmon," Butch said.

"What do you mean?"

"See, some salmon bite and go right into the landing net, meek as lambs. Others will jump a few times. But that one . . ."

Butch looked out over Monashka. "That humpy's a true salmon. He didn't deserve to be someone's supper or put in a can on a shelf somewhere. He won't be food for bears, seals or eagles, either. Your true salmon is like that—different from the others, somehow. He's meant not to be caught, but to live his life out all the way, his own way, doing his thing, being him. He's one of them that make it all the way upriver, to where he came from.

"That's why you tail-hooked him. You weren't supposed to bring him in."

"Oh yeah," Ray said as he popped a Lucky. He took a drink and waved at the spruce trees around Monashka. "I got it now, Butch."

Ray gestured with his beer can. "It's all part of God's grand tapestry of life, the splendid canvas in which He creates His masterpieces, day after day."

"Shut up, Ray," Butch said. "He's cold. You said so yourself. Let's get him into town. A rum toddy or two at the Pot will do him a world of good, and it won't do you any harm either."

*

The canneries had filled up again with the new crews coming up from Seattle each week. These Filipino contract workers reminded Billy of photos he had seen of Confederate soldiers at the end of the Civil War—half of them fourteen year-old boys and the other half seventy year-old men. The story was that many of the Filipinos who came to Kodiak were illegal immigrants sent up to Alaska by some Manila-based underworld boss. This boss had a feud going with the canneries and so he made sure that only the dregs in his workforce would be shipped up to the island. Some of them only stayed a week and then took a cab out to the airport with their first paycheck and tried to fly back to Washington. One man, "Old Sam," who must have been eighty and could not read or speak English, went back and forth three times in two weeks. Each time Roy Brumfield sent him down to Seattle, Old Sam would come back a few days later on the four o'clock. Finally, Sam returned to Seattle for good.

Billy's shrimp job at the *Queen* was unloading and working one of the four peelers inside. The peeler work was nothing, just standing around at the top of the sixteen-foot rollers, picking out bits of crab shell or the occasional bullhead that had the misfortune to be caught in the nets, but the unloading part was much tougher than crabbing. The four-foot square hatch cover was winched off, revealing a hold topped with chunks of dirty ice. One or two unloaders stood on the shrimp, armed with short-handled pitchforks; then each unloader placed his fingers between the tines and jammed the fork into the ice, moving it out onto the deck until they could reach the shrimp. He picked up a twenty- to thirty-pound scoop of shrimp and dumped it into the unloading tub. Gradually, the unloaders worked their way down in the hold, lower and lower, deep into the boat. The pitchfork stuck fish, octopus, crab, all dead of course, but a nuisance, since the unloader had to stop and pick the carcasses off the tines. It was backbreaking work, especially the first two or three weeks, until a man's back and leg muscles became used to the new routine.

The *Aleutian Queen* used four unloaders. Besides Ray and Billy, there were two new hires, Hector Estrada and Marse Grimes. Both of the new unloaders had come from a cannery at Sand Point, down on the Alaskan Peninsula. Hector was a horny Filipino boy of about seventeen who believed that he lacked only one component for a successful marriage—a woman. By the time he reached Kodiak, he had suffered rejection from all of the single females he could contact on the Peninsula, and was now scanning classified ads in the Anchorage newspapers.

Finding a bride was Hector's obsession. One day, after they had cleaned the *Lin J* out of shrimp, Hector approached Billy and Ray as Marse winched out the last tub.

"Look this one," he said to Billy, pointing to an ad from *Alaska Magazine*: "Japanese Women Make Wonderful Wives."

"Look. I got to get a wife," Hector said. "I got to *para-para* them."

"*Para-para?*" Billy asked.

"*Para-para.* You know what that is. You a man. You know."

"Oh." Billy grinned. "I got it now."

"So, what you think?"

"I don't know. What do you think, Marse?"

Billy looked over at Marse, whose real name was Matthew. Everyone called him Marse because he was always quoting Marcel Proust. Marse never went anywhere without a volume of *Remembrances of Things Past* crammed in his jeans back pocket.

"Let us leave pretty women to men devoid of imagination," Marse quoted.

"Well, I got to get me one. Get a wife." Hector looked at Billy. "You got to get one too. Can't get a white woman, get yourself an Aleut girl."

"Hector," Marse said, "believe me when I tell you in all sincerity that there is no woman in God's glorious kingdom— Inside or Outside, native or white, rich or poor—who would have you for a husband."

"Man, you cold," Hector said as he guided the thick wooden hatch cover down onto the hold. "You see, though. I get me a wife. Then you best man at my wedding."

"I'll look forward to that. In fact, I will count the days, Hector," Marse said.

Marse was one of those people who had 110 volts passing through them at all times. He simply couldn't sit still. He hopped around the cannery as if the concrete was hot coals, unloading the boats, running the retort, helping out on caseup, taking the flatbed down to the city dock for supplies, and always with the book in his back pocket. He told Billy that the only thing that kept him reasonably sane during his four years at the Sand Point cannery was reading. He could get any book he wanted by mail from the Portland library, and had ripped through much of Henry James, Dickens, George Sand, a smattering of Joyce and some of Eudora Welty, but he always came back to Proust.

"William," he said, "I believe that Marcel Proust will be all I'll ever need from the world of literature."

"I think I read some of him once, in a *Classics Illustrated* comic. The pictures were nice, I remember." Billy said.

"Very amusing. You may be smarter than you look. Or perhaps not."

When he wasn't reading or working, Marse played chess. He had read *Bobby Fischer Teaches Chess* several times, and had ongoing games with several people Outside, to whom he faithfully sent his moves through the mail and then patiently waited for their counter strategies to arrive at the Kodiak post office. He and Billy played each day on a small magnetic board during their lunch break. Though Billy knew how to play, he was no match for Marse, who often won by taking Billy's king with a pawn, pausing to say with a dramatic flourish, "Now you have lost to a pawn, the lowest piece on the board. How does that make you feel?"

He was hopelessly outmatched every time he played Marse. Except once.

That was the day Billy first saw Laura Patterson.

CHAPTER 16

"Check."

Billy couldn't believe it. He had never come close to checking Marse's king before. He had taken one of Marse's knights with his queen and for once, he had a real chance to win the game.

"Check."

He said it again, with great satisfaction.

Then Marse lost a rook and his other knight. His game, always so forceful and confident, was now in shambles. Billy had laid waste to Marse's chessmen and was now pushing his advantage.

"Check."

It felt even better saying it for the third time.

One more uncharacteristic error and after studying the board carefully, Billy uttered the word he thought he would never be able to say to Marse:

"Checkmate."

As he said it, he reached over and flicked his index finger out. The half-inch-tall black king toppled face down onto the magnetic board.

Billy had won.

He looked up, but Marse wasn't paying attention at all. Instead, he was staring across the break room at two women sitting together on one of the corner benches.

Billy followed Marse's eyes over to the bench. The two women couldn't have been any more different in appearance. One was a squat, beefy brunette, at least forty pounds overweight, with the build of a football player; "A Dick Butkus with tits," Ray said later.

It was the other woman who drew Marse's attention.

She had hair the color of cornsilk in August, with pretty, cobalt blue eyes that seemed to carry him away somewhere. Billy could also tell that she had a fine body under her sweatshirt and jeans, although somewhat on the thin side.

"Who *is* that?" Billy whispered.

"That's the gossamer girl."

"The what?"

"I call her the gossamer girl," Marse said. "You know, that wispy fabric? You can see right through her. Her name's Laura, Laura Patterson. The other woman's Angela something or other. You never see one without the other. They're inseparable. They commenced working here last week."

"She looks so frail."

"Doesn't she? Oh, yes. She looks as if a slight breeze would break her right in half."

"Is she sick or something?"

"I don't know."

"God, she's beautiful," Billy said. "I've got to try and talk to her."

"Well, you'd probably be the seventh man today, not counting Hector, who tries all of the time, but go right ahead. Be my guest."

Billy stood up and clomped across the break room, feeling self-conscious about the noise he made.

Standing in front of the two women, he tried to think of something to say. The older woman, Angela, watched him with a look of disdain while Laura simply stared at the floor.

"Hi," Billy finally said. "My name's Billy."

"Beat it, kid," Angela said. "She doesn't want to talk to you."

Billy ignored her. "Hello, Laura."

Slowly, the girl raised her head. Her eyes were the lightest shade of blue he'd ever seen, a pale agate color that flashed as she turned her head away from the light.

He couldn't think of anything to say for several seconds.

Finally he said, "You have pretty eyes."

Angela stood up. "I said, get lost. She doesn't want to talk to you."

She gently put her arm around Laura and helped her up. "Come on, honey. Lunchtime's over. We have to go back to the pickbelt."

The two women left the break room and went down the steps to the processing area.

"Struck out, I surmise?" Marse said, tapping a cigarette against his thumbnail as Billy rejoined him. "I'm not surprised. A fellow like you. On the other hand, while I've yet to approach her, I'm reconciled to the fact that she is unobtainable."

"Why?"

"Well, if you must know, she's had a hard go of it. Evelyn Brower told me all about it. She works next to Angela on the belt."

Marse took a drag of his cigarette. He only smoked Gauloise Caporals, ten dollars a pack from Anchorage; the same brand that Proust smoked.

"It seems that Laura and Angela were hitchhiking up from Seattle two years ago. They were on the Alcan, between Fort Nelson and Whitehorse, when it happened."

"When what happened?"

Marse lit his cigarette.

"Some trucker in a silver Peterbilt picked them up. He waited until they were at a rest stop, then he hit Angela over the head with a Thermos bottle, knocked her unconscious, and dragged Laura into the woods. He raped her, came back, and raped her again. He left her for dead. When Angela woke up, Laura was half-naked, huddled up against a spruce tree. From what Evelyn says, the poor woman hasn't spoken again since."

"Did they ever catch him?"

"No. One would think the haulers would know who was on the routes at that particular time, but no, nothing."

He took another long drag off his cigarette.

"So ever since then, Angela has been watching over Laura. She's with the poor girl every minute. Never leaves her, as far as I know. She's her guardian angel."

"Do you think they're lesbians?"

"No, I don't think so. That's because I myself have seen Angela in the company of Max the Moose from Alaska Packers and you know what a Lothario *he* is. In any case, Evelyn says these two have worked in almost every cannery on the island from here to Karluk: Alaska Packers, Whitney-Fidalgo, and Galactica—all of them.

"That's all I know about the gossamer girl. That, plus the fact that every male hominid in this cannery except yours truly has tried to converse with Laura but without any success."

Marse looked down at the chessboard.

He frowned.

"Is that my black king? Why is it knocked over?"

"That *is* your black king. *I* knocked it over. Checkmate."

"Checkmate? What do you mean, checkmate?"

"I said it. I'll say it again because I love the way it sounds: checkmate. You just weren't listening."

"I can't believe it. No, I refuse to believe it. You've actually won. You've beaten me."

"Clean and proper," Billy said. "And you know what?" He stood up. "I like this. I could make this a habit."

"Don't get used to it. It won't ever happen again," Marse said grimly. He carefully put the pieces away, folded up the chessboard, and stuffed it into his back pocket.

CHAPTER 17

The snowcaps on the mountains were long gone with the rest of July as the shrimp flowed into town. The work was steady and hard but Billy still had a few hours here and there to steal away to tie into the humpies with Ray and Butch. And he could see Laura, his gossamer girl, every day, twice a day if he sneaked into the plant between the shrimp buckets. Laura always stood at the same spot by the pickbelt with Angela by her side. In fact, Angela was always with her. She worked next to Laura on the belt, and walked with her to and from the cannery. Even though he couldn't get close to her, he loved watching Laura's delicate fingers working on the belt, picking out small bits of shell. He liked seeing how her body moved as she floated over the line.

Hector Estrada was also watching Laura. He had realized that the chances were slim of finding a wife anyplace else but right here on Kodiak. Furthermore, she was right in front of him, his future wife, on the *Aleutian Queen*. Hector had decided that he would concentrate all of his matrimonial efforts on Laura Patterson.

"Billy, I found her. She right here at the cannery. Her name is Laura. She the one."

One day when the unloaders were finishing up, he found an octopus that had been caught in the nets. He knew that women liked jokes, so he gathered up the sticky purple carcass and tentacles and brought the whole mess up the steps to the pickbelt, where thirty women were working.

He burst through the double doors holding the octopus high over his head.

"LADIES," he yelled over the machinery noise. "LOOK AT THIS."

He ran down the belt line, thrusting the octopus in each worker's face.

All the women screamed except for Laura.

"Oh, it's just octopus. Look at him. He don't hurt nobody," Hector said. "See, girls? He dead."

Hector walked over to Laura and held the octopus up to her.

"Look, Laura. See? You can see. He dead. He won't bother nobody."

Laura looked around wildly. For once, she was by herself as Angela had gone for a drink of water.

Laura swayed a little bit and backed up against a wall.

Hector grabbed a tentacle and waved it in front of her.

"Ooh, look at me. I'm gonna get you. I'm gonna get you."

Laura's knees buckled and she slid down the wall.

"Hey, what's the matter with you?"

Billy was right there.

"Leave her alone, Hector."

"Aw, I was just having some fun." Hector grinned and waved the dead octopus in Billy's face.

"See? He won't hurt nobody. He dead."

"It's not funny."

"Yeah, it is. Is funny."

"No, it's not. Stop it. Right now."

Billy took a step closer to Hector. The Filipino boy looked at Billy for a few moments, then turned away.

"Aw, man," he said, as he threw the octopus into the dump tank and walked away.

Billy tried to help Laura back on her feet, but she recoiled when he touched her arm.

"Are you OK?"

"She's fine," Angela said, and pushed past Billy to Laura. "We don't need any help. Come on, sweetie, let's get you a drink of water."

Angela put her arm around Laura, and the two women walked over to the drinking fountain.

"What's going on here?" Roy asked. He reached under the belt and pressed the red STOP button. "All the shit's getting through."

"Don't worry about it, Roy," Evelyn Brower said, "Hector just brought an octopus in to wake us up, that's all."

"Get back to your jobs, goddamn it. We got to finish the *Jody* this morning. The *North Star*'s coming this afternoon."

He waited until all of the women were on both sides of the pickbelt, then he hit the green button. The belt lurched and started up again. Roy grunted with satisfaction and went back up the stairs to the unloading dock.

Billy savored his small, glorious moment. He had made contact with her. Now she might remember him and separate him from the hundreds of no-name cannery bums in town.

The next day, out at the mouth of the Buskin, Butch Edwards took a big slug of Mateus. He was up on Pine Ridge again with his wine bottles.

"So how are things going with the blonde girl? Any luck yet?"

"Shut up, Butch," Ray said. "It's not that kind of deal."

"It's not?" Butch asked. "Well then, what kind of deal is it?"

"You know the story with her."

"Oh, yeah," Butch replied, as he put the bottle down. "Yeah, yeah. I've heard it. 'Course, you don't have to worry about that since you got a wife to come home to every night—not like us tomcats."

"She *is* different, though," Billy said. "She has some kind of special glow about her."

"Oh yeah," Butch scoffed. "I've seen the same thing in the eyes of a whitetail buck, sitting in the crosshairs of my Springfield 30.06."

"You don't know what you're talking about, Butch," Billy said.

"Uh-oh," Ray said. "Looks like Billy's in love."

"Get lost, Ray."

The men fished for a few minutes in silence. Then they heard a faraway rumble that became louder and louder until they saw one of the Coast Guard C-130s lift off from the base airstrip, head out over the harbor, and bank left toward the mainland.

"Uh-oh. One of the shrimpers must be in trouble," Ray said. "Happens whenever there's been a strike. Some skipper pushes his luck, gets a little cocky or overloads, and then, bang, right down to the bottom. Ten minutes. That's what you have in the water, maybe fifteen minutes tops. That's why I don't like being on a boat anymore. I hate going out."

"Friend of mine, Eddie Majeski, took a ride in a king crab pot once," Butch said. "It was on the *Norma J.* We'd been working for thirty hours straight, and you know how after that much time without sleep, you get sloppy. I guess Eddie wasn't paying attention. His rainjacket wasn't buttoned up all the way, and he didn't notice it. When we dumped the pot, his jacket got caught in the door somehow, it closed on him and over he went, right inside the damn pot."

Butch took another drink, remembering.

"I saw him on the surface, struggling to get out. Then he looked over at me and down he went. Took about five seconds from beginning to end."

Butch sat down next to his pine board full of wine bottles.

"I can still see his face to this day. That look of terror. It's something that I can't ever forget."

"Well," Ray said, "that's not stopping you from checking around for a boat for king crab season."

"No," Butch replied. "When your number's up, it's up. No sense worrying about it. I know how it all works. It's a big card game, and you just ante up each time you go out."

"Is it really worth it?" Billy asked.

"Hell, yeah, it's worth it," Butch said. "If you two had any sense, you'd be trying to get on a king crabber right now. Hell, everybody in town is trying for a boat, except for Sally Perdido's whores. And you don't know what Kodiak town is like when it's king crab season. Those boats come in, loaded down with crab, and then as soon as the holds are emptied, the crews run down Shelikof into the heart of town, ready to get drunk before it's time to go back out again."

"But sometimes the boats don't come back," Ray said. "You forgot that part."

"So what? Like I said, it's a poker game. You toss in your ante. Sometimes you get called on it."

"Hey, fish on," Ray said calmly.

A salmon had slammed into his Kroc. Ray played it expertly and after a few more jumps, he had it out in the tall grass, admiring its shimmery sides.

"Nice fish," Billy said, lobbing his orange and silver Pixie at a jumper's shadow; but his mind was elsewhere. He was thinking of Laura, and how to find the time and the place to talk to her.

Then he had an idea. Since it was no good trying to talk to her at the cannery, he would find out where she lived. Then perhaps he could find a way to talk to her without Angela.

The next day, he found out from one of the older Aleut women on the pickbelt that Laura lived in the trailer park on Rezanof Street past Bartel. So after he and the other unloaders had clocked out, Billy went home and changed from his rubber cannery boots to hiking boots, put on his best flannel shirt and walked up the Rezanof hill. At the top of the street, he turned around as he always did and looked across the harbor to Barometer and the other emerald-colored mountains that ringed the bay.

He thought about what Rudy Cabigon told him the day that Hector brought the dead octopus over to the pickbelt.

"An octopus is considered good luck in the Philippines."

Perhaps the old man was right.

Billy continued on, past the robin's-egg blue domes of the Russian Orthodox Church, and clumps of houses with oars, buckets and even a few tanner crab pots in the front yards, until the pavement ended and the gravel road began. Several pickup trucks passed him, their slab sides covered with the standard Kodiak paint job: gray dust, right up to the window line.

He cut across a vacant lot to Ole Larsen's trailer park, a mess of campers, VW vans, and doublewides set down with no apparent grid or plan. He stood at the driveway by the office, looking for a clue as to where Laura's trailer might be located. Walking around the park several times, he could see that all of the trailers looked the same—dust-covered, ragged aluminum siding with a few broken windows here and there.

He was about to ask at the office, but then he saw several red and blue bandannas hanging on a clothesline, waving slightly in the breeze. A pair of black cannery boots flopped over by the door.

Billy took a chance. He climbed up the three steps and knocked gently on the door.

There was no answer.

He knocked again. Nothing.

As he turned to go, he saw something move inside. A small hand slid the curtains back and he saw a pair of blue eyes watching him warily.

"It's OK, Laura," he said through the door. "Don't worry. You know me. I work with you at the *Queen*. You've seen me there. My name's Billy. Billy McCord."

She looked at him for more than a minute. Then he heard a key turn and she opened the door, but only a crack.

"I saw you the other day, remember? With Hector and the octopus?"

No response.

"Would you mind if I came in for a few minutes? You'll be safe. It's OK."

Laura said nothing, but took a hesitant step back from the door. Billy decided to take that as an invitation and walked in.

The inside of the trailer was furnished in basic yard sale, with junk scattered everywhere. An old broken-backed rocking chair was in one corner with a shawl tossed over it, a few cracked plates hung crookedly on one brown paneled wall, and in the kitchen was a half-finished needlepoint of a cottage with the words "HOME AND FAMI." The blackened stove was covered in grease, and the refrigerator next to it was an old monitor-top Kelvinator from the '30s.

He sat down on one of the two red plastic kitchen chairs. Laura picked her way through the room and settled into the saggy green couch.

Neither one spoke. Finally Billy said, "Do you live here by yourself?"

Laura just looked at him.

"Did she go into town?"

Laura nodded slowly.

"Do you have any tea or coffee?"

Silently, she stood up and lit one of the burners.

Five dead minutes went by as the water in the teakettle began to boil. After it whistled, Laura made him a cup of tea and sat back down on the couch.

Then he heard a hollow clomping sound outside as someone's boots banged up the steps. It was Angela with a bag of groceries.

"What the hell are you doing here?" she snapped.

"We're just sitting here talking. No big deal."

"Well, get the hell out. We don't want to see you. Do we, Laura?" As Angela said this, both she and Billy looked over at Laura, whose eyes were now focused dully on the brown shag carpeting.

Billy stood up and drained his cup.

"Thanks for the tea, Laura. I'll see you down at the *Queen*."

He opened the door and left, as Angela called out after him, "And don't come back. I mean it. Nobody gave you a special goddamn invitation."

But Billy came back three more times that week. Each time, Angela was there, and each time she refused to let him inside. Each time, he walked back down the hill to town.

The shifts were tough that week; long slashes of motion. Jump down in the hold, all sweaty from shoveling, kicking out the little dead fish that were caught in the nets and dumped with the shrimp, working down past the chunks of ice, the sensation of the black gloves squeezing around the tines of the pitchfork as he lifted another 20-pound load of shrimp. Then finally seeing the wooden boards peek through as he and the other unloaders shoveled the last bits of shrimp into the wide steel bucket.

Clock in 5:00 am, coffee break; 9:45; lunch, 11:30; clock out at 6:00 pm, but this was the big push toward the end of the shrimp season so the unloaders worked until 11:00 to finish up the boats. The boats refueled and headed out, while others took their places, and the process began all over again.

Then came Friday. That day belonged to Hector.

CHAPTER 18

Billy woke up at 4:15 that Friday, dressed quickly, crept downstairs past Jan Day, asleep in her armchair, slipped on his boots and then walked out onto Rezanof as the morning sun burned off the fog, past the Island Maid bakery, cut through the grocery store parking lot, and swung onto Shelikof and the darkened canneries. On mornings like these, he felt he was the only person on the island, as he never saw anyone else until he came to the cannery.

He turned left into the black gravel parking lot of the *Queen*.

Hector was waiting for him.

He stepped in front of Billy.

"Hey, Hector."

Hector had a big grin on his face. "I walk the line, man. Johnny Cash."

"What?"

"I walk the line. You show me up. I'm looking for a wife, and you show me up. Make them all laugh at me."

"What do you mean?"

"The octopus. With Laura. The blonde girl. My wife. You remember."

Hector looked down at his right hand. It was as if Hector's hand was a separate entity unto itself, opening and closing around the black-handled Bowie knife.

Both of them stared at the hand.

Hector smiled and crouched down. He was in control and he liked that. He shifted the knife from his right to his left hand and back to his right hand again, just as he had seen in the kung fu movies.

I'm going to die now, Billy thought, right here on Shelikof Street.

Hector circled around Billy. He smiled broadly, showing two rows of misshapen teeth in the dim morning light.

Billy heard the generator click on at the *Roxanne* next door.

"I want to get married, man," Hector said. "I'm Johnny Cash, the man in black. I walk the line."

"Hector, take it easy."

"Nobody wants Hector to get married."

He feinted at Billy with the knife hand.

"Nobody wants Hector to be happy. Nobody gives shit about Hector. Not Billy, not Roy, not Mr. Lynch, nobody. But now, somebody gonna pay this time."

He moved toward Billy.

Billy threw up his right hand to block Hector but he was too late. The knife cut across his palm.

He cried out with the pain.

"Got you now," Hector said with his crooked smile. "Now, this time, I bury this in you, so you won't *para-para* Laura or any other girl."

But before Hector could move in again, two strong arms grabbed him from behind, pinning down the Filipino boy's arms.

It was Ray Griebling.

"Drop the knife, boy," Ray said calmly, and moved both his hands down to Hector's knife hand.

"I said drop it or I'll tear your goddamned fingers off."

The knife clattered onto the rocks.

Ray picked it up and tossed it into the water.

"Now get out of here, Hector."

Hector hesitated.

"I said, get out of here."

Hector ran past Ray down Shelikof.

"Let's take a look, partner," Ray said as he held Billy's arm out. Blood was running down Billy's arm, staining his white thermal undershirt.

Billy watched the weave in the shirt changing from white to a dull red.

"Shit. That crazy bastard Hector did you up real good. I better get you over to the clinic."

He loaded Billy in the Bronco and they drove downtown.

Dr. Alvarado smiled when he saw Billy.

"You look familiar, son. Have you been here recently?"

"Yeah, " Billy replied. "I helped you stitch someone up about a month ago."

"Well," the doctor said as he cleaned the wound with saline, applied a little local anesthetic, and began putting the stitches in, "you fellows better learn to stay away from those boys and their knives. One of these days, you're going to come in here horizontal instead of vertical. I can't do much for a man whose insides are on the floor."

He threw in twelve stitches, patted the wound with a 4X4, and taped a fresh gauze pad over it.

"I'd take it easy for a few days. What boat are you on?"

"We aren't on a boat. We work at the Queen as unloaders," Ray said.

"Shrimp season still going, right?"

"Yeah," Ray said. "Almost done. Just a few weeks left."

"OK," Dr. Alvarado said as he stripped his gloves off, "you're all set, son. I don't want you to do any lifting for a week. You'll pop those stitches. Here's a prescription for the pain."

They walked out of the clinic as it began to rain.

"I'll clock in and tell Brumfield that he's gonna be short two unloaders. That's two down, because if I know Hector, he won't be back today. Old Roy's not gonna like that," Ray said with a grin.

He took Billy to the drugstore for the pain medication.

"Where can I take you now? Jan Day's?"

"Take me up to Larsen's trailer park off Rezanof."

"What for?"

"Unfinished business," Billy said.

They pulled up outside Laura's trailer.

"Looks like nobody's home."

"That's all right," Billy said. "I'll wait."

So he sat there on the porch for most of the day, listening to the rain as it banged down on the rusty corrugated roof. It was one of those all-day Kodiak specials, maybe an inch or so every twenty-four hours, the island socked in all the way to Three Saints Bay.

No mail plane today, he thought.

The ravens and eagles were flying, though. They always did. He could see them wheeling around in the sky, circling something at the other end of the trailer park. The eagles were magnificent, with their stark white heads and tail feathers, while the ravens screeched and cawed and flapped their wings, trying to fly as smoothly as the larger birds.

He grew very sleepy. As the painkiller spread through his bloodstream, he nodded off.

When he woke up it was four o'clock in the afternoon. His body was stiff from sleeping in the chair and his hand throbbed.

The birds were gone now but the rain still came down hard, splattering in the dirt road as Billy ticked off the minutes. At four-thirty, he could almost hear the time clocks clicking as the unloaders shoved their cards into the slots all along the row. The pickbelt women would be right behind them, hanging up their yellow aprons on the hooks and soaping up their hands to kill the shrimp smell. He knew that the women would soon be on Shelikof, dispersing through the town as they made their way home.

And sure enough, here were Laura and Angela, trudging up the hill to the trailer park. He watched them turn off Rezanof and cut across the lot.

Now they saw him.

Angela took a few steps in front of Laura.

"How many times do I have to tell you?" she shouted. "Get off our porch."

Billy stood up, and both women saw the bandage on his hand.

"Jesus Christ, what happened to you?"

"Hector got me with his knife."

"Those Flips," Angela said. "Well, Jesus, come on in. You look like you could use something to drink. God knows I could."

She opened the door and Laura and Billy entered the trailer.

"We got tea, we got coffee and we got Everclear."

"Coffee for me," Billy said.

Angela lit the gas stove and put the teakettle on.

"It's instant."

"That's OK."

"Want some tea, Laura?"

Laura nodded.

"Coffee and tea. Well, that's fine for you two, but I'm an Everclear girl. Mind if I take a snort?"

Angela unscrewed the cap and tilted the bottle.

"Ah," she said, "there's nothing like some good hooch in the afternoon."

She raised the bottle again.

"To happy times," she said, as she took another long pull from the Everclear.

The teapot whistled and Angela fixed the coffee and tea.

The three of them drank in silence for a few minutes.

"Shit, I forgot," Angela said. "I was going to go over to Max the Moose's house to, uh, look at a Dodge half-ton he's got."

She looked at Billy.

"You want to come?"

"No, thanks. I don't know much about trucks."

"Neither do I," Angela said, and gave Billy a wink. "I'm just a girl."

She stood up and put the Everclear on the shelf behind the stove.

"You all right?" she asked Laura.

Laura nodded.

"You sure? OK, sweetie. I'll be back in a little while."

"So long," Billy said.

"Bye."

Angela slammed the screen door and tromped down the steps. Billy heard her boots crunching across the gravel lot.

He didn't know what to say at first. The words were flying around just over his head but he wasn't sure which ones to pull down and use.

The two of them sat silently for a few minutes.

"Laura, I . . . " he began, then trailed off. He reached for his coffee and took a sip.

"Look, Laura," he tried again, "I know you don't know anything about me. I could tell you a thousand things about me, that I'm from Ohio, that I'm twenty-three years old, that I used to feel my life was over. Then I get Inside, and everyone starts telling me about the money and that was the big reason for being in Alaska. They said the pipeline was coming, and I'd be fool not to try to get on it. Then I came to Kodiak and everyone said that it was crazy not to get on one of the boats. But that's not why I came here. I came because I could start over, because I needed to try again . . . "

Billy stopped talking.

Laura's lips were moving, but there were no sounds coming out of her mouth.

"I'm sorry, what did you say?"

"H . . . hands . . . " she said with considerable effort, jerking the word out of her mouth.

" . . . His hands . . . they were cold. Cold."

"Whose hands?"

"*His. His* hands . . . I remember," she said. "I remember . . . hands. And I remember . . . lying there . . . in the sharp pine needles . . . under the trees."

She closed her eyes.

"I don't remember . . . anything else . . . I've tried and I don't remember what . . . happened after that."

Her pale blue eyes began to fill with tears.

"It's all right," Billy said. "It's all right."

He moved over next to her and put his arm around her shoulders. She flinched.

Billy slowly brushed back her long blond hair away from her face as she began crying. Tears ran down her cheeks onto his hand.

"I was with Angela," she said in a low voice. "This man picked us up in a big silver truck."

"Shhh. It's all right. I know. You don't have to talk about it."

"You don't understand. He . . . waited and . . . he had cold hands . . . and . . . there were pine needles everywhere. Sticking me."

"Yes."

"And . . . he touched me. And when it was over, Angela . . . was there and she said she would always protect me."

"I know, Laura."

"No, you don't. You . . . don't know anything. You don't know anything at all."

She cried for a few more minutes. He began to hear raindrops spattering again on the corrugated roof.

Billy shifted his weight on the couch.

"Laura," Billy said slowly, "Listen. Before I came to the Rock, I worked at a hospital Outside. Last year, a woman came in for a breast biopsy. Her name was Jackie Catullo and she was about twenty-two or twenty-three years old.

"She's in the OR and all of the other doctors and nurses are outside the room for a minute. It's just the two of us in there and she looks at me with the same kind of fearful eyes that you have.

See, she didn't know whether she would wake up with a small scar from the incision or with her whole breast gone. With a biopsy, they test for cancer right there and then do the mastectomy if they need to. Anyway, they gave her the pentothal and the nitrous, and they took both breasts. Right down to the chest wall. Then the case was over and I didn't see her again.

"I didn't think about it until I read the paper four months later and found that she had died. I remember walking to the Ohio River, watching the current take all the driftwood and everything else away and thinking how I wished I could float away in the muddy water and how I would never feel that way again. I knew I never wanted to see that fear again, the fear I saw in Jackie Catullo's eyes."

"But why . . . why are you telling me this?"

Billy leaned forward and took a sip of coffee. "Because when I saw you in the break room," he said softly, "I saw that same look of fear. I knew I wanted to help you somehow."

"You can't, Billy. No one can help me."

"Maybe, maybe not. It's just that . . . I can't explain it any more than that. I just want to be with you, to try to protect you, that's all."

She raised her head up so she could see him better.

"Look, Billy. You don't understand. You can't."

"I don't need to understand. I don't need to know anything else."

"You don't understand," she said again. "You don't understand. It's . . . "

The rain slammed down harder on the roof.

"Look, let's just stop talking for a few minutes and sit here for a little while and listen to the rain. We don't have to do anything else. We can just stop thinking," Billy said quietly. "That's the easy part. Do you know how to stop thinking? I've done it a few times. You just disconnect your brain."

Neither one spoke for several minutes.

The rain beat down over their heads, a steady, soothing rhythm.

Laura fell asleep in his arms. He felt himself fading as the rain began to sound far away and tinny to him.

He didn't hear Angela come in.

"Jesus Christ, Laura," she said as she stomped her boots on the doormat. "What's he still doing here? I thought he'd be gone by now. Well, shit, Billy," Angela said with her hands on her hips. "It seems like we just can't get rid of your ass. Here," she tossed a pillow at his head. "Might as well stay the night. You'll get soaked going back to town."

Billy stood up.

"I've been wet before."

"Shut up," Angela said. "You got no sense. Never met a man who did."

Laura went into one of the bedrooms.

Billy watched her walk away, then sat down and stretched out on the couch, wrapped a blanket around himself and fell asleep.

Angela fished out the Everclear. She took a shot and then watched his face for a long time.

Then she touched his hair. Billy didn't move.

"Such a young boy," she said. "So goddamn young."

She drained the Everclear and pulled the blanket up around Billy's shoulders.

CHAPTER 19

The foreman studied Billy's face carefully. Then he looked at Billy's right hand.

"Bullshit," Roy said.

"Well, that's what the doctor said. You want me to pull off the bandage and show you the stitches?"

The foreman reached into his back pocket for his Copenhagen. He took a pinch and jammed it behind his lower lip.

"Well, the whole thing stinks."

Roy spat into the water.

"Now I got me a real problem. Ten days to go in the shrimp season and here I am, down an unloader. No—make that two. Hector's gone. He hasn't clocked in since last week. There ain't any more unloaders around. The whole town's tight now, and here I stand, stuck on stupid."

"I didn't plan on getting you stuck."

"Maybe so, but that doesn't help me any."

Roy was watching the *Jody Ann* come in, its hatch cover already off, filled to the top with shrimp and ice chunks.

"Probably have you back for king crab," he said. "That's two weeks away."

"I could work earlier."

"No, you just get better. And watch out for Hector."

"OK," Billy said. He tried to be serious, but found himself stifling a laugh as he thought of Laura and the warm, wonderful feeling that burned inside him. He left the cannery and spent most of Saturday in the town library and at the Pot.

Ray and Butch showed up at the end of the workday.

"Hey, iceworm," Butch said. "How's the hand? Boy, I'll tell you, Bob. Some people will do anything to get out of work."

Billy grinned. They couldn't touch him.

"Six-pack him," Ray said. "That'll wipe that stupid look off the boy's face."

"No, no," Billy said, and put his hands up. "I'm just here for one drink. I'm off to Larsen's."

"Oh, yeah," Butch said. "I heard about that—you and the blonde girl. Getting any yet?"

"Shut up, Butch," Billy said, still smiling.

"Huh. I didn't think so. Well, one thing's clear anyway. We know that Ray's not getting any because he's married."

"Kiss mine, old man," Ray replied, taking a swig of his Lucky.

"Old man? You're eighteen months younger than I am. Besides," Butch said, "I am not interested in chasing any tail at this particular moment. I got bigger fish to fry. I'm still trying to get on a boat for crab season. If you two had any sense, you'd try too."

"I'm not interested in getting on a boat," Billy replied.

"I always knew you had no sense," Butch said. "Now it's been documented."

"Sure, Billy's got no sense," Ray said. "That's why he hangs around with you."

"I think this is the part of the movie where I came in," Billy said.

He slapped a five-dollar bill on the bar.

"Keep it, Bob. See you both later."

"Wait until I get on a boat. I'll be in here every day, ringing the bell," Butch said. "Drinks on the house. Good stuff, too. Johnnie Red. And then we'll go visit Sally Perdido, and when we get tired of her and her girls we'll fly over to Anchor-town and blow what's left there. Those massage parlors on Fourth won't know what hit them."

They were still talking when Billy left. He wanted to be waiting on the porch of Laura's trailer when she came up Rezanof and across the gravel lot. They shared an awkward embrace and then she let him inside and made him some special oolong tea that her sister had sent up from Oregon. Laura was still finding her way back, but he could sense that she was becoming more relaxed. Her shoulders dropped when he held her, and she even smiled slightly when he made some small joke about Ray and

Butch, her lips parted momentarily to reveal beautiful white teeth, complimenting her pale china-doll complexion. He hadn't thought he would ever be able to feel this good.

*

Billy wandered around town on his days off, stopping off at the Post Office, the library, hitching out to Monashka Bay, waiting for the silvers run. Sometimes he would go to the city dock and watch the town kids jig for flounder. And always at the end of each day, he had Laura.

On August 15, he was there as usual on the porch when she trudged up. This time, she smiled before he spoke.

"How was it today?"

"Good. The last of the shrimp boats came," she said as she eased by him and let him inside. She lit the gas stove and put some water in the teapot.

"Did Roy find any other unloaders?"

"Yes, but when they don't show up, he grabs a pitchfork himself."

"I'd like to see that."

He could hear the water sloshing in the kettle as it grew hotter.

"You know, Laura, they took the stitches out yesterday. I'm going back to work tomorrow."

Laura nodded. "Good," she said, and took two teabags from the box and dropped them into the cups.

The teapot began to make a low whistle. Laura waited a moment so it wouldn't splash when she poured it into the cups.

She sat on the couch and pulled off her cannery boots. Then she tentatively reached over and brushed Billy's hair, which curled down his back in an unruly mess.

"You need a haircut," she said, as she picked up a kitchen chair and moved it to the center of the living room. "Sit down over here."

Billy was puzzled. "Are you sure?"

"Just sit down. It'll be OK. I've done this before," she said as she picked up a pair of scissors.

He felt a flash of fear, wondering for a split-second if Laura might want to get even at her Canadian attacker, but he let it go. Billy did as he was told and sat in the chair.

Laura disappeared into the bedroom and came back with a striped sheet. She wrapped the sheet around him and tucked it in below his neck. The sheet was soft from hundreds of washings.

She bent over slightly to cut his hair, and then straightened up again.

"Wait a second," she said, and went over to the old record player. She flipped through several albums until she came to one she liked, placed it on the turntable and carefully selected one of the tracks.

It was *Mandolin Wind* by Rod Stewart, one of Billy's favorite songs.

The words floated around the room as she cut his hair:

I recall the night we knelt and prayed,
Noticing your face was thin and pale.

She moved around him, her hair occasionally brushing his face, which made his heart jump. Each time the song ended, she stopped and reset the needle at the beginning of the track.

The third time the song played, Laura brushed his lips with her hair. Billy reached up, gently gathered her hair in his hands and kissed it.

She pulled back slightly and looked at him.

Slowly, he leaned toward her, eyes closed. Then he could feel her breath and in another moment, her lips, warm and moist.

I know you can't play
But I'll teach you someday
Because I love you.

He wasn't in Kodiak, Alaska anymore. He didn't know where he was. When he opened his eyes he saw that she was looking at him, her fear gone; then he stood up and moved to her and brushed her lips gently with his. Her breath moved across his face as a warm breeze. They shared another kiss, a slow and gentle one.

"Laura, I . . . "

"Don't talk. Please don't talk right now, Billy."

He hugged her and stood up. Some of his cut hair fell all around him.

"I wonder if this is how Samson felt?"

She smiled and brushed his hair back from his forehead.

"If you're Samson, then I'm Delilah. I'm beginning to feel stronger already."

They kissed again as *Mandolin Wind* played again on the old turntable.

CHAPTER 20

"You are a sight for sore eyes," Roy Brumfield said when Billy showed up at the cannery.

"Thanks, but it's not my *eyes* that are sore. They took the stitches out of my hand yesterday. I'm ready to go," Billy said.

"That's good. That's real good. The *Teaser* is coming in from Dutch any time and Dick Szymanski came over the radio and says he's up to his scalp with king crabs. The *Vansee* is right behind her. You ready to work your ass off?"

"Sure."

Billy went past Roy into the galley, where Leonard Ives, the cook for the cannery live-aboards, was sitting at the table, smoking a cigarette.

"Hi, Billy."

"Hey, Leonard. Got any coffee?"

"Just made some."

Billy reached up for a mug and filled it.

"Did you hear about the fight in town last night?" Leonard asked.

"No. What happened?"

"Oh, those goddamn Natives. They can't hold their hooch. It started outside the Breakers and spilled over to Solly's Office. Then the Flips got into it. They filled all the beds in the clinic last night—I'll tell you that. Doc Alvarado was working all night, that's for sure."

Leonard took a long drag on his cigarette. "You know, I don't care if any of those greasy sons of bitches kill each other off. Do this town a favor. But if they come after me, that's the last mistake they'll ever make. I'm ready."

He lifted his apron and showed Billy the butt end of a revolver.

183

"Jesus, Leonard."

"That's right. It's a .38 Police Positive. Like I said, I'm ready for 'em. Just let 'em try to start something with me."

Leonard sat down at the galley table across from Billy. The cook's arms were milky white below his T-shirt sleeves. He never went outside, except to the bars at night, and as Ray said, "Nobody ever got a suntan under 60-watt bulbs."

"I know about Hector. You got to sleep with your eyes open from now on."

"Yeah."

"Tell me if you need any protection. I can get you a gun from the Coast Guard base with no numbers on it. Untraceable. A nice one—nine mm automatic, Smith & Wesson revolver, whatever you want."

Marse came into the galley.

"Gentlemen," he said as he took a mug down from the rack.

"Hey, Marse," Billy said.

"Well, William, I heard about your little contretemps. Are you sufficiently healed from that dust-up to begin unloading the venerable *Paralithodes camtschaticus?*"

"My hand's a little sore, but otherwise I'm ready to go."

"Good," Marse said.

"What are you reading?"

"Oh, the usual. *A la Recherche du Temps Perdu.* I think you should try it sometime. It might broaden your horizons."

"You've said that a hundred times. I will—sometime," Billy said.

"I have an extra copy. It's in my bunk upstairs."

"Thanks, but I don't think I'll have much time right now."

"All right. I'll see you in the hold then," Marse said, and walked out the plastic door to the cannery barge next to the *Queen,* to check the temperature level of the cooking trough.

Billy smiled at the way Marse moved. Marse was the only cannery hand Billy met who never made any squeaking noise with his boots. He meticulously lifted one foot above the other when he walked.

Leonard left to start dinner for the live-aboard workers. Alone, Billy poured himself another cup of coffee. It was pleasant to sit there as the *Queen* rocked slightly in its moorings, creaking with the current against the tall wooden pilings in the dark blue water. From his chair, he could peer out one of the portholes across the harbor to Near Island. Big whitecaps were marching across the harbor today; it's probably a rough haul in from the Bering Sea, he thought. Gulls, cormorants, and pintail ducks bobbed in the water around the cannery, waiting expectantly for the boats to come in. Billy saw a bald eagle wheel high above the harbor, its white head brilliant against the blue sky. He watched the birds on the water split as the *Resolution* steamed by—that was the big Alaska Department of Fish & Game's patrol boat, coming back home after a run looking for king crab season-jumpers or any Japanese trawlers that might have "accidentally" strayed inside the twelve-mile limit.

The *Resolution* must have had a successful trip; a boat was following it, but Billy couldn't see the stern and didn't recognize the white and green Bender wheelhouse. It looked like about a 110-footer, and as it steamed by he saw two glum crewmembers standing on deck, smoking cigarettes in front of a stack of large rectangular king crab pots, the ropes wound neatly inside. The captain and crew were facing a stiff fine, possibly some time in jail, but worst of all, the impounding of their vessel. Now their season was over before it had even begun. Billy wondered which was worse—the punishment the crew and skipper would face or the degradation of being dragged into port past the entire cannery row. Now everyone would learn about it, if they didn't know the news already. Nothing moves faster than gossip in a fishing town.

The birds moved back into their positions in the water again. Watching them for a few more minutes, Billy could see more gulls perched on top of the corrugated metal roof of the *Skookum Chief* next door.

He drained his coffee cup and walked back across the galley to the window opening where Leonard was washing the dishes. Billy slid the cup through to Leonard, who picked it up and plopped it in a sink full of soapsuds.

"See you later, Leonard."

"Yeah, take it easy, kid, and remember what I said about a gun if you want one," Leonard said, and plunged his pale arms into the hot, steamy dishwater.

Billy walked down the corridor and bumped into Bonner Lynch, the cannery owner. Lynch was a wizened little man with a pockmarked face who always used a yellow cigarette holder, which he clamped in his teeth at such a jaunty angle that he reminded Billy of a sawed-off Franklin D. Roosevelt.

"Well, son, the first king crabber should be here any moment. Be ready to work straight through. No stopping until it's done." The cigarette holder bobbed up and down as Bonner spoke.

"You bet," Billy said with as much enthusiasm as he could muster.

"Are you ready for the long shifts?"

"Yes sir."

"Good man. What's your name, son?"

"Billy."

"Billy, have you ever worked with kings?"

"No."

"Unloader?"

"Yes sir."

"Watch out for those claws. The sons of bitches will take your finger right off."

"I will."

"Good, good, good. Well, I have to go topside. Make some money for me, son."

Lynch went around the corner and Billy could hear his boots clattering on the metal ladder outside the *Queen*'s wheelhouse. Now he could hear something else as well, the low throb of a large diesel engine which grew louder and louder, until he felt a gentle tap against the *Queen*. He knew it was either the *Vicky C* or the *Teaser*, inbound from Dutch with its first load. Billy followed Lynch up the ladder so he could see Ron Knight, the skipper of the *Vicky C*, bringing the boat portside, maneuvering it expertly into position as if it were an extension of the captain's body. Two crewmen lobbed the docking ropes up to the *Queen* and the *Vic* was tied up in within a few minutes.

"How much, Ronnie?" Bonner Lynch yelled down from the *Queen*'s bridge.

"Maybe forty thousand pounds. Enough to keep you busy for a while. I already pumped the water out. They're all set."

"Goddamn. Goddamn," Lynch said as he rubbed his hands together. "Well, pop that hatch, boys. Let's take a look at all that money."

Ray Griebling fired up the crane and lowered the hooks into position. The *Vic*'s crew connected the wire to the hatch lid as Ray pulled one of the stalks and the crane's motor whined away.

Billy inched forward for a better look inside.

He couldn't believe what he saw.

It wasn't the hundreds of enormous king crabs, a mass of spiny, dark purple bodies piled high, some of the oxygen-starved ones blowing bubbles. No, that wasn't what caught his attention, because on top of all the king crabs, spread-eagled, were two large men, in matching brown Carhartt overalls.

At first Billy thought they were dead, but then he heard one of the men grunt. They aren't dead, he thought; they're just asleep.

Ron Knight cursed and yelled, "Wake up," but the two men in the hold did not move. It was not a practical joke, Billy thought. They really were sleeping, right on top of the crabs.

"Goddamn it. Wake those stupid shits up," Knight hollered. "Drop the bucket on their fucking heads."

Billy thought the skipper was going to climb out of the *Vic*'s wheelhouse and jump right on top of them himself.

A crewman turned on a hose and sprayed water down in the hold.

The two men sputtered and sat up, rubbing their eyes.

"Hey, what the hell did you do that for?" the redheaded one asked. "I was having the first good sleep since we left Dutch. I was dreaming about an Aleut girl I met."

"Shut the hell up. Just shut the hell up," Knight yelled. Billy could see the veins in the captain's neck sticking out. "Get off of those goddamned crabs."

"Lower the bucket down," Bonner Lynch said quietly.

Ray ran the steel bucket down and the two men hopped in. He expertly arced the bucket over the *Vicky C*'s deck to the *Queen* and gently put it down topside.

The men climbed out of the bucket and stood next to Billy. They were tall, raw-boned, and powerful-looking, each at least 6'3" and well over 200 pounds. One man had a filthy yellow Caterpillar hat on, the other had a tangled mess of red hair.

Billy grinned. "You boys must have been tired."

"The man asks if we were tired, Eunice," Red Hair said, as he stretched his arms up and moved them in big circles over his head. "All we've been doing is sleeping. We found all the bars in Dutch and closed 'em down, which wasn't hard because the whole town is about a hundred feet long. Say, you ever been to Dutch Harbor?"

"No, I . . . "

"Don't ever go. It's the sorriest place you'll ever see. Sorrier than A-town, sorrier than Fairbanks, sorrier than Nome. It's got absolutely nothing—no good bars, no women at all, no nothing."

"It's got Mount Ballyhoo," Caterpillar Hat said.

"Oh, yeah. It's got Mount Ballyhoo."

"I always liked the name of that. Ballyhoo," Caterpillar Hat said. "Ballllllyyyyyyhoooo."

"Don't start with that shit again," Red said, and pointed a warty index finger at the other man. "I told you if you started with that again I'd knock your teeth out."

He turned back to Billy. "Anyway, here we are. We got a shit-pot full of money coming to us and we aim to spend it all. Right here in downtown Kodiak. Compared to Dutch, I bet this place is goddamned Times Square."

"Well, I know that the bartenders will take your money the same as in Dutch. I'm Billy."

"I'm Howard Fehlin, but everyone calls me Red," the man said as he grabbed Billy's hand. It wasn't a hand that grabbed him, it was a pair of vise-grips.

"This here pitiful excuse for a human being is Jimmy Whitaker. Now, tell me, Billy, what is the poontang situation around here?"

"The same as anywhere else Inside," Billy said. "Sad."

"Not really," Ray said from the crane seat. "Billy's got a woman."

"Now *that's* interesting," Howard said. "Where's she live?"

"You won't get that out of Billy," Ray said. "You'd have to pull out his fingernails one by one to get that out of Billy. Isn't that right, Marse?"

"That's right," Marse said.

"Well, I'd love to set and chat with you old ladies all day, but Jimmy and me got to go." Howard offered his arm to Jimmy and the two walked over the gangplank onto the barge.

"Hey,"Ron Knight said. "Come back here. You still have some work to do."

But the men pretended they didn't hear the *Vic's* skipper. Arm in arm, they disappeared behind the crab cookers.

"Worthless sons of bitches," Ron muttered. He turned to the cannery owner.

"Worst mistake I ever made, Bonner, hiring those two. Work like hell once they get started, but you have to light a stick of dynamite under each one's ass to *get* 'em started. And you have to watch 'em every goddamned minute. They're always pulling some crazy shit like this.

"You know what they did at Dutch last year? They climbed up Mount Ballyhoo—this was in December, right before Christmas—lit a fire and took off all of their clothes. Danced around until they nearly froze to death. Said they were Druids, and that it was the winter solstice and their goddamned religion told them to celebrate. Had to chopper their frozen blue asses off Ballyhoo and over to the hospital for frostbite."

Bonner wasn't paying attention.

"Hey, Ray, let's go. Start unloading."

He gestured to Billy and Marse.

"Hop in the bucket and get that money, boys."

The two unloaders clambered in and Ray winched them down into the hold to the deck of the *Vicky C.* Billy climbed out of the bucket, careful not to break any of the crabs' shells.

He picked up two purple bubblers, remembering what Bonner had told him, watching their big right claws, each one about as big as a man's fist. The crabs moved in slow motion, their gills barely fluttering; their brains, which were about the size of the tip of his little finger, were fatigued and stressed from the ordeal they'd been through. Billy hefted the crabs, bending his arms slightly; they must have weighed about ten to fifteen pounds each, with legs at least two feet long from one tip to the other.

He swung the two kings over his head and dropped them into the bucket. It was tough work, and it would take eighteen straight hours of non-stop work before the *Vic* was ready to make another run out for king crab.

CHAPTER 21

As soon as Marse banged the last crab into the steel bucket, Billy was already out of the hold and up onto the *Queen's* deck, jumping over the chains to the gangplank and hurrying past the processors to the gravel parking lot. He climbed up into Ray's Bronco and drove down Shelikof Street past the *Roxanne* and the *Skookum Chief* canneries, smelling the pungent protein-laced steam of the cooked crab.

He filled up the tank at the Chevron and hustled back to the cannery, just in time to pick up Laura.

Perhaps it was his imagination, but he thought he saw some color rise in her pale cheeks when she saw him.

Angela gave him a thin, stony smile.

"Where you two going?"

"Oh, there's a break between boats and I thought we'd drive out to Pasagshak."

"I'll be careful, Angela. Don't worry."

Laura climbed up into the Bronco and closed the door gently.

"Whose truck is this?"

"It's Ray's. He said I could borrow it for the rest of the day."

"That's nice of him."

"Yeah. It is," Billy said, and shoved the Bronco into gear. He turned left onto the airport road and drove past the wall of crushed cars that kept the rocks from sliding down Pillar Mountain. The mountain itself was now covered in green vegetation with blue sky behind it and Billy remembered how brown and dead everything had been when he arrived in Kodiak in April.

The paved road wound down around past the East Point cannery and then the *Galactica,* the 1930's-era ferryboat with the streamlined hull. After the *Galactica* there were a few more curves in the road, with the town peering back at them through the hill cuts, and then they saw Pyramid Mountain. They crossed Buskin River Bridge Number 2 now, in the deep shadow of Barometer. Billy pulled off the road and they walked over to the river. The humpies had finished their run. Now there were just a few stragglers in the river and the shallows and pools held hundreds of fish carcasses.

A bald eagle came down from its aerie and pecked at a dead salmon. The fish was a male, its hump a good four inches high. Laura turned away as the eagle's hooked beak tore into the gray rotting flesh.

"Eagles can be scavengers, too, Laura. At least that's what Butch says."

"Yes, I know, but I don't have to look at it, the way it tears into the fish."

She looked around at the dead salmon scattered around the riverbanks.

"Why don't the fish have eyes?"

"That's the first thing the gulls eat."

"Why?"

"I don't know," Billy said. "Come on. We have a ways to go yet."

They pulled back onto the road, past the Coast Guard base and around Womens Bay as Billy showed her the broken concrete ramps that the seaplanes used during World War II and the overgrown pillboxes scattered along the shoreline facing out. Away from the base now, the asphalt road turned into gravel past Bell's Flats and the Russian River, and then wound past Cliff Point and Middle Bay with its Saltery Cove road.

"These mountains are beautiful," Laura said. "What are their names?"

"They don't have names. They don't really need them."

"How much farther is it?"

"Probably about ten, fifteen miles."

"It's so pretty. I wish it would go on like this forever."

"So do I."

"But it won't. It never does."

"It can if you want it to," Billy said.

They drove down the Pasagshak Road, through the river valleys at Lake Rose Tead, until Billy pulled the Bronco over next to a herd of brown cattle.

"There they are. There are the Beatle cows."

"What?"

"You know, the Beatles. See—look over there."

Billy pointed at a herd of cows a few yards away. They were light brown in color, and all of them had bangs down over their eyes so when Laura looked at them straight on, they did indeed look somewhat like bovine Beatles.

Laura laughed.

"What kind of cows are they?"

"They're Scottish Highlanders. They belong to a guy named Si Zentner. He has a ranch here. I don't know how he does it, how he takes care of them with all of the bears around."

"What do you mean?"

"It's a real problem, Laura. The bears eat the cows."

"I never would have guessed it," she said.

"Yeah. See how that one's looking around? The bears come down from the hills and pick 'em clean, right down to the bones. Meat on the hoof," Billy said.

"How did you learn so much about Kodiak?"

"I hang out with Butch and Ray. They never stop talking. They know everything about the Rock."

Billy turned and watched the light play off of her face.

"Say, listen," he said as he turned to her. "Would you mind if I kissed you?"

She turned and swept her blond hair away from her face.

"No," she said. "I mean, I wouldn't mind."

He leaned over and their lips brushed together.

"Billy?"

"Yes?"

"I'm glad you asked first."

"I'll always ask if you want me to."

"I do want you to."

"All right," Billy said. "I can do that. Here, right here on the Pasagshak Road, in front of Si Zentner's Highlanders, I swear to you that I will always ask if I can kiss you."

Laura giggled. "Will . . . will you ask me again?"

"Yes," Billy said, "I'll ask you. In fact, I'm asking you now."

They kissed again, and then Billy started up the truck and they drove the rest of the way to Pasagshak. They parked on a sandy overlook and walked down to the black sand beach as the foamy water pounded the shoreline.

"How cold is the water?"

"There's only one way to find out."

They sat down on the sand and took off their rubber boots and thick wool socks. Billy rolled up his jeans and then hers. They held hands as they walked into the foaming water.

Laura gasped and squeezed his hand hard.

"Oh, Billy. It's so cold."

"I know it. The crabbers tell me you wouldn't last ten minutes if you fell overboard."

The icy water rushed between them, wetting their bare legs to the knees. Billy looked down and watched the black sand rushing away from their ankles as the water made small indentations by their feet.

"Oh no," Laura screamed, and broke free away from the surf.

Billy stood there for at least another minute, a living testament to the male ego, until he started to lose the feeling in his toes.

He ran back to her.

"I'm going to ask you for another kiss," he said, out of breath.

"Yes."

They kissed on the black sand beach and Billy felt the mountains behind him break loose from their granite bases and begin to swirl around the two lovers slowly in a dizzying dance.

He opened his eyes and saw that Laura was crying.

"Billy," she said. "I don't know if I can do this."

"It's OK," he said. "I understand."

She reached over and gave his hand a small squeeze. "I'm glad that you do."

He wiped the tears away from her cheek. "Anyway, we should be heading back soon."

"What time is it?" she asked.

"Ten."

"I'll never get over how the sun is so high in the sky this late at night."

"Yeah," Billy replied, "that's Alaska summer for you. Besides, the sun won't set until I tell it to."

He looked around.

"I wonder if this is how God felt."

"Really?"

"Yeah, on the day after He made the mountains and the sea."

"Let's go back now. Angela will be wondering where I am."

"OK, but before we do, turn around for a second."

Laura turned toward him.

"Look behind me at all this beauty and tell me how it could all be in one place like this."

"I don't know."

Billy turned and said, "I want to take a picture of this," and raised an imaginary camera to his eye.

He snapped off a photograph.

"There," he said. "I've got it. Now I'll always have it."

"Can you make a copy for me?"

"Sure."

"I hope it lasts. Photos turn brown after awhile."

"This one won't," Billy said, as he started the truck.

In a few minutes they were bouncing on the gravel past Si Zentner's cows.

"I'm so hungry," Billy said. "I wish I had some money. We could stop at the Rendezvous for something to eat."

"I'm hungry, too," Laura said. "Wait a minute."

She reached into her jacket pocket and pulled out a small bag of M&Ms.

"I forgot I had this. Here," she said, and tearing open the bag, took out an M&M and put it in Billy's mouth.

"Everything tastes so good when you're hungry," Billy said.

"Yes," Laura replied. Her face brightened. "I'll bet I can make this little bag last us all the way back to town."

"How?"

"We'll make a game out of it. One at a time. I'll dole them out slowly. And for every red one, I'll give you a surprise."

"A surprise? What kind of surprise?"

"It wouldn't be a surprise if I told you," Laura answered with a smile as they passed the Chiniak Road cutoff.

She moved over next to him. Every so often, she reached into the bag and took out two M&Ms. She slipped his into his mouth and he loved the crunchy sweetness of the candy on his tongue.

"Don't bite. If you suck on them, they'll last longer."

"All right."

She leaned over and kissed him on the cheek.

"What was that for?"

"It was a red one."

"Oh—is that the surprise?"

"Yes."

The miles clicked by as they made their way back to town. When they left the gravel part and reached the asphalt by Bell's Flats, he asked her, "How many are left?"

"About four or five."

"We're going to make it."

"I told you we would," she said. "Oh, here's another red one. Let's celebrate when we get to the Buskin River."

"We're already celebrating," Billy replied.

"You're right."

She kissed him again.

They rounded the curve by Gibson Cove and saw the town shimmering under the rising moon.

"Look at Kodiak shining. It's The Emerald City, right from *The Wizard of Oz*," Laura exclaimed.

"Kodiak's never looked this good before to me. You know, Laura," Billy said, as they passed the crushed cars of the avalanche wall, "I used to think that everything was dead, and that the world had gone away somewhere. But now when we're together like this, everything is new again."

"I'd like to believe that."

"Why can't we? No one says we can't."

"You're speaking for yourself. Not me."

"I'm telling you that we can. It's a fresh start. Look, I met you, didn't I? That's a sign."

Laura looked out over the harbor.

"Do you think that's how God works? He sends us signs?"

"Of course, Laura."

"I used to think like that."

They pulled into the *Queen*'s parking lot.

Billy looked up and saw Butch Edwards standing by the outside hoist, watching them. He came over to them as Billy switched off the engine.

"Where the hell were you two?"

"On the Pasagshak Road."

"Well, it doesn't matter. Good news, boys and girls."

"What is it?"

"Ray and I are on a boat," Butch said. "We leave tomorrow."

*

They dropped Laura off at the trailer park and drove back down to the Crab Pot. Butch rang the brass bell.

"Drinks all around," he yelled over the Friday noise. "I'm a highliner now."

He pushed his way through the crowd with three Oly long-necks and sat down at a table where Ray was waiting.

"What happened?" Billy asked.

"You won't believe this shit," Butch said. "You know those two morons from the *Vicky C?* The ones who came in asleep on the load of crab?"

"Sure," Billy said. "The Ballyhoo boys. The unloaders."

"Yeah. They got into it over at the Breakers last night with a couple of Aleuts. Guy said something about their matching overalls and got his jaw busted with a goddamned *elbow.* Yeah, the two of them are just sitting there with their beer and these natives came up and start in on how cute they both look in their Carhartts and the red-headed guy doesn't even look up, he just swings his elbow out and busts the guy's jaw.

"So anyway, down goes the Aleut, and his buddy comes storming up and the second Dutch guy cracks his beer bottle right over the guy's head, and down he goes. And Freddie Solomon, the Breakers bartender, is trying to figure out what to do when Redhead reaches over and takes a swing at *him.*"

Butch leaned back, satisfied. "So I don't need to tell you what happened next. Freddie's got his Louisville Slugger out, chairs flying all over the place, beer bottles in the air, and when the dust settles, poor Freddie sees bodies everywhere. Aleuts, Flips, whites, scattered all over the place. Now the town jail's busting at the seams."

He took a swig of his beer and gestured with the longneck. "So the *Vicky C* has to leave port tomorrow and the poor little Dutch boys are downtown in the jug. And Ron Knight's going nuts. He doesn't want to bail 'em out. Hell, he doesn't even want to *look* at 'em again. He asked Lynch if he knows anybody that might want to go out crabbin', and old Bonner looks around and guess who's standin' right there? Yours truly, plus Ray.

" 'Well,' Bonner says, 'I know that these two guys work hard, and they've been on boats before.'

"Ron looks us up and down. 'You boys been out before?'

" 'Oh, yeah,' I said. 'I was on the *Vansee* and the *Pacific Lady,* and Ray here was on the *Conquest*—that's a boat out of Petersburg. So we know which end of the rope to hold.' And that was that."

"I don't know, Butch," Ray said. "I really don't want to go out again. You've heard me say it a thousand times."

"Well, you heard *me* tell *him*. It's a done deal. We're shipping out tomorrow. Yep, and we're gonna come back with so much money at the end of the season it'll be just plain sad."

"Butch already has it stacked and counted," Ray said, looking glum. "Besides, we still have to find the crab, have to hoist 'em out of the water first and then make it back. At least that's the part that I can remember. The hard part."

"Ray, why are you so down all the time? Ron Knight's a highliner. He knows all the good spots for kings. He knows the Bering like I know Rosie Escobar. It'll be a piece of cake."

"I don't know," Ray said. "Maybe you should have asked Billy."

"Hey, come on. Don't get cold feet, Ray," Billy said.

"Yeah, Ray. It's not like you're gonna puke all over the deck or anything. It's not like you're gonna make a fool of yourself," Butch said. "You've been out before."

"No, it's not that."

"Well, what? Honest to God, Ray, after all this time, I can't figure you out."

"I don't know. It's been a few years. Maybe I'm just nervous is all."

"You'll do fine. It's gonna be great."

Bob the bartender brought another round of Olys.

"From Harry in the corner," he said.

The three men raised their new longnecks from the bottle forest on the table.

"Thanks, Harry," Billy and Butch said in ragged unison.

"Good luck, guys," Harry shouted from across the bar.

"You know," Butch said, "they say that the crab a highliner catches looks different. It isn't purple at all. It's green. Comes out green like glacier water—the money color."

"I never heard that," Ray said.

"Well, it's true. See if it isn't. Tell me what you think about it when we come back through the pass with a hold full of crab."

The three men said nothing for awhile, drinking their beers. After the fourth round, Billy drained his longneck and stood up.

"Well, I have to leave. I'm tired," he said.

He shook hands with Butch and Ray.

"Knock 'em dead, Butch. You too, Ray."

"We will, Billy boy," Butch said. "See you when we get back. We'll have such a big party, they'll have to call in the troopers."

Billy walked out of the Pot and trudged up the hill to the boarding house. Pausing for a moment, he checked his watch. Midnight. The stars were just beginning to come out, flickering far above the harbor, and he thought he heard a loon from way off somewhere, maybe around Three Sisters Mountain. Billy thought he could, at that moment, see and hear everything on the island—the bears crunching around in their dens, the eagles in their aeries, the trout holding steady in the river current, all settling down.

He remembered all of the details of the day that he'd had on the Pasagshak Road with Laura, and how everything was coming into focus. Billy wanted the feeling to go on forever. Before he fell asleep in his cot, he pictured the cold ocean, with whitecaps marching past Shelikof Strait, all the way out to the Bering Sea.

CHAPTER 22

Three more boats came in on Saturday and Billy was so busy he saw himself coming and going. The *Peggy Jo,* the *Polaris* and the *Oakland* were lined up in a row, all inbound, and the foreman had hired two local sixteen year-old twins to take the place of Ray, so Billy, Marse and the two boys worked without hardly stopping, lifting the heavy crabs into the buckets hour after hour, day after day.

"Come on, come on. Keep going, boys. Work for that money," Roy urged, as they moved down into the hold, until gradually the steel hull and the wooden planks peeked out between the purple crabs until all of them were loaded into the *Queen*'s white tubs. Billy was so tired that at the end of each day he couldn't lift his arms above his chest. But of course now he had Laura, and he saw her whenever he could steal a few minutes away from the boats. She looked beautiful even in her faded jeans, a gray sweatshirt, and a plastic apron as she worked the line. He'd take a break and wait for her and the two of them would climb through the narrow doorway onto the *Queen*'s bow and look at the mountains around the harbor, watching the eagles wheel about high above the cannery's steam vents.

Even Marse was harried, hopping back and forth from unloading to running the cooker. Now his boots squeaked across the floor. He had no time for reading and his face was always flushed with effort as he hoisted the big purple crabs into the cookers.

Then it was a Tuesday, the 18th of September. Billy was in the hold of the *Lin J* finishing off a load when he heard the bells tolling—the bells of the Russian Orthodox Church, ringing out over the harbor and down Shelikof Street. He hopped into the bucket with the last few king crabs and was winched up onto the deck.

"What is it?" he asked Richie Basler, one of the *J*'s crewmen.

"Trouble. One of the boats out on the Chain somewhere. Skipper's on the sideband now."

Billy climbed up to the wheelhouse. The captain was crouched over a bank of radios and CB's, listening intently.

"It's one of the Sikorskys from the base," he said. "Some guys were swept overboard by a rogue wave. Out around False Pass. Boat's on its side, and all of the wheelhouse windows are busted out. They found one body facedown in a kelp bed."

"Which boat?" Richie asked.

"Let me see," Al Pryor, the skipper, said, and keyed the mike. "Say again the name of the vessel, please?"

Static through the speaker, then, "*Vicky C.*"

Billy felt his heart slam shut.

"What boat did he say it was?" He could barely say the words.

"The *Vicky C.* It was just here a few days ago, I think. Wait a second. Let me try another channel."

The *Lin J* skipper flipped the dial and put on his headphones so he could hear better.

"The chopper is coming back to the base now. They've called off the search for the other guys. Wait a minute. There's four men missing. Ron Knight was the skipper, then there's Paul Dowdell and . . . I can't make it out. Hang on."

He switched radios.

"Hey, it's Pryor from the *J*. Did anyone out there copy the names of the other two guys? I got Knight, Dowdell . . . "

There was a long silence as the static bounced around the Lin J's wheelhouse.

"Yeah," a voice said weakly. "The other two guys were named . . . Griebling and Edwards . . . Griebling's the one they found in the kelp bed."

Billy didn't wait for any more. He jumped onto the *Queen* and started running. He ran down cannery row and cut across Mill Bay to the Pillar Mountain Road. Running up the dirt mountain road in his clumsy rubber boots, his heart hammering away, boots kicking up the dust, he struggled to keep moving forward, sweat pouring into his eyes.

He stopped at the summit where the dirt road ended. Bent over, clutching his jeans with his fists, he gasped to catch his breath. The blood pounding in his head, he cried and cried as if there were no end to his tears, weeping for Ray and Butch.

Far below, he could hear the church bell tolling again, the sound ringing out from its blue, onion-shaped domes as if it were going to go on forever, echoing across the town and up the mountainside, over to Three Sisters behind him.

Billy straightened up. His breathing slowed down, and he looked out across the town to the archipelago and out over the ocean, watching the blue rollers break across Crooked Island. Far off, he could see Woody Island and Long Island, and then the gulf. He didn't want to look in the direction of Barometer, the mountain where he had so many memories of his fishing trips with Ray and Butch. He had been thinking about the silver salmon run on the island, but now there wouldn't be any more season for him this September; the salmon would still run up the rivers all right, all around the island, but the silvers would not be for him. He had lost that now.

In a daze, he stumbled back down the mountain road into town and bought two one-quart bottles of Everclear, the first of which he drank under a Sea-Land trailer behind the hardware store. He smashed the empty bottle against the truck wheels and passed out on the black rocks.

When he woke up, it was 3:30 am. It was still dark. His head ached and the rest of his body was sore from sleeping under the truck.

Billy walked back to the *Roxanne's* live tanks. The cannery was deserted; the night shift must have finished early. He walked down the long drive back to the live tanks and rested his head against a rusty wall. The condensation from the cold water in the tanks ran down the wall and helped cool his throbbing head. He hopped up on the angle iron and looked into the black water and the thousands of pounds of king crab in the tanks; he could barely see them three feet down, but they were there, scuttling from one side of the tank to the other, menacing each other, all ravenously hungry.

His mind was freewheeling. As he had done five hundred times before, Billy raised the lever on the live tanks, and the water began to gush out through the boards as it splashed down to the harbor thirty feet below. Within a few minutes all of the water had drained out.

Billy looked around. There was no movement anywhere in the cannery. The lights inside were all turned off. He fired up the crane, winched the bucket down gently so it hung a few inches over the crabs, and climbing down gently into the first tank, began dropping them into the bucket. They made a dull clanging sound as they hit the steel sides. When the bucket was full, he climbed out and walked over to the crane. He sat down on the crane seat and pulled one of the four levers. The bucket full of kings—608 pounds worth, the scale read—moved slowly over to the side of the dock. Billy hopped down and calmly walked over to the bucket and flipped the two U-clips that held it upright, one on each side. He rocked the container, which flipped upside down, and the crabs tumbled out and dropped into the harbor with a satisfying splash.

He reached out, locked the U-clips into position, and winched the bucket back over to the tanks until it hung just a few inches above the crabs' spiny carapaces. Billy slipped as he climbed back down into the live tank. He remembered to walk gingerly on the shells. He filled the second bucket, and stripped off his flannel shirt and then his T-shirt as the rivulets of sweat ran down his back and soaked his jeans. Fifteen minutes later, he had the next bucket filled and dumped several hundred more pounds of crab into the dark water.

Three more trips into the tanks, and in a little more than two hours he had emptied the live tanks down to the bottom. He lowered the bucket onto the dock and shut down the crane motor. The silence around him was deafening. He wondered if anyone had seen or heard him, but there was no one else. Billy could feel the dock spinning under his feet as he walked rather unsteadily down the long drive to Shelikof Street. The street was deserted, as the bars had closed a few hours ago; the town was finally asleep. There were no cars on cannery row. It was a little before 5:45 am, according to his wristwatch, and he could see a rosy glow over toward Chiniak. The first shift would be coming down Shelikof soon. Stumbling out onto the street, he found the second bottle of Everclear and cracked open the cap. The 200-proof slid down his throat and warmed his stomach. He moved past the hardware store, watching the boats bobbing in the harbor, listening to their hulls creaking against the wooden pilings.

Except for a few lights on Mission Road, there was no sign of anyone being awake. Billy heard a dog barking way over off the town road toward Monashka Bay, and then he heard somebody's truck engine turn over and catch as he headed up the hill to Jan Day's.

He stopped outside the house and sat on the front steps for a few minutes. His head hung down, he rested his elbows on his knees and fell asleep.

Billy woke up an hour later, sore and tired. The sun was peaking over the harbor mountains and for the first time he could see a dusting of snow on their green tops.

Termination dust, that's what it was. Butch had told him that once. It was the first snow, the time when all cheechakos took their last paycheck and boarded the ferry for home.

Billy walked over to the trailer. The inside was dark, which was odd, since Laura and Angela should have been getting ready for their shift.

He knocked on the door and waited. There was no answer.

Billy pulled a rusty shopping cart over to one of the windows, stood the cart on its side and climbed up so he could see peer in through the yellowed curtains but it didn't take more than a few seconds to see that Laura and Angela were gone. The broken chairs were pushed against the wall, the kitchen was cleaned up and the half-finished HOME AND FAMI needlepoint that had hung on the wall was missing.

Billy climbed down from the cart and sat on the porch, feeling sick, trying to think. Then he ran over to the trailer office, where Ole Larsen lived.

Billy banged on the door. A light came after a minute and Ole shuffled over and unlocked it.

"What? What is it?" he said.

"Where's Laura and Angela?"

"Who?"

"Laura and Angela. Where are they?"

"What trailer are they in?"

"Twenty-four."

"Twenty-four? Oh, yah, they left last night. They lost their deposit, but they don't care. Took the ferry, I think."

"They're gone?" Even though he'd seen it for himself, Billy was incredulous.

"Oh, yah. They gone. They gone away. Somewhere off the island."

"Did they say where?"

"Nope. The big one just kept saying over and over, 'It's time. It's time.' And now they lost their deposit, and they don't care."

"I can't believe it. I just can't believe it," Billy said.

"Well, you *better* believe it. They gone."

Billy stood there for a few minutes, and then walked down the hill to the dock where the ferry had left the night before. Two boys were fishing with handlines for flounder. Neither one looked up as Billy walked past them.

He sat down next to one of the wooden pilings and looked out at Near Island. Something caught his eye. It was a large raven, circling over the harbor. Billy watched the bird make larger and larger circles; then it glided over some spruce trees on Narrow Cape and disappeared.

Billy sat there for a long time, listening and watching the water lap against the pilings. After a while, he stood up.

He walked through town to the harbormaster's office.

A man with a bright orange hunting hat was reading the *Mirror*.

"Are you the harbormaster?"

"No, he's over at Sutliff's."

The man lowered his paper and looked at Billy.

"Jesus, Mary and Joseph, what happened to you? You look like shit."

"Nothing. Nothing happened to me. "

"Well, you ought to get cleaned up. Take a shower or something."

"I said I'm OK. Hey, tell me. You know about the ferry?

"Sure."

"Where's the farthest you can go?" Billy asked.

"Homer or Seward, I guess. Or Anchor-town."

"What about the other way? Out on the Chain? Who goes that way?"

"The Chain? The state ferries don't go there. You got to fly or take a boat."

"I want to go out to Dutch."

"Dutch Harbor? Jesus Christ, that's a long trip."

The man took a drink of coffee from a chipped cup.

"Besides, you know what they say about the islands out on the Chain: 'There's a woman . . . ' "

" ' . . . behind every tree in the Aleutians.' Yeah, I know. I've heard that one."

"Tell you what," the man said, as he folded his paper, "if you want, I think I can find somebody who can take you. Jensen's going out on the *Chief* tomorrow. I can get him on the CB and see if he has an extra bunk. But before I do, listen. I got to tell you again. I've been out to Dutch and I know. There is nothing there."

"Fine," Billy said. "That's exactly where I want to go. Where there's nothing. Absolutely nothing at all."

The End